WHY
OF
THE
BEHOLDER

WHY

OF THE

BEHOLDER

ERIC PORTER

No part of this publication may be reproduced, distributed, or transmitted in any way, including photocopying, recording, or other electronic or mechanical methods, without the prior written permission of the publisher, except as permitted by U.S. copyright law. For permission requests, contact Puzzledust Media LLC (service@puzzledustmedia.com).

Hardcover: ISBN 978-0-9984919-3-6
Paperback: ISBN 978-0-9984919-2-9
eBook: ISBN 978-0-9984919-1-2

Library of Congress Control Number: 2024910517

All names, characters, and incidents portrayed in this work are fictitious. No identification with actual persons (living or deceased), places, buildings, and products is intended or should be inferred.

Edited by: Erin Young and Sara DeGonia

Book Cover and Interior Layout by theBookDesigners.com

First edition 2024

Puzzledust Media LLC
service@puzzledustmedia.com

This book is dedicated to my wife, Audrey, for her strength, patience, and unwavering support and to my daughter, Ashlyn for reminding me to find my creative voice and to show poise during times of adversity.

CHAPTER 1

NOT LONG BEFORE he shut his eyes for the final time, the old man's best friend had referred to these as the wasting years, where one's circle of friends faded into the background until they passed on to the next world. It was a pessimistic view, but the old man found it difficult to refute as he rested in his wheelchair, a blanket across his lap. It had been only about a week since the stroke, and he was grateful for the break in therapy sessions.

He scanned the pond as he sat beneath a bright but unwarming November sun. Tossing a small pebble into the water, he imagined the ripples were rings on a tree, marking the years of his life as they traveled to the pond's edge. Since arriving at the Bryn Wood rehabilitation center, he found he seldom had alone time. As a widower, having been on his own for several years, he had grown accustomed to silence, the only chatter being that which lived inside his head. The outside world appeared familiar momentarily, a peaceful oasis from the daily hustle that had become ubiquitous in his temporary home.

Pulling the blanket closer to his waist, he noticed a man parked on a bench across the pond. The old man wondered why he had not seen him initially, as if he magically appeared as a figment of his imagination, perhaps a side effect from the painkillers he had been taking. The man was engrossed in his newspaper, never raising his head to make eye contact. He appeared to be wearing a badge with a retractable lanyard attached to his belt. A bagged lunch remained undisturbed on the seat beside him.

The old man snapped a mental picture of the stranger, a practice he'd adopted many years ago from his time in the military. He could tell he was on the shorter side, perhaps in his late thirties. His full head of wavy brown hair may have had a bit of grey mixed in, but the old man couldn't be certain from that distance. The stranger's dark-green fleece nearly matched the conifers that enveloped him. The old man could not know it then, but this nameless figure absorbed in his periodical would be his vessel to share a terrible secret he had been holding onto for far too long.

"Chuck," one of the nurses called from the doorway leading out to the koi pond. "Your granddaughter is on the phone."

The old man smiled with delight. There was no more important person in the world. The nurse flipped off the brake on the old man's wheelchair and guided him back to his room.

He knew how important these calls were for both of them. Cassie credited him with saving her many times in more ways than could be counted. Telling him she would never have seen her thirties had it not been for his watching over her. He wasn't sure about that but knew he would do everything he could to keep her safe.

"Hi, Grandpa."

"Hi, angel."

"How are you feeling? Have you started much of your rehab yet?"

"Not too much, yet. I think they want some of my strength and balance to return before putting me through the gauntlet."

"Hmm. So, do you feel stronger?"

"I think so, but they are playing it safe, no doubt in fear of lawsuits. I have never seen so many fall risk signs in my life. You'd think people were toppling over like dominoes in this place."

Cassie chuckled. She filled him in on the latest in her online coursework at Copper State University.

"I'm so proud of you for going back to finish your degree."

"As they say, better late than never. I was precariously close to never." Cassie chuckled.

"Nobody could blame you, Cassie, not after everything you went through."

A brief silence filled the void, as if both parties were unwittingly playing back a tape in their minds.

They talked for several more minutes before a certified nursing assistant interrupted, entering the room to take vitals.

"I better go. They need to retake my blood pressure, you know, in case it has changed dramatically from fifteen minutes ago." He looked at the CNA and flashed a sheepish smile.

"Don't forget I am coming on Sunday," Cassie said. "I will bring you *Shadow Divers*, that amazing book I told you about."

"Can't wait, Cass. So long as you come with it."

"Bye, Grandpa."

"Bye, angel."

CHAPTER 2

AT SIX-FORTY, the alarm went off for the first official day of a new job and a new life for Dr. William "Bill" Taggart. After a fierce battle of willpower to get out of bed, Bill recognized that the consequences of falling back to sleep outweighed his so-called choices. He showered, shaved, grabbed a Nutri-Grain bar and a large cup of coffee, and started on his way to work. The drive to work was beautiful, filled with endless rolling hills, the occasional winding stream, and tiny country homes dwarfed by the mountains. As the miles accumulated, being both nervous and excited, he felt the butterflies slowly building.

Dr. Taggart's first day at Maybrook Psychiatric Facility, often referred to by those who spent time there as the motel for the permanently fucked, or MPF for short, began in a typical way. Upon checking in at the front desk of the administration building, Janice Hoffman, an executive assistant, escorted him to a room where he filled out the familiar paperwork, followed by the ceremonious pee into a plastic cup. As he aimed, he hoped the cup was large enough to contain a morning's worth of coffee. It's a good thing coffee isn't considered a drug, he thought. I am practically pissing espresso.

Janice introduced him to the human resource department, accounting, and a couple of other departments that he forgot as quickly as the names of those who made their nine-to-five at the facility. Not surprisingly, the administration building sat isolated from the rest of the patient buildings on campus, both geographically and symbolically. The administrative staff had limited interaction with patients, their knowledge of the mentally ill rarely extending beyond the popular media's portrayal in Saturday matinees or the occasional front-page newspaper article.

Bill spent most of the day touring the individual units of the Maybrook facility, starting with the children's ward and ending in the stabilization unit. On his first pass through the buildings, he noticed the settings were similar to those from his work in Florida: the whiteboard constantly shifting to reflect bed assignments, room restrictions, suicide precautions, and the all-important smoking privileges. The nurses busily paged through medical records and made notations for meds while answering the patients' numerous requests or, in most cases, demands, often accompanied by various insults, defamations, and irrational diatribes.

The happenings in each patient's room he passed were as unique as those calling them home for their short stay. Some lay on plastic and rubber mattresses with their weathered and flat pillows. Many appeared to be in a lengthy slumber, tranquilized by the gripping mix of depression, addiction, and psychotropic downers. Others found comfort in writing their feelings down in the hope that they would reveal a truth about their lives that, to this point, had eluded them.

Of course, one could not miss the token patient on the phone demanding a spouse, brother, sister, parent, or anyone who would listen to sign them out of the "hellhole." The dual diagnosis unit where he would primarily be assigned had eighteen bedrooms—nine on each side of the hall.

None of these things were new to Dr. Taggart. They could be found in any inpatient center across the country. Nevertheless, a few patients stood out like a white tuxedo at a black-tie affair. For example, thirty-nine-year-old David Tenor, a once gifted medical student from Baylor University, who, at twenty-nine years young, suddenly and inexplicably experienced a psychotic break during his first year of residency. While most psychotic breaks associated with schizophrenia happened in one's late-teen years, this man's illness had been making up for lost time. David spent most of Bill's orientation pacing the hall, mumbling incoherently to relentless voices that echoed in his head. He walked with a stiff but hunched posture; index finger of his right hand pointed to the ground as if it were a pistol hunting the demons that plagued him from the hell below.

A large, out-of-breath woman interrupted Bill's unit tour, calling him from down the hall. At first, he thought there was an emergency but realized she was merely a grossly out-of-shape nurse who wanted to introduce him to some of the unit's staff.

The nurse led him down the long, narrow hall, stopping to unlock a door between the two last rooms in the unit.

"This is where we have our change-of-shift meetings to discuss the chaos of the last eight hours and properly sap the confidence out of the crew taking over." This was met with some smiles and a few chuckles in the room. "Here we have Ruben Keller, Allison Baker, and Linda Merris, the mental health technicians for this shift. Mary Brodsky is the sole nurse on duty. She will administer the meds. Oh, and Tom Zimmerman, the certified addictions counselor, is also here, but he is sitting in on the AA meeting down the hall."

The group exchanged pleasantries with Bill and welcomed him to the group. He could not help but feel they were placing bets with the bookies in their minds on how long he would last. After all, Bill knew of the transient nature of inpatient settings. Most psychologists just marked time until they could assimilate into a private practice where it was much easier to leave work at the office.

"Nice to meet all of you. I didn't catch your name," Bill said.

"I'm sorry." She paused to take a breath. "My name is Barbara, but you can call me Barb or Barbara. Just don't call me Bitch." A large grin appeared out of the corner of her mouth. "Some patients get Bitch and Barb confused, it seems."

Bill could see that she was tough and let things roll off her back. He had just met her but could already tell he would like her. With that, the shift meeting began.

"Let's see, Jonathan Knight is on CI," Barb said.

"Again? He was on CI just two days ago," said Allison, strangely surprised.

"Yeah, well, he was late for the morning agenda meeting, and when confronted, he decided to skip the remaining groups."

"Patricia and Jennifer have been in their rooms all day; they are new admissions from overnight. Both are heroin addicts with major depression. Jennifer is with co-occurring psychosis. They both have fevers and diarrhea from withdrawal and probably won't start with groups until tomorrow at the earliest."

With that, Barb pushed the binder across the table to Mary. It contained the patients' names by room, with shift notes scribbled by the tech assigned to shadow them during the last eight hours.

Mary got up to pour herself another cup of tea. Her feet were heavy, like those of a battle-fatigued soldier heading back to the lines. "Okay, let's hope for a quiet shift."

It was Bill's third job in the field since receiving his PsyD in clinical psychology at Gulf Southern University in Miami. He had loathed the lack of seasons, the torrid heat, and the vapid cultural scene surrounding the university. He finished first in his graduating class and published his doctoral thesis on society's prejudice toward the mentally ill and how it affects treatment outcomes. It proved controversial as he argued that many therapists enter therapeutic relationships with a strong confirmation bias and preconceived notions about their patients. The thesis created a stir that reached deep into the American Psychological Association's hierarchy. By the time he'd completed his thesis, he had championed a seat in social isolation, albeit at the front of the class.

"The search for truth is never easy, nor should it be. If you don't ask more questions in seeking it, you are not a true scientist of behavior," went an often-repeated line in Bill's head. They were words of encouragement from Dr. Peter Hample, one of his mentors. "Remember this, William, and you will make a fine scientist and, more importantly, a fine therapist."

The axiom helped sustain Bill through a challenging five-year doctorate program, one filled with plenty of work and little money to come by. Bill Taggart was thirty when he was awarded his PsyD, and in all the ways that mattered, he was alone.

The first two years of practice following graduation proved to be a difficult adjustment for Bill, and he imagined it to be so for other graduates. He discovered that innocence had no home in the world of mental health, not among the staff and certainly not among its patients. It was like being born inside a snow globe, a fixed environment where childhood was stolen and its captives left unaware that a world existed outside: a healthier world, one with different possibilities, actions, and results.

He saw more weird shit in his first two years than most people would witness in a lifetime. Such as the time he was drinking a Diet Coke in the hospital cafeteria when a seven-year-old girl approached him, laughing and chanting, "You like to suck cock." The girl, hospitalized for stabbing a schoolmate with a pencil and trying to bite her teacher when she attempted to intervene, was a victim of her father's sexual abuse. Bill did a residency with children but found it impossible to handle the mental anguish of working with them. A child's mind was like a tape, always recording its surroundings but without the ability to edit out the garbage.

He remembered watching the cute seven-year-old with a rabid temper and filthy mouth returning to her seat with her breakfast tray and how he pictured her in some hospital somewhere as an angry, depressed adult, and it sickened him. He remembered his days at Gulf Southern and the controversy his thesis created and was amazed at the triviality of his education. It was a world he could not relate to then and even less so now. Reality was disturbing in his chosen occupation, and to search for the truth, he knew he committed himself to this world on a level few would find possible.

Upon exiting the shift transition room, Bill made his way to the group room diagonally across from the nurse's station. Taking care not to be seen, he peered through the wooden door's thin, vertical windowpane. An AA meeting was in progress. A bushy-haired, large man adorned in a ragged pair of jeans and a Dale Earnhardt T-shirt played with his empty Styrofoam cup, staring into it as if in disbelief that he was out of coffee and perhaps out of second chances. He had the full attention of his peers, a diverse bunch that would not likely congregate anywhere else. A room full of lawyers, accountants, truck drivers, homemakers, and homeless patients locked in on his every word as he shared a story that could've easily been their own.

Bill kept his opinion to himself but found the effectiveness of these meetings highly questionable. They never seemed to work for his brother, Colton. His road to recovery only came from reaching rock bottom in the form of a car chase with the police in an attempt to avoid a DUI. To save himself from drowning, Colton mustered the will to push one last time in hopes of reaching the surface for a lifesaving gasp of air. From Bill's experience, while the depths might look different, everyone faced a potential turning point where they'd either seize the moment to change or take one last breath underwater, marking an end to their suffering.

CHAPTER 3

AS DAYS TURNED TO WEEKS, Bill settled into his new job. He never minded the commute, even in the heart of winter. The car, where he was free from the distractions of the workday's chaos, was always an excellent place to catch up on thoughts. However, at times, the flood of information came uninvited, disregarding his desire for moments of peace.

It was the end of the week. A fickle mixture of snow, sleet, and rain slowed the journey home from work. The intermittent brake lights ahead of him stirred a childhood memory from deep beneath the surface.

He found himself sitting in the back of his father's Ford Taurus, watching as the van in front of them stopped at a red light. The journey itself was unremarkable. It was one he had made several times before as a young teenager. The view alternated depending on the season and the part of the country they found themselves traversing. Oddly, journeys such as these exposed him to much of the beauty of the eastern United States, more so than the sparse family vacations he could recall.

The sun had almost set, nearly complete with its retreat on the horizon. The sky was gorgeous, on fire with a blend of oranges, yellows, and reds. The hills rolled endlessly in all directions, dotted with old farmhouses and grain silos. Like before, they were on their way to drop some things off to Colton, who was starting another stint in drug and alcohol rehab. As was typical, the facility was situated where time stood still, the only rare change being the occasional fresh coat of paint on the road and some new vinyl siding on the ranch houses. The car radio fizzed an AM news station as it passed in and out of range. His father paid no mind. In retrospect, the broken transmission perfectly symbolized the conversation that would follow.

They were about five minutes from their destination when his father looked in the rearview, waiting for his son to meet his gaze.

"I am proud of you," he said. "You are not a problem." These two phrases could not have been more different in their connotation.

Bill knew he had good intentions but would never be able to reconcile them. They were two equal truisms from his childhood, two sentences that perfectly summed up his role within the family. His family life seemed to sway from praise to scorn.

When they were both in elementary school, the relationship with his older brother, Colton, was typical. They were best friends. Bill could picture his brother asking his mom if his sibling could sleep over. While this meant simply moving a sleeping bag from one bedroom down the hall to another, to the Taggart boys it seemed like an adventure, a special occasion, no matter how many times it was repeated.

In the summer, they would stay up late watching the fireflies they had captured and released in their room, anticipating where the light would appear next. The memories began to cycle like slides on a slide projector. Images flashed of playing video games on the Atari 2600, making them celebrities as the first family on the block to secure one. So many hours were surrendered to *Combat*, a game where three small fighter jets battled against one huge but slow bomber. The contest was pointless as the bombers' inability to escape the speedy fighter squadron was exacerbated by its sheer size, making it impossible to miss. Colton always allowed Bill to be the jets, delighted by the joy and pride in his younger brother's triumph.

Sports were a big deal in the Taggart household, with both boys trading in a soccer ball for a hockey stick and then a baseball bat as they followed the calendar. They were blessed with a neighborhood that had experienced its own baby boom. Almost every other house had a boy or girl within a few years of each of them. Entire teams could be constructed for a contest without leaving the block. The highlight was an annual Wiffle ball game set up and run by the older kids. A backyard was selected to be the diamond. Old shutters made up the home run fence, adorned with unevenly painted distance markers in left, right, and center fields. The chalk lines were carefully laid with large bags of flour. A random collection of lawn chairs was scattered down the right field line. The town's entire population could be found in this one place on a warm summer afternoon in June. If anyone wanted to scout the neighborhood for a robbery, this would've been the ideal time. The event cost each family $3, which was given to the local children's hospital.

One particular Wiffle ball game stood out in Bill's recollection. It was a perfect early summer day, a sweet spot in the calendar, right after the brief warm and sunny days and the cold and rainy ones that characterized spring but right before the scorching, humid, and stormy afternoons that dominated the better part of summer.

The Taggart brothers' team led by a single run entering the bottom of the ninth. Their opponent's first batter reached third base with a triple off the faded, black, left-field shutter painted with a recently dried "80-foot" marker in white. The following two hitters could not drive in their teammate. One struck out after the five-strike rule applied to the younger kids, while the other hit the ball straight back to the pitcher for a line drive out.

That brought up the best athlete on the team, a bigger-than-usual fourteen-year-old. He was awkward, tall, and thin, his girth not yet catching up with his lanky frame. His ball cap was pulled down, perhaps in a failed attempt to disguise the pimples that had recently made themselves known. He took the first two pitches as if waiting for the perfect ball for him to drive out of the park, a feat he had accomplished earlier in the game. The next offering fluttered over the plate, appearing as big as a beach ball; he would not need to wait for anything juicier. He connected with the meat of the barrel, driving a screaming line drive toward the center field wall.

The younger Taggart instinctively raised his hand as if eager to answer a question in Mrs. Bagley's third-grade class. To everyone's amazement, he closed his hand on the ball as if it were almost a protective reflex. The crowd cheered. Even the batter smiled, raising his hands over his head in an "oh well" fashion. Bill's teammates mobbed him. Colton, reaching him first, lifted him on his shoulders, allowing him to absorb the abundance of glory offered by the neighborhood. It was his own "World Series" moment, and his brother was there to ensure he relished every second of it.

Like most siblings, the brothers had their fair share of scuffles. Bill could hold his own for a while, but the outcome was never in doubt. Most fights ended the same way, with his older brother putting him in a headlock for no other reason than to demonstrate his control. Once Colton felt satisfied that his point was made, he would release his grip and retreat to his room to blow off steam. Usually, what followed was the thumping of heavy music, Ozzy's "Crazy Train" or Def Leppard's "Rock of Ages." The China in the living room below would gently vibrate as if dancing to the tune, shifting ever so slightly in the hutch.

Bill would curl up on the living room couch to read *Sports Illustrated* or, if feeling intellectual, an old copy of *National Geographic*. His father had a subscription for many years before having children. Bill needed a chair to reach the top two rows of periodicals. He was unconcerned with the dated material. He found it interesting to read and contemplate whether they were still valid today. Was the red panda still endangered? Had it gone extinct or made a recovery? Since the internet did not exist, these questions often went unanswered. He used to ask his parents before realizing they rarely, if ever, had any answers.

Worldly enough, like most parents, their knowledge was reserved for what they had to know to raise a family, pay the bills, and get promoted at work. His father's free time generally consisted of listening to Phillies games on the radio while catching up on paperwork, which was done while sitting at a card table in the driveway in the spring and summer. He would gather small rocks from the yard to act as paperweights as he created separate stacks of paper that, to a passerby, looked like organized chaos. In time, Bill realized his father's obsession with paperwork was a ritual, a man seeking refuge from his family drama. Bill would come to appreciate how he did much the same in his own way.

"You are not a problem," kept repeating in Bill's thoughts as he signaled to pass a car in front of him.

While it could never be proven through one of his graduate school-controlled experiments, Bill remained convinced it was middle school where things began to change for the worse for Colton. Grade six was a melting pot of confused preteen adolescents. Three elementary schools in the area merged into a single middle school. Suddenly, a large population of fifth graders was lifted and shifted from a position of seniority to the bottom of the totem pole. They went from being the lords of their realm, watching over the tiny kindergarteners, their partners in the school's buddy system, to serfs in a new kingdom of power-hungry older kids. Not unlike the gangs of New York during the height of immigration, jockeying for a position would become a struggle of life and death, not in the literal sense but in terms of shaping whether the next few years would be avoiding the bullies, becoming the bully, or, if fortunate, simply disappearing into the background.

The first month or so of middle school was a strange vacuum where children clung to cliques from their prior schools, like gangs in a prison. While there was security in numbers, something would have to give. Groups had to decide if they would merge or overtake one another. Would the jocks from one school combine with those from the others, or would they seek to change the labels of their new peers? This applied to all groups: nerds, thespians, brainiacs, punks, metalheads, musicians. Some would have a more natural affinity with one another. In general, the lower the value of the group, the more likely they were to join forces, seeking strength in numbers. In a methodology whose criteria would never be able to be measured, the jocks and more powerful kids sorted who would be part of the new club or pushed down a rung or two in the ladder. Being on the top of the pyramid ordained its tenants as predators while all other groups would become lesser degrees of prey. True to the laws of the universe, the geeks, nerds, or simply strange kids were the bottom feeders, the minuscule fish at the pet store whose only purpose was to feed the insatiable appetite of those with higher status.

Nobody in middle school was happy, whether the bully or the bullied; all were insecure, living in an in-between existence. While only three years long, middle school was an eternity for anyone at the bottom of the caste system. It was plenty of time to damage an impressionable young person's self-esteem for years. The onset of puberty presented an additional cruelty, creating a mixture of emotions and hormones that exacerbated the self-doubt. Some would suffer unnecessary years of isolation in high school, college, and beyond, thinking themselves unworthy of the love of another. The more logical the child, the greater the suffering. Science textbooks could explain some of the rules of the universe but seemed not to apply to their own lives.

Colton was a perfect use case for what the social science experiment known as middle school could do to someone. Entering middle school, Colton had several good friends, kids going places despite the label they would be given for the next few years. Colton and his friends were easy targets. They were not especially good athletes, got good grades, and were a potpourri of acne, slim frames, incongruent features, and just enough shyness and self-doubt to form small fissures ready to be cracked open by opportunistic bullies.

The bullying came fast and furious. Books were scooped off Colton's desk and thrown in the trash at the front of the room with everyone watching. Some laughed because they were part of the group; others laughed out of nervousness, glad they were not the target; and some did not laugh as they looked down at their books before them, feeling disgusted but unable to assist. In place of physical contact, bullies often resorted to psychological abuse. Those unfortunate enough to be on the receiving end would agree that while sticks and stones would break bones, words, contrary to the saying, did lingering damage.

The minutes Colton spent staring in the mirror at home grew longer as bullies focused on the size of his nose. The acne was bad enough. While he knew he had a slight curve on the top of his nose, it had never occurred to him until then that it was noteworthy. Being the shortest kid in school did not do him any additional favors.

In middle school, the schoolchildren would walk across the pedestrian bridge to the high school to take a swimming test. The fog of chlorine permeated the air surrounding the green-tinged indoor pool. There was so much chlorine that the air irritated Colton's eyes while he stood with arms folded, waiting for his turn to complete the test. The exam was mainly about treading water for a certain amount of time. A long list of kids with "doctor's notes" lined the bench along the wall. The number of ear infections seemed to correlate conveniently with these swim sessions.

Swimming was an exercise in humiliation. Standing in swim trunks, Colton was embarrassed by his diminutive stature. Some boys had begun to sprout in the seventh grade, leaving him further behind. The fact that there were girls in bathing suits, many of whom Colton had had a secret crush on at one point or another, made it even worse. He tried to keep his arms crossed, covering the moles that, like a Lite-Brite set, dotted his body with no distinguishable pattern. Colton successfully passed the test, no surprise given that he had been swimming at the public pool practically all summer since he was five years old.

An additional week of gym class was scheduled at the pool. The entire pool requirement seemed to exist only to bookend the hellish experience known as middle school. In yet another stroke of evil genius, the game of choice was often water polo. Colton lost count of the number of times he almost drowned. Defending and dunking was a fine line that bullies took full advantage of. Then came the required showering after class. While everyone kept their trunks on, it presented one final trial. After trying but failing to wash off the potent smell of chlorine, kids had to navigate the slimy and slippery floor back to their locker to change. This entailed turning a couple of corners, which was the perfect cover for bullies lying in wait.

They called it the car wash. Kids would be whipped with a tightly spun, soaking-wet towel. As Colton rounded the corner, he covered his eyes. The bullies had enough sense not to go for the face, but that did not mean they didn't miss the target now and then. Colton sucked in his stomach so it was nice and tight. Thwack! The sting of the towel transferred energy to his skin. On a couple of occasions, he managed to avoid the beating. He would be the last to turn off the shower, then wait quietly beneath the showerhead for several minutes. The evaporating water from his skin made him shiver, but it was far better than what awaited him around the corner. Thinking that everyone had received their unjustified punishment, the bullies would return to their lockers.

No single event or proverbial fork in the road could be identified as the time and place where things began going off the rails for Colton. It wasn't that his parents didn't see the warning signs. They started attending weekly therapy sessions with a child psychologist. Colton received the typical diagnosis of generalized anxiety disorder. A classification that likely pertained to almost everyone in middle school, even those in positions of power. The medication and hour-long weekly therapy sessions were no match for the hours spent feeding a building self-hatred. Colton's grades started to slip. He began to have trouble concentrating in class, and homework was replaced with time spent listening to heavy metal music, like "Am I Evil?" by Metallica, on heavy rotation.

Colton stopped hanging out with the friends he had known since elementary school, slowly gravitating to a group of deadbeats, kids that would raid their parents' alcohol cabinet when the opportunity presented itself. For Colton, misery indeed loved company. It was unclear whether his former friends pushed him away or vice versa.

As seventh grade led into eighth, things got worse. Colton had all but forsaken his studies, pulling straight Ds with an occasional C when his raw intelligence overcame negligible study habits. Bill's hardworking father began slowly building resentment toward Colton as he took the lack of effort personally. By contrast, Bill's mother began to hover over Colton, which only drove him further away. Bill himself did not know how to help. He watched as his once close brother, the same one who only a few years earlier he would have sleepovers with all but ignored him. One evening,

Colton received another poor report card with grades bad enough to threaten his ability to graduate middle school. Bill's father, who had the day off, stared at the news as he counted the hours waiting for his son to come home from school. As the hours passed, the script in his head changed, becoming more emotional and angrier. What started as a speech filled with questions and a tone of concern had been replaced by unconstructive, pure anger. Colton finally walked through the door at just past seven. His dad had not moved from the table the entire night. Colton discarded his book bag as he walked into the dining room. It hardly made a sound. He generally left his books in his locker as he did not make any use of them at home.

"Where have you been?" His father's tone indicated it may have been rhetorical, a means to begin the diatribe that would follow.

"Nowhere," replied Colton, a fully expected response consistent with the level of information sharing that had become commonplace in the last couple of years.

"Your guidance counselor called. You are on the verge of not graduating to the ninth grade. Did you know that?"

"Makes sense," Colton said in a dismissive tone that further fueled the building bonfire.

"Do you know how much we spend on you? We pay a lot of money for your therapy and medication. We send you to the best schools. All you have to do is make an effort, and you can't even do that. Why can't you be more like your brother?" That was not the first time a comparison was made with Bill, and it would not be the last. The doctor was convinced it was the catalyst for the adversarial relationship that would form between the once close brothers.

"You are just a walking wallet! That's all you care about. That's all you are to me!"

With that, his father left the room and disappeared upstairs.

When he returned a few minutes later, he carried the sound system he'd bought Colton for Christmas.

"I am done throwing money at you. You ungrateful shit."

He grabbed a pair of scissors from a junk drawer and cut the speaker wires and power cord. Saying nothing else, he carried the receiver and small speakers outside. The curtains were drawn, but the sound of the electronics dropping into the aluminum trashcans was unmistakable. There had been several arguments like this, but they never led to anything as overt as destroying property.

When he returned to the house, he stared at Colton and, slightly under his breath, said, "Now you don't have a stereo either. Since money doesn't mean anything to you, you shouldn't miss it." Not wanting to give his father satisfaction, Colton attempted to hide his surprise. It was then that Bill started crying.

The tears started slowly, but when Colton met his gaze and said, "It's OK," he began crying uncontrollably. In what would become the last brotherly olive branch extended by his brother for several years, Colton reached over and pulled his younger brother toward him in a tight embrace. Through his hysterics, Bill eked out, "Why are we so fucked up?"

"It's OK. Lots of families are fucked up," Colton said.

With that, Colton scaled the stairs to his room, never turning around to acknowledge his parents. For the next few hours, Bill's parents argued over the right approach to handling Colton. Bill knew enough to understand they were not on the same page, leaving little chance that things would improve before they got worse.

Bullying in high school had all but vanished. Kids went from beating the differences out of their classmates to simply ignoring them. But for Colton, the damage had already been done, bringing with it new opportunities for self-destruction previously out of reach.

Colton fell into a new crowd that shared his anger, the source of which differed from peer to peer. Some were angry from physical, emotional, and even sexual abuse at home. Some were soaked in rage from tragedy. The anger of others was anchored in undiagnosed and untreated mental health conditions—ADHD, depression, anxiety, OCD. The one thing they all had in common was that their pain could be forgotten, even if only temporarily, through the magic of alcohol and drugs. While marijuana proved more challenging to access, getting their hands on beer and liquor came relatively easy. What they lacked in effort when it came to schoolwork, they made up for in finding more inventive ways to secure substances.

Living relatively close to impoverished towns made it easy to buy beer. They didn't even have fake IDs. The bartenders at the run-down corner bars would smirk when they put the Colt 45s and Old English on the counter, money from suburban wannabes gladly taken. The police had their hands full with rampant street crime, and looking the other way meant avoiding the hassle of paperwork and dealing with angry and potentially powerful parents who would often get charges dropped or reduced through their lawyers.

Bill grew to appreciate that there were two types of drunks: those who became carefree, silly, and reckless, and the others who seemed to tap even further into a well of anger. His brother was the latter type. During the week, his brother would isolate himself in his room, cranking his stereo that had since been replaced. On weekends, on more than one occasion, he came home drunk and angry. The family dynamic had long since morphed from an environment where people had the best intentions to one where everyone had accepted that avoidance was the best recipe. Bill, not yet having a driver's license, would ride his 10-speed bike to friends' houses and stay late, limiting time at home as much as possible.

The relationship between Colton and his father had deterio-rated to total hatred. After unsuccessfully trying to convince Colton to join the military, something he would never have imagined him-self encouraging years before, his father had written him out of his life. Colton had become a tenant that, in due time, his father knew he could evict—though Colton's mother would not allow it. The deeper Colton fell, the more desperate she became to manage his life and addiction. She worried to the point of exhaustion, staying up late into the evenings, gazing out the window and wondering if it would be the night he would not come home. Colton resented his mother's hovering but knew he could not survive without the life-line she provided, a fact that only increased his self-hatred. Colton's father's resentment was fed by the obsessive attention Colton got from his mother. He blamed Colton for ruining his life, sapping his financial resources, impacting his marriage, and redefining a good day as the inverse of a bad one.

It was after 7:00 p.m. when Bill Taggart finally pulled into the entrance of his complex. It would be a good night for a hot bath to help wash away the stress of his day at the MPF.

CHAPTER 4

THE MPF WAS tucked away in a valley twenty minutes from the nearest Walmart, a fixture in rural areas that had come to be synonymous with "civilization." The center could not be seen from Interstate 80, which passed only ten miles to the south. One had to leave exit 23 and drive for another fifteen minutes before the campus came into view. The town of Maybrook could not resist the grants that came with the proposal to repurpose some agricultural zoning to make room for the new facility.

The endless hills and valleys of the local farms made the campus's proximity a nonissue, and the mind-your-own-business sentiment of the town's people manifested as indifference. With the addition of the MPF, the community now had a Turkey Hill gas station/convenience store, two bars, a sizeable Goodwill center, and a mental health facility. Like most small towns, Turkey Hill had become a local hangout for teens, many of whom could frequently be found around the *Centipede* arcade machine between breaks to step outside for a smoke. So often, smoking would be picked up out of sheer boredom rather than an attempt to look cool or rebel against one's parents.

Maybrook was a man's man type of town with a long history of farming and coal mining. Much like towns throughout the mid-Atlantic region, what mining and manufacturing jobs once existed had vanished years before. Mostly, all that remained was a mental health treatment center ready to serve anyone from the local population primed for a possible spell of depression and alcoholism exacerbated by the high unemployment that rested over them like the heavy fog that sat for days in the valley.

It had been precisely sixty days since he started at the MPF. As he pulled into the long, windy entrance, Bill wondered how beautiful it must look in the spring, with the winding creek rolling alongside the drive until it suddenly turned sharply into several acres of woods on the facility's east side. Twenty-foot maple trees dotted the windy road, evenly spaced from the sign at the entrance to the front parking lot. He looked forward to the warmer months when he could take in the beautiful natural setting of the MPF and use its walking trails. For now, it was all just potential, like the many addicts behind its walls. Spring would come for the flowers, trees, and rolling creek. The certainty comforted him as he knew the same could not be said for some of the facilities' inhabitants. If only the human mind could count upon such laws of nature.

Bill scanned his badge, entered his ID, and heard the familiar click of the power lock releasing. The unit was quiet, with only the shift supervising nurse, Barbara, and tech, Ruben, at the nurse's station. It was 8:00 a.m., and the patients were in their morning kickoff meeting, where the day's schedule was reviewed before they headed to the cafeteria for breakfast. "Hey, Barb. Any new admissions last night?" asked Bill.

"No, too cold last night. Even addicts wouldn't brave that to get their score." Barbara giggled. "And since some of them probably sold their jacket for a hit, braving the cold was probably even less appetizing."

"Interesting theory, Barb. You should see if the local university will give you a grant to study the correlation between all three factors."

"You are such a wiseass, Dr. Taggart."

"I know, can't help it." Dr. Taggart had grown fond of Barb.

At her core, she cared deeply about her job and the patients in her care but never lost her sense of humor or, more importantly, herself in the job. Bill was convinced that this made her the most effective practitioner on the unit.

"I am going to review the prior shift recording. Be right back," Bill said.

Dr. Taggart retreated to the shift change office, hit play on the ancient but reliable tape recorder, and poured himself another cup of coffee. Thank God coffee is not such a bad addiction, he thought. If it were, I would probably be selling my body by now for my next hit of beans. He smiled as he contemplated such a world. As he listened to the tape, he thought, Nothing much out of the ordinary.

Almost immediately upon exiting the office, he saw one of his patients, sixteen-year-old Kyle Madsen, flirting with a teenage girl who laughed and appeared to be loving the attention. Bill understood that Kyle was cool in ways that only mattered during one's youth. Most kids in the doctor's care were not especially known for their good judgment. Like Kyle, the loudest and brashest kids were often mistaken as the most confident. In time, he was certain Kyle would be left to wonder what happened as his followers grew up while his pranks only grew old.

As Bill passed, he reminded Kyle that they had an individual session in twenty minutes. Kyle made eye contact but did not hear him or, more likely, chose to ignore him. While Kyle's behavior was ubiquitous with other teens on the unit diagnosed with oppositional defiance disorder, he had seemed to master the art of subtlety when portraying the message that authority figures were unworthy of his time.

Kyle walked into Dr. Taggart's office three minutes late—not late enough to warrant non-compliance per the rules but sufficient to send the message that if there were a line drawn, he would find a way to approach it and even cross if he were reasonably sure he would get away with it.

"You're late, Kyle," Bill said, shuffling some papers.

"My bad." Kyle shrugged, glancing at the generic mountain landscape on the wall.

"Look, Kyle, you have been here a few days now. You barely participate in group and seem to do everything you can just to mark time in our meetings. You do realize why you are here, don't you?" Bill asked.

"Um, isn't it obvious? Do you always ask questions you already know the answer to? Is that what you learned with your degree? Money well spent." Kyle leaned back in the chair.

The doctor did not respond. He shuffled his notes, wondering how he would fill forty-five minutes with a kid who would do everything in his power to waste time as if it were a competition.

"So, do you want to tell me about those burns on your forearm?"

"What burns?" Kyle crossed his arms, covering them from view.

"Kyle, how are we supposed to help you if you won't open up to us?"

"You already know how I got them. So, why are you wasting your time asking me? I'm sure there are all sorts of juicy bits in that binder about me. Let me guess, it probably says something about some kind of attachment disorder, anxiety, or maybe even some PTSD bullshit. I'm fine. Why don't you ask my stepfather how he is doing? He's the one who needs to get a new Beamer." A sheepish, satisfied smile crept across his face. "You know, I bet it still works if you don't mind sitting on extra crispy seats."

Everyone suspected that the stepfather was responsible for the cigarette scars on Kyle's arms, but it remained unproven. Since the object of Kyle's fury didn't always align with those who wronged him, it was hard to be confident about the culprit. Kyle's mother remained silent, something she learned as a means of survival during her first marriage to Kyle's biological father. She managed to get away from his violence when, fortuitously, he did not come home one day after work. He now had a new, younger girlfriend who kept him warm at night when he returned from the bars. Not long after, Kyle's mother met who would become Kyle's stepfather. The security that came with Kyle's stepfather's money led her to ignore or rationalize his destructive behavior. It would be hard to judge her. Since Kyle's father walked out, finances were tough. The job she picked up as a waitress barely covered the rent of their new apartment.

Kyle's stint in juvenile detention for his act of arson was short-lived. In a nod to irony, his stepfather used his knowledge of the system and pull as an attorney to get the state to let him attend inpatient therapy in place of more time in detention. Kyle knew it was simply a way to influence the authorities not to look too deeply at the cause of the nearly perfect circles etched on his skin. Nobody was itching to give Kyle, who was relatively well known to the township police, the benefit of the doubt.

There was no denying it. Kyle got under Bill's skin in a way that few other patients ever could. The doctor cycled through the various techniques and approaches he had learned from this training. Each met a dead end. Kyle's responses, a string of "Yeses," "Maybes," and "Not reallys," were as curt as Bill's dwindling patience.

"Are we done here?" Kyle said as he yawned. Bill thought: You must be drained from such deep introspection.

"That depends. Are you going to talk to me?" Bill asked.

"Look, doctor, it's not personal; I just have nothing to say. You're wasting your time."

Bill's anger was rising to the surface. His mind drifted to his childhood, his head spinning with frustration at a level he had not felt in some time.

"I've got an idea," said Colton to his ninth-grade buddy, Noel Bridges, his perfect partner in crime, someone who could match his anger-fueled sense of danger. It was mischief night, and Bill was tagging along, something he did less and less as he drifted further from his brother. The three tossed toilet paper rolls into the tree branches; a harmless tradition practiced all around town. Bill loved how the long streams looked under the full moon.

After running out of supplies, Colton led the three boys back to the Taggart house, disappearing inside before returning a minute later with a bar of soap. Without saying a word, he grabbed a bucket from the garage.

"Follow me," Colton said.

The boys followed him to the back of the house, where Colton filled the bucket a quarter of the way under the spigot before dropping the bar of soap into it.

"This is gonna be great." Colton's eyes expressed excitement at what was about to take place.

"What's the soap for?" asked Bill, fearing he would not like the answer.

"I'll show you."

Bill considered making an about-face and returning to the house. In the end, peer pressure and fear of relentless teasing won the day. The boys walked several blocks from their home. Colton was smart enough to know that someone would be less likely to recognize them should they be discovered. His intellect was wasted mainly on fueling ever more creative nefarious activities.

Colton found a mostly dark home, save for a soft light over the porch door. He slowly approached the driveway, handed the bucket to Noel, and pointed to a Pontiac 6000 parked by the two-car garage. The three boys crouched and slowly approached the driver's side of the car. Colton carefully tried the front door. A smile came across his face as the door opened with a slight squeak.

"Bucket," he said, his hand extended in Noel's direction. "Soap, please."

Bill could see he was imitating a doctor doing surgery.

Opening the door just far enough, he rubbed the corner of the bar against the cloth seats. Unimpressed with the result, he moved to the dashboard, steering wheel, and even the light on the interior roof. The bar left a thick residue. He finished by writing "Happy Halloween" across the front driver-side window.

Noel was impressed. "That's brilliant! Let's do that house," he said, trying to contain his excitement as he pointed across the street. "I think that douche Dalton Crawford lives there."

Bill knew it was the wrong house. The "douche's" younger sister was in Bill's art class. He didn't even live in the same part of town. He couldn't think of any reason the two would have a grudge against Dalton. He thought they might have even been casual friends. He said nothing.

"Here." Colton handed the bar of soap to his younger brother.

"That's OK. It's Noel's turn." He hoped Noel would spare him by taking the baton.

"What, are you afraid? What's the big deal? Don't be a loser." Colton laid into his younger brother. Noel was silent. He knew he would have his opportunity soon enough. He preferred watching the conflict unfold. Against every fiber in his body, Bill grabbed the soap and made a few random patterns on the windshield. He dropped the bar back into the bucket, resulting in a splash that got all three wet.

"There," Bill said. "Happy?"

"Really?" Colton was unimpressed.

He took the bar of soap and below Bill's abstract work, wrote, "Next time, lock your car, DUMB ASS!"

The guilt and fear rushed through Bill like water through a

storm grate suddenly freed of debris. Would they be caught? Would they know he was involved? Would he get suspended from school? He knew how angry his parents would be. They would expect this sort of thing from Colton, but not from him. While their potential anger was scary enough, their disappointment in him would really sting. Of course, most of their vitriol would be aimed at Colton for spreading the disease, which was his unyielding desire to break down order wherever he could.

Nobody ever fingered the boys for their minor acts of vandalism. Colton and Noel took pride in outsmarting others and effectively covered their tracks. Wisely, most of their mischief was reserved for the middle of the night when they could move in darkness, their only witness the creatures who could be heard but never seen.

"Are we done here?" Kyle brought Bill back to the present.

"So, you won't talk to me?" Bill asked.

"Like I said, Doctor, it's not personal. I just have nothing to say. Let's not waste one another's time."

"Kyle, whether you return to detention is based on our recommendation to the disciplinary board."

Kyle uncrossed his arms. "Is that some kind of threat?"

"Not a threat." Bill repeated himself, "Not a threat," as if trying to convince himself that was the case. "Just the truth."

Maybe serving some time would do Kyle some good. If his brother Colton had faced more consequences earlier for his transgressions, he might have straightened his life out sooner, sparing the family and himself from at least some pain. Kyle was being given a gift of a second chance he didn't deserve, and he was wasting everyone's time. Bill had all but written him off. He had no intention of going to bat for him.

Bill ended yet another unproductive session and returned to the break room to get water from the cooler.

CHAPTER 5

THE WORST PART of winter had passed. While spring had not quite arrived, the crocus flowers would soon make an appearance, more often than not prematurely, resulting in their untimely death from an unforeseen frost. Bill took advantage of the improving weather by taking short drives to escape the MPF. He would find a mostly empty parking lot to eat lunch and catch up on reading, something he could not stay awake for following a long day at work.

It was perfectly random and spontaneous when he decided to turn down a road he had passed by many times before. The road twisted repeatedly without reason. There were no boulders, streams, or hills to warrant its inefficient route, even if the occasional tree appeared on one side of the road or the other. The dogwood trees were beginning to bloom, their beauty further emphasized by the red buds of the maples that had not yet opened. There were no other cars, houses, or people to be found. He drove one mile, followed by two more, before finally coming upon a dark oak sign with the words Bryn Wood Rehabilitation Hospital carved ornately in large yellow cursive letters. There were two floodlights, one of which flickered intermittently despite it being the middle of the day. The facility and its sprawling campus sat back from the windy road. There appeared to be plenty of open space, which made the facilities seem small and out of place, as if the intention was to continue expanding until the funds ran out.

He decided to make a quick pass around the perimeter of the campus. It was a sizeable ellipse with several turnoffs into parking lots well marked for visitors, caregivers, security, and maintenance. It was a spoke-and-wheel layout. He noticed a walkway that parted large evergreen trees on both sides. In the distance, he could see several benches circling what appeared to be a large pond with a fountain. He mentally noted its location, imagining dropping a big red pin into one of those online maps. Oddly, the hospital offered a feeling of tranquility that was the antithesis of the treatment center where he worked. He thought the setting could be a worthy place to read and write on his lunch break. As he was about to rejoin the main road again, he noticed a worker walking alongside a patient, slowly driving his scooter along one of the walking trails. Awkwardly, he waved at the two, but neither seemed to notice.

He thought, Leave it to me to visit a Rehab Center when I have nobody there to see. Unbeknownst to Bill, that would only be the case for a little longer.

CHAPTER 6

WHAT HAD STARTED as a spur-of-the-moment decision had become a ritual, a brief respite from the heaviness that often cloaked the MPF in dense fog. While they were both healthcare facilities separated by a mere ten-minute drive, the similarities ended there. Bill had no responsibilities at Bryn Wood Rehab. He was a spectator, a man without a name, without a backstory.

He had made a few visits before discovering a couple of benches facing the far side of a koi pond, a series of tall evergreen trees framing them. A ghostly, high-pitched hum emanated from the branches as the wind passed. The discarded pine needles sat in layers beneath, partially covering the benches. Having forgotten his novel, Bill was pleased he had a copy of the local newspaper, *The Mill*, in his bag. Generally dominated by the results of local high school sporting contests and people trying to pawn their "antiques," it seldom reported anything interesting. Despite the droll and predictable journalism that graced its pages, Bill often skimmed it just the same. As a bonus, the paper served well as a brush as he made quick work of the needles covering what he had decided was now his domain.

About 150 feet in diameter, the oval pond was surrounded by cattails. Not being a green thumb and having no land to garden at his townhouse, he could only identify the yet-to-bloom coneflowers and black-eyed Susans that hugged half of the pond's perimeter. A fountain in the pond's center spurted multiple symmetrical arches several feet into the air. The splashes radiated outward, pushing small waves toward the pond's edges. Directly across from him was a large deck that butted out several feet over the pond. The water disappeared under the structure, making the water feature appear more extensive than it was. The deck was well maintained, as it was a frequent stopping point for patients and therapists. Regardless of the method—scooter, wheelchair, walker, or cane—all the inhabitants seemed to use the tranquil setting.

On more than a few occasions, Bill watched as residents tossed small pieces of bread into the water, creating a disturbance incongruous with what only seconds earlier had been a tranquil scene. Several fish would rush toward the offering, their heads fully visible as they broke the surface, an almost cartoonish mass of mouths opening wide, begging for their share. While chaotic, Bill noted the fish did not seem to be aggressive with one another, similar to how a hoard of commuters may crowd the subway platform with an unspoken understanding that those closest to the doors when the train rolls to a stop have won first rights to any available seats.

One day, Bill noticed a gentleman across the pond. He sat in a wheelchair under a beach tree several yards from the deck at the pond's edge. The man sported a beard dominated by gray patches, except for his chin, which had a patch of white as if it were a birthmark. The odd random red hair poked through the forest of gray. The crow's feet had long since settled along the edge of his deep blue eyes, eyes that, unlike the rest of the man, had not aged. They briefly met each other's gaze. While he couldn't quite put his finger on it, his eyes revealed an odd blend of sadness and confidence. As part of his training interpreting nonverbal behavior, Bill had come to rely upon the shift of a shoulder, the avoidance of eye contact, the shuffling of feet, or the twirling of fingers as much as a person's words.

The old man scanned the trees, attempting to locate the chirping, which seemed to be coming from a cardinal. His forehead had three definitive, nearly parallel lines. The one in the middle became more prominent as he squinted to locate the song's origin. His white hair streamed from the back of his John Deere hat, stopping short of his shoulders. He wore a blue button-down shirt covered by a light sweater vest. His slacks, one size too big, were held in place by a belt that used the last hole or a new one punctured into the leather. His brown leather shoes were scuffed and in need of polish. The antique large silver watch on his wrist appeared to match his age. After briefly attempting to locate his feathered friend, his eyes returned to the pond. A giant koi in the pond surfaced, showing off its bright orange and red splotches. The random pattern made it look like two buckets of paint were dumped over its back. Even one of its eyes had traces of orange in the cornea.

Seeing Dr. Taggart mesmerized by the fish, the old man leaned slightly forward in his chair. Without taking his eyes off the fish, he said in a low but clear voice, "They call them living jewels." He leaned back in his chair and made eye contact with Bill. The mannerisms of the older man made it hard to tell if a response was being elicited. The old man broke the brief silence.

"You know they live forty years or more. It's funny because you can pick them up right out of the water. They don't seem to have any sense of danger." He broke an unsalted saltine in half and released it into the water as if he were throwing a Frisbee or attempting to skip a stone. A flurry of fins splashed at the water's surface, making it difficult to see who captured the meal. Just as quickly, the fish resumed their slow glide near the water's surface in a way that suggested there were no winners or losers, no ill will from those who did not seize the opportunity. Bill imagined that could be one of the reasons for their longevity and something he could try to emulate.

"You don't say," Bill replied. "They are beautiful."

"I've seen you here before. Pretty sure you don't work here. You visiting a patient?"

Bill considered lying since it was a bit weird that he frequented a rehab where he had no ties.

"Umm, no, I just come here sometimes on my lunch break."

Bill felt embarrassed, wishing he'd trusted his instinct to make up a story.

"Huh, must have a stressful life to find solace in watching a bunch of washed-up, decaying old fogies tossing stale bread into a pond."

Bill smiled. He wasn't far off.

"My name is Chuck." The older man tipped his cap.

"Nice to meet you, Chuck. I'm Bill. Bill Taggart."

"You work at the psychiatric center?"

"How did you know that?"

Chuck pointed towards his waist and said, "Your badge. Can't make it out, but it's the only institution or company in these parts."

Bill blushed. "Of course."

He was impressed with the man's eyesight. The glasses hanging from his vest pocket must have been only for reading.

"I'm a psychologist. I just come here for some peace on my lunch break."

"Knowing your occupation, it makes sense. Seen my share of shrinks over the years. Wish I could say they helped."

Chuck said it in such a way that it did not come across as judgmental, as if he were reading a fact from the almanac.

"I hear ya. Sometimes, I wonder how much it helps."

"Admirable work either way." He tipped his hat again.

"Well, gotta get back. It was nice meeting you . . ."

The old man paused momentarily, searching his memory for Bill's name. "Bill," he said while pointing back at Bill. "Yes, of course.

My legs no longer work so great, but my mind is still sharp. Just never been good with names."

Bill chuckled. "Me neither, Chuck. It was nice meeting you."

Chuck nodded, spun his chair, and headed toward the building. Dr. Taggart glanced at his cell phone. Time to get back, he thought.

CHAPTER 7

AS BILL RETURNED from his break, he heard some excited chatter coming from room four. The door was open a few inches, and he decided to check to see what was happening. Upon peering in, he saw sixteen-year-old Steven Bishop. The psychiatrist had been working on getting his meds right for over two weeks with little success. Upon looking at Steven, one could quickly draw the wrong conclusions about his health. Standing at six feet, he was skinny, but his muscle tone was starting to catch up with his lean physique. It had made him a two-sport star in baseball and football and was already garnering the attention of college scouts. Like so many others in the Rust Belt, Steven came from a broken home with broken hopes. He spent most of his formative years with five siblings and a single mother working two jobs. His deadbeat father rarely made good on his court-ordered child support payments. The authorities often did not know his whereabouts as he seemed to blow whichever way the wind was strongest at the time, more often than not into fast drugs and loose women. His father only recently resurfaced when he caught wind of his son's potential future.

The under-reported norm was Steven's mother: strong, independent, and loving of her children. Steven's mother managed to keep Steven and his siblings away from the many temptations of drugs and violence that plagued the area. Steven was a nearly straight-A student. On occasion, Steven would look at his friends out on the streets doing what they wanted without so much as a word from principals or parents and wondered from his bedroom window why he was not with them. His mother reminded him that his way out and hope for a better life was through education. Deep down, she knew better. There was little chance he would get a sizeable academic scholarship, and she knew she was on borrowed time before his younger siblings picked up on that. Her carrot would be gone, and there would be little to keep them from being swept downstream by the flood of temptation.

It frustrated her that she could not point to herself as an example of the benefits of hard work; working two jobs, she still could not provide for her family and remained dependent on food stamps and the WIC program. Nothing aggravated her more than the talking heads who liked to paint a picture of people experiencing poverty as lazy and unwilling to pull themselves up by their bootstraps. Each time she handed in food stamps at the store, she forfeited a piece of her pride along with them.

She knew Steven's best hope was a full ride to college on an athletic scholarship. Even his deadbeat father recognized that and ensured he stayed on the periphery, ready to swoop in if and when he saw personal gain. Everything looked very promising until the final four games of the football season. Steven started to lash out at coaches and teammates for incomprehensible and trivial reasons. During his most recent game, he was reminded to get his mouth-piece before returning to the field. He responded by slamming his helmet on the ground and kicking it a good ten yards.

What he said next shocked the coaches; even the adolescent football players stared in disbelief, absent the expected immature response of laughter. There was no ridicule, just a stunned sideline.

"I knew you were in on it. You trying to control me with your fucking messages through that thing. I won't wear it. I don't care if your God says I have to. I can't keep building the tower. You build the fucking tower, why don't you do something?"

Three hours later, Steven was at the MPF. Only a day before, he was in the cafeteria, riding his friend about shaving his jersey number into the side of his head. During his admission, Bill asked his mother how long he had been hallucinating. *Hallucinations*, the word set in like a poison taking effect. No, it could not be. Her son, who had fought off so much adversity and stayed the course, was now being brought down by an invisible force and one that she did not know how to fight. She rolled her fingers as if trying to squeeze the life out of the air. It was not long before the tears started to flow.

"No, Doctor. He has done everything right, everything. He has sacrificed so much. You need to fix this. Do you understand me? You need . . ." Her voice gave out to tears, congestion, and exhaustion.

"I am going to do my best to help your son. I promise you that. I know you are tired and a bit shell-shocked, but I need to get as much information as possible so I can provide the best solution."

"Solution . . . so he can be fixed?" asked Steven's mother with a moment of hope that just as quickly was overtaken by more tears.

"There are many things in our arsenal we can use to help," said Bill. Of course, there was no guarantee that any of them, in isolation or combination, would provide the key to unlock the door that would lead out of his personal purgatory.

"When did you notice this . . . I mean, when did you first start noticing odd behavior from Steven?"

"I work two jobs . . . I-I . . ." She managed to fight off another avalanche of tears. "I see him staring off into space sometimes, but I thought he was just daydreaming. He left the last five answers on his chemistry test blank last week. He didn't even guess. I figured he was tired. He said he was not feeling well. I knew I shouldn't have pushed him so hard with school and all the pressure of school and sports. He is only sixteen. He never got to be a kid. It was not fair of me to put so much on him. He has had to be the man of the house and look after his younger siblings. He has a heart of gold, and now I have made him sick. I just wanted him to escape all of this." She let out a big sigh.

This was one of the two extremes often seen by Bill: parents who blamed themselves for their children's situation and those who did not know or even care. Being a parent was unfair. Years of schooling, advice on handling your financial portfolio, and making a perfect knot when putting on a tie were all covered. There was no handbook for raising a child or definitive answers like those in mathematics. How do you know when to rescue your children versus letting them fall and get back up? Sometimes, helping can hurt more than the fall itself.

"It's not your fault. I can assure you," Bill said.

His mind temporarily pictured *Good Will Hunting* when Robin Williams said something similar to Matt Damon and hoped she did not make the same connection.

"You should know that this is a chemical, biological illness. It has been there all along. It is not uncommon for it to surface in the late teen years. There is nothing you could have done outside of what step you have made just now. You got him into treatment."

Seeing Bill peeking in through the door, Steven excitedly showed him a photo from the *Cosmopolitan* magazine he was holding.

"Hey Doc, did I ever show you a picture of my girlfriend?"

The picture was of a scantily clad, beautiful brunette with the headline, "10 Ways to Make Your Man a Tiger in the Bedroom."

"I see," said Bill. "Hey, why don't you put some clothes on, Steven? Can you do that?"

"Sure, Doc, sure." He leaped from the bed to the floor.

"Hey, I gotta game later today against our archrivals. You coming?"

"We'll see, Steven. We'll see."

There was no game in Steven's immediate future, if at all, but it showed that brief rays of the sun of his reality could occasionally break through the clouds. Bill began to rifle through a catalog of drugs in his mind, trying to assemble a new recipe to discuss with his psychiatrist. He continued eliminating drugs and combinations, and as the list began to shrink, he could feel his anxiety rise.

CHAPTER 8

AFTER ENJOYING a long weekend binging streaming services and catching up on his reading, Bill pulled into his reserved parking spot at the MPF. He felt obligated to use it despite the spot being closer to the children's unit than his own. He had hoped that an extra day away from the center would have refreshed his attitude, returning some much-needed optimism. Any such benefit, had it existed, vaporized upon entering the unit.

Bill checked the whiteboard to get the lay of the land and to see who, if anyone, was on room restrictions. He proceeded to his office, sat in his chair, and took a deep breath. It was time for his session with Kyle, an event Bill looked forward to as much as going to Sunday school as a child, which is to say, not at all. He half hoped that seeing his name on the board was a mistake and that maybe one of the MHTs had forgotten to erase it. It wouldn't be the first time. Bill glanced at the clock opposite his desk. Kyle was now ten minutes late. He could feel his anger rising as ten became fifteen and fifteen became twenty. Fuck it, he thought. I'm not budging; I am not chasing down the little shit. After half an hour passed, he lost his nerve to wait him out. It was clear he wasn't planning on attending.

Bill went down the hall, his fury growing with every step. Kyle's door was slightly ajar. Bill knocked softly.

"It's open," Kyle said. Even his casual response irked Bill.

"Kyle, were you planning on showing up for our session?" Bill was sure it was the most unintentional rhetorical question he'd ever spoken.

Kyle was lying on the bed, folding a paper airplane, fittingly out of one of the brochures on Oppositional Defiance Disorder. Kyle responded under his breath, "Busy." He then shifted his body such that Bill was no longer in his peripheral vision.

The exchange jettisoned Bill back to high school. He was sitting in study hall working on some chemistry homework, attempting to complete it well before the due date. Unlike most of his peers, who used the hour to catch up on wasting time, he used the period to get things done early. He was interrupted by Colton walking through the door. Bill remembered how odd it was, given that it was already fifteen minutes into the period and Colton did not have a study hall. He wondered where he had been during that time and where he was supposed to be. As usual, he was doing a poor job executing his mother's request to keep an eye on his brother and report back. Colton pulled up a seat.

"Whatcha working on, nerd?" Colton excelled at combining questions with insults.

"Nothing." Bill closed his book, knowing that his productive time had passed. Colton began drawing something on the desk with his number two pencil, which was finally being put to use.

A couple of minutes later, Colton's English teacher appeared at the door. "Colton! Why aren't you in my class? Let's go."

Colton said nothing. He did not make eye contact. He simply raised his open hand in her direction. His English teacher froze, incredulous at the lack of respect. He shooed her away, providing the ultimate insult without uttering a word.

Bill felt embarrassed. He wasn't sure for whom. He only knew he wished he could disappear. Making matters worse, as would sometimes be the case, he would have the same teacher two years later.

He found himself trying to shed the reputation he was assigned by association. His resentment toward his brother grew the more he found himself digging out of the holes placed before him.

Bill had reached his breaking point with Kyle. While he recognized this was partly due to transference from his relationship with his brother, his frustration won the day.

"If you like your bed so much, why don't you stay there? I'm putting you on room restriction."

"You can't do that," Kyle exclaimed. "Take a look at my points sheet. That's only my first warning."

Bill walked over to the dresser, grabbed the wrinkled behavior tracking sheet, and circled both warnings.

"There. Now you are on restriction."

"You can't do that, asshole."

"Can't I?" Bill said. "Look, if you want to waste my time, that is one thing, but I'll be damned if you are going to impact other people's treatment."

Kyle was fuming—not because he was quarantined to his room; he preferred it. His only concern was that he would not be permitted to go on smoke breaks. Bill had removed one, if not the only, effective carrot in controlling behavior on the unit. It was an acceptable irony: a treatment center using a drug as a motivator.

As Kyle's discharge date approached, Bill had a choice. He could recommend that he be transferred to a two-month-long residential treatment program for troubled teens or return him to juvenile detention. Bill slumped into the loveseat in his office and stared at his official letterhead. He rolled the pen between his fingers, a useless skill he'd picked up over the years. Staring out the window, he watched as a snow squall passed through. While it looked impressive, he knew it would barely leave a trace upon its exit. It was not unlike Kyle's stay at the MPF: all bark and little bite. He put pen to paper, keenly aware of the power he held in his hand. He believed Kyle was unlikely to change his ways without a shock to his system.

"Hello, Dr. Taggart," said Barbara, peeking into his office. Mesmerized by the thick white flakes now exploding in intensity, Bill was caught by surprise.

"Hi, Barb. Sorry about that. Was somewhere else for a moment."

"Hopefully, far away from here." She smirked. "So, what's the verdict?" Barbara asked.

"Verdict?"

"Kyle's fate."

"Oh, just writing it up now." He angled the notepad toward Barbara.

"I see." Barbara's tone made it clear she was not on the same page.

"You disagree?"

"Maybe I do, but you're his doctor," Barbara said.

"Come on, don't give me that. You're never shy about speaking your mind. Now you choose to go quiet?"

"Fine." Barbara took a seat on the couch across from him. "Look, we both know the kid is kind of a dick. But if you send him back to detention, you pretty much doom any chance he has to turn things around. That place will just make him angrier and harder."

Bill rebutted, "But it could also scare him straight. He did nothing here to help his case. His participation in the group was practically nonexistent, and it would be generous to say he shared a paragraph's worth of relevant content with me. What has he done to deserve another chance?"

"I can't argue with that on paper. He may never turn things around. But if our job is to help, maybe it's less about what these kids are owed and more about our responsibilities to put that aside and give them the best chance, whatever that may be."

"And you think some tough love won't give him the best chance?" Bill dug in his heels.

"I don't know, Doctor. I think he may not be ready to change. He is still a kid. I guess I believe that nine times out of ten, mercy is a better serum than punishment. I realize it's easy for me to say. I didn't have to deal with him as much as you, and I don't have to make the call."

Barbara stood and put her hand on Bill's shoulder.

"I'm going to start prepping the med cart."

The doctor put down his pen and peered back out the window. The squall had stopped.

CHAPTER 9

AFTER ANOTHER NIGHT of limited sleep, Cassandra Ripley pulled into the nondescript strip mall in search of the comfort of a simple cup of coffee. Its dependability starkly contrasted with the people who seemed to come and go from her life, sharing moments of intimacy in the night only to be followed by a quick exit in the morning. She sometimes wondered whether their brief presence was merely an apparition or the contrails of a dream.

The coffee shop stood out from the rest of the tenants, its faux stone and stucco front with distressed bone white shutters contrasting with the typical gray vinyl siding, large rectangular windows, and automatic doors of its neighbors. The entryway was a gate like those found on a western ranch. Along the top, the words "The Crescent Café" were burned into the wood in the style of a cattle brander. A tin, pale-yellow crescent moon with a mischievous grin and a winking eye was nailed at the end. A large oak barrel, which doubled as a trash can, sat against one post while a wagon wheel, missing a few spokes, was bolted to the other. She took note of the poster board fastened to the door with "Help Wanted" written in black Sharpie. Someone had opportunistically stuck stickers to the free space on the sign, advertising who knows what.

She'd recently started taking courses again, this time at Copper State University. Despite having a modest safety net from the insurance policy that became hers when she turned twenty-one, she made an earnest effort not to rely on it for fear that it would not be there when she most needed it. She dipped into it once when she first attended college and again last month when she finally decided to return. She let it sit in low-risk, interest-bearing mutual funds to grow like a slow tumor. Yet, the hours she worked at the student bookstore were insufficient to cover her condo payment. It couldn't hurt to inquire about weekend hours at the coffee shop. She figured it could double as a place to study. Entering the café, she was assaulted by the pleasant aroma of ground beans and freshly baked croissants. It dawned on her that she never felt sad in such a setting. Several dark oak tables were marked with natural, deep, irregular grooves, each surrounded by wooden benches and chairs. Their unique and uneven surface was a nod to the distressed theme of the place. There was an inviting, weathered, burgundy leather couch in front of a gas fireplace and a steampunk glass coffee table adorned with coffee beans sealed within the glass mold.

At one table, an older man with a shiny bald spot and surrounding streaks of white hair dealt cards to other seniors—three men and two women. They carried themselves with a confidence that suggested they were regulars. She imagined they must have been from the retirement community behind the shopping center. It seemed like a solid business plan as it offered an escape for the two-hundred-plus elderly that called it home. Two girls appeared to be working on a school assignment at an adjacent table. One wore an odd mismatch of summer and winter clothing, complete with camo shorts, purple Chuck Taylors, and a black sweatshirt accompanied by a gray scarf. The other donned a long-sleeved concert shirt with "Circle Jerks" on the front and another long-sleeve tee tied around her waist. Her jeans had too many holes to be from wear and tear. Long strands of thread hung from the open space around the knees.

Walking up to the counter, Cassie was greeted by a barista with enough ear piercings on both ears to trigger TSA alarms at the airport more than thirty miles away. She flashed a genuine smile, and her blue eyes sparkled, a sharp detour from the message transmitted by her nose ring and dyed pitch-black hair.

"What can I get for you?" the barista asked, her smile stretching even further.

"Um, can I get a cappuccino and a slice of the berry pound cake to go?"

"Sure, will that be all?"

"Yes, I think so," Cassie said, scanning her phone to make the payment. She returned her phone to her bag and followed the barista to the cappuccino machine. "Actually, there is one more thing. I saw a 'help wanted' sign. Are you still hiring?"

Without responding but indicating she heard the question, the barista walked to the back and quickly returned with a sheet of paper, handing it to Cassie with a blue Bic missing its cap. Cassie was surprised to see it was just a blank piece of paper. Seeing her confusion, the barista informed her that she had no idea where the applications were, adding that she would be surprised if they even existed.

"Just put your name, email, cell phone, and, I guess, the hours you're available. I'll let the owner know you stopped in, but if it were up to me, I'd hand you an apron today." Looking back at the stack of mugs waiting to be washed, she added, "We could use the help."

The café had only one other worker, who was busy wiping down tables. The barista handed Cassie her cappuccino, directing her to the nook where they stored the cream and sugar. Cassie was pleased to see a little heart with a smiley face in the foam. In her experience, such a touch usually correlated with the coffee's quality. Taking a sip, her theory was reconfirmed.

Cassie slid the paper with her contact information to the barista. "Thanks much," said Cassie as she walked toward the exit, ready to bite into her pound cake.

"Have a good day," the barista said, her head down, cleaning the machine.

Cassie made the ten-minute drive back to her condominium, stopping at the entryway to collect her mail from the community mailboxes. Her unit was on the second floor of a two-story building. It was new construction, modern, and had a small footprint compared to the other properties in the area. It was one of the selling points when she conducted her search early last summer.

Upon walking through the door, the light in the foyer flicked on, a slight touch that was greatly appreciated for those times when she entered carrying a few bags of groceries. She dumped her keys on the end table beside her couch and scanned her mail: junk, junk, junk. But the last piece of mail gave her pause. It appeared to be handwritten with no return address. She opened it. As expected, it was more junk mail disguised in a way that made the recipient open it out of fear of missing something important. She dumped the mail in a blue recycling bin she kept by the door next to the coat rack that was mainly bare save for her winter coat and a couple of umbrellas, which, based on her track record, would soon be left on a train or park bench somewhere.

Living alone, Cassie rarely saw the point in using her stove. Her freezer, more congested than the fridge, was full of Lean Cuisines, orange sherbet, and bags of microwaveable vegetables.

She grabbed left-over penne vodka from the previous night's takeout and put it in the microwave. While waiting for it to heat up, her cell vibrated against the small granite kitchen island.

"Hello?"

"Hi, can I speak with Cassandra?" the voice inquired.

"Cassie, that's me," Cassie said, sounding more annoyed than she intended.

"It's Shayna Thompson. I own the Crescent Café. I understand you were looking for a job."

"Yes, actually, I am going back to school. I have a part-time job but am looking for additional hours if you have any openings."

She always made a point to say she was going back to school. Since she was approaching thirty, most people assumed she was pursuing her master's rather than still working on finishing the undergraduate degree she abandoned so many years ago. To her surprise, people seldom inquired further, saving her from having to tell them she lacked a degree. Purposely vague, her résumé referenced her Copper State University program of study with a single start date. There was no mention of a degree, but she hoped some employers would assume she had graduated from how it was presented. She had completed just shy of three years' worth of credits before dropping out. Her fault was not with stopping but instead deciding to start in the first place. At the time, it was simply an effort to keep moving, to put her past in her rearview as quickly as possible. It took her a couple of years to understand that no matter where she went or the cacophony of distractions around her, she could not escape herself and the memories that took residence between her ears.

"Do you have any experience?" asked Shayna before stopping herself. "You know what, doesn't matter. When can you start?"

"Next weekend," Cassie said.

"Great! Stop in at 9:00 a.m. on Saturday, and we can go through some things. Oh, and by the way, on Thursdays, Fridays, and some weekends, we host an open mic night, and a couple of Saturday nights a month, we have local singer-songwriters play. Are you OK working a double on those days if needed?"

"Absolutely."

"Great, then we'll see you on Saturday. Bye now."

Cassie hung up the phone. Despite only being a part-time job, she saw it as a sign that maybe things were starting to turn around for her. Retrieving her meal, she poured herself a glass of pinot grigio from her boxed wine and moved to her familiar spot on the couch. Turning on the satellite radio, she kicked off her Uggs as the familiar chorus of Edie Brickell's "Circle" kicked in.

CHAPTER 10

CASSIE DISCOVERED SHE liked working at the Crescent much more than at the campus bookstore. She knew she could add hours at the café but wanted to keep her other position for the discount on schoolbooks and supplies. Cassie liked all her coworkers but grew especially fond of Abby, who had given her the pseudo-application. Despite being only twenty-three, they seemed to have much in common. Abby followed a similar path in that she was on and off again with her education. The difference was that Abby seemed more patient and comfortable with uncertainty. She would tell Cassie that she did not know what she wanted to do with her life but figured she had plenty of time. When she first dropped out of college, Cassie felt like a loser, and while she knew she was having trouble focusing on academics, not being in school seemed to validate her uncle's disparaging remarks. Maybe he was right that she would not amount to anything. Looking at her résumé from the last ten years, it was hard to argue.

After years of working as a cashier and attending twice-weekly therapy, Cassie finally felt whole enough to return to school to finish what she started. She liked to think that going back had nothing to do with proving her uncle wrong. She knew she would always carry some guilt for what happened so many years ago, but she hated the thought of him having power over her choices now that he was out of her life.

Abby was infinitely more social than Cassie. She seemed to lack Cassie's insecurities. Cassie could see how it sometimes led to the occasional foot-in-mouth situation for Abby, but the positives of such an approach far outweighed the negatives. Occasionally, Abby's boyfriend would stop by. He worked at a pharmaceutical company downtown. Abby tried explaining his job to Cassie, who did not fully understand and lacked the desire to inquire further. He was a nice guy enamored with Abby and her free spirit, natural, makeup-free beauty, and quirky facial expressions.

Cassie was most comfortable interacting with the poker-playing senior citizens who frequented the Crescent every weekend, taking the time to sit with them during lulls in customer traffic. She listened intently to the stories they would tell of their youth. It reminded her of her grandfather, who was being treated at Bryn Wood Rehab following his stroke. There was nobody she loved more in the world. She made sure to visit him whenever possible, always bringing him goodies from the café, sometimes sharing some of the poker players' stories. Being of a similar age, she thought he could relate. Like her grandfather, one of the regulars had fought in the Korean War. Not surprisingly, her grandfather did not recognize the name. He was in the Air Force, whereas her grandfather was in the infantry. When either of them told her stories of the war, she was at her most focused, shutting out the world around her, hanging on to every word. Having lived through so much trauma, hearing how they lived in constant fear, not only for their safety but for their brothers in arms, it reminded her how there was always someone who had it worse.

She occasionally heard the regulars gossiping about some of their neighbors from the retirement community. It always made her smile, realizing they were not much different than a bunch of high school kids chatting away about classmates.

In particular, Cassie loved the singer-songwriter nights. There was little work to do after she showed the concertgoers to their reserved seats, leaving her to stand behind the counter to take in the harmonies and turn off her racing mind. It was its own kind of therapy, another perk of working at the café.

CHAPTER 11

A FEW DAYS LATER, Bill returned to the pond. As had become a habit, he swept the pine needles from the bench before taking a seat. He stared into the water, watching the koi casually make laps around the edge. Occasionally, without any apparent reason, a few koi would change directions, leading some to follow. This pattern repeated, guiding Bill into a trance.

"Sea-gills," he heard a voice say from across the pond. It took him a few seconds to place the source of the comment.

"Excuse me?" Bill said.

"Sea-gills." Chuck pointed at the circling fish. Seeing Bill look confused, he clarified. "Sea-gills. You know, like seagulls, only the fish version." Not wanting to leave any doubt what he meant by the analogy, he elaborated. "They are true scavengers, waiting for a bunch of broken old people like me to feed them saltines or pieces of Wonder Bread. Don't get me wrong, they are beautiful. I see why they call them living jewels, but they seem ill-equipped to make it in the real world. I guess it's just foreign to me." Making eye contact with the doctor now, he touched the tip of his John Deere cap and nodded. "Sorry to bother you. Don't mean to interrupt your peace."

"No, that's OK," Bill said, indicating he was happy to engage further.

"Psychologist, eh?" Chuck said, scratching the gray-and-white stubble on his chin. "Not easy work, I imagine."

"No. No, it's not," Bill said.

Chuck repositioned the brim of his cap again before expertly navigating the pathway to join Bill. "At least what you are doing is admirable. At least you are helping people. Just like the people here. Not enough helpers in the world. Easier to tear things down than to build them up. I should know."

Bill wondered what he meant by the last comment, which almost seemed to leave his lips unintentionally as if the words betrayed him.

"I guess so. I don't know how much we help, though," Bill said. "It's more like we make a dent. The more time passes, the more dents we make, but that's all. It's hard to say how many dents are needed to break through. Once patients leave, we rarely find out what happens to them . . . well, except for the ones that don't . . ." He left the thought unfinished.

No elaboration was needed. Being no stranger to death, Chuck knew what that meant. "In any case, you have my respect."

"Thanks," Bill said, slightly uncomfortable with the attention.

Chuck's crow's feet grew as he squinted in the midday sun. Despite being restricted to a chair, he looked healthy. His thick gray eyebrows, high cheekbones, and line of wrinkles across his forehead made him look wise. He had an aura that suggested he was at peace with himself. His deep blue eyes remained youthful, but Bill sensed pain lived just beneath the surface. The older man placed his hands on his knees and lightly kneaded them. He had large hands, more considerable than expected for his skinny, five-foot-eight-inch frame. Bill noticed Chuck's right hand bore an uneven diagonal scar, which started in the fold between his index finger and thumb and ended halfway across the back side of his hand. He figured the fault was indicative of a poor stitch job long ago.

An aide approached from the path leading from a side door of the rehab facility. The younger woman, likely a recent graduate, smiled at Bill as she approached Chuck. She had long, blonde hair that curled as it reached her neckline. She had dark hazel eyes and a round, kind face that seemed fitting for her chosen position.

"You about ready?" she asked as she approached Chuck's chair.

"Would it matter if I wasn't?" said Chuck in a tone that made it clear he was messing with her rather than being genuinely obstinate.

"No, I guess not. You could always lock the brakes on the wheels if you want to stop me." She giggled.

Chuck smiled, enjoying the harmless game of cat and mouse.

As she grabbed the handles and turned him around to head back into the facility, Chuck cupped his hand around the edge of his mouth. "Hey, seeing that you have adopted this place, tell you what: I will give you access to my pond if you agree to bring me a coffee next time you come." With his back now facing Bill, there was no reply necessary.

Not knowing Chuck well, Bill was not sure if he was being serious. Bill reached into his leather briefcase and pulled out his turkey sandwich and thermos, which, fittingly, held hot coffee. He quickly finished his lunch, saving a small piece of the bread to toss into the pond. A swirl of activity rushed toward the offering, several mouths breaking the surface, opening and closing at the air. Some fish missed the target and ended up sucking the side of other fish. Others were pushed beneath the surface by larger fish bolting in from behind. Bill had no idea who won the competition. As he put back his thermos and Ziploc bag, he nodded, smiled, and said, "Sea-gills."

CHAPTER 12

ON HIS NEXT VISIT, Bill was happy to see Chuck sitting at the edge of the pond. A light, misty rain was falling, making tiny circles on the pond's surface. The fish broke through as if searching for food gifted from the sky. Curiously, several koi were suctioning the edge of the pond. Bill couldn't be sure but imagined they were trying to eat the worms brought to the surface by the saturated earth.

Bill waved across the pond to the older man, who returned the greeting with the familiar touch of his hat's brim. Bill walked past the bench where he usually sat and circumnavigated the pond, crossing the wooden arched bridge. A small stream ran under it into a smaller pond designed to handle overflow. He approached Chuck, revealing a cup of Dunkin' Donuts coffee in each hand.

"My penance to use your pond," Bill said, extending his left hand to Chuck, who looked surprised.

"I was kidding when I said that."

"I know that. Guess you don't want it," Bill said, pulling back the offering.

"I didn't say that," Chuck said. He reached out, revealing that the scar on his hand continued across most of his palm. Chuck nodded as he clutched the cup.

"Oh, yeah," Bill said as he fished through his fleece jacket pockets, revealing individual creamers. "Cream? Sugar?"

"Just creamer, please," Chuck said.

"Good, because I forgot the sugar. So, you don't have coffee here?"

"No, we have coffee, if you want to call it that." He dumped three half-and-halfs into his coffee. "Problem is that they have those non-refrigerated individual flavored creamers and that powdered crap you mix in your coffee, which is more like parmesan cheese."

"Am I gonna get in trouble for this?" Bill asked.

"Doubt it. I will make quick work of it, just in case," Chuck said, taking another big gulp. Continuing the running joke, he looked Bill straight in the eyes and, with a serious face, said, "You are welcome to my pond anytime, sir."

Bill laughed. "It's a deal then. I will have my attorneys review the contract."

Chuck pointed to a nearby bench on the patio that jutted over the pond.

"Do you want to sit for a moment?"

"Sure." Bill instinctively reached to wheel Chuck over to the patio.

"Not necessary," Chuck said in an assertive but nonabrasive tone. He tucked the coffee in his cupholder and followed Bill onto the patio.

"I can't get the vision of flying koi out of my head ever since you called them sea-gills," Bill said as he rested his hand on the fence's banister.

"Am I wrong?" Chuck asked, taking another gulp of coffee.

"No, I guess not," Bill said, taking another sip.

Chuck made quick work of his drink.

"Hand it over; I will hide the evidence," said Bill, quickly putting the cup back in the Dunkin' bag.

Bill extended his hand.

"Should I call you Dr. Taggart? After all, you put in a lot of time to earn that title."

"I would appreciate it if you didn't."

"Fair enough."

After the two chatted for several minutes, Bill took out his iPhone.

"I need to get back. I have to get some gas before going back to work."

"No worries," Chuck said. The casual phrase seemed odd coming from his lips as if he had heard the lingo from someone and was trying it on for size.

"Tell you what," Bill said. "You want to meet here on Wednesday and Friday for coffee, you know, like a regular thing?"

"I would love that. Don't get many visitors here."

"It's a deal then. See you next week."

CHAPTER 13

BILL COULDN'T PUT his finger on it but was drawn to Chuck. Was it a father-figure thing, considering he had lost his from type 1 diabetes almost ten years ago? He couldn't be sure. Whatever the reason, he felt comfortable in his company. He was sure they could talk for hours if not for other obligations tearing them away. The conversation flowed like wine from an oak barrel, flavorful and voluminous. Even the pauses in conversation lacked the awkward silences that plagued typical interactions, each quiet moment only adding atmosphere to the discussion in the same way short pauses between beats made songs more memorable.

He was running about fifteen minutes late and found himself stepping a bit harder on the pedal than usual. He had been a member of the community long enough to know the stakeout spots for the local police, where he would lay off the gas accordingly. It was a particularly windy day. As he approached the old wooden sign for the treatment center, the cattails around the stormwater collection pool swayed wildly in every direction as if fighting with one another. The occasional gusts were ready-made for dispatching the hats of those lulled into complacency.

After parking, Bill made his way along the path that led to the pond. His heart sagged a bit when he noticed Chuck was nowhere to be found. Bill immediately thought the worst: Had something happened to him? After all, he was in a treatment center for a reason. He just as quickly pushed aside the worry, realizing that the hours spent bathing in the suffering that permeated his profession were clouding his judgment. He delicately positioned the two coffees on the bench, sitting down and crossing his arms to protect himself from the circling winds. The ghostly sounds emanating from the tall conifers around him were louder than usual, creating an eerie symphony. The pattern of the sun's rays danced across the landscape in accordance with the swaying branches. It would have been a warm day if it had not been for the wind's chill.

He had only waited about two minutes before the automatic door opened, and the older man appeared in his chair. More appropriately dressed for the fickle weather, he wore a thick burgundy fleece with tan slacks. His usual John Deere hat was replaced with what appeared to be a military veteran cap. It had the emblem of the Marines and read "Veteran of Foreign Wars." Catching Bill's gaze, he waved to join him at their usual spot on the deck by the pond. As Bill approached, Chuck apologized for being late.

"Don't sweat it. I just got here myself."

He handed him the coffee.

"Careful, it seems hotter than usual. I added the cream myself. Figured I'd save you a step."

Chuck smiled.

"So now I am too old to prep my own coffee?"

"Something like that," Bill said, testing the beverage's temperature on his lips. "So, been meaning to ask you unless it's personal. What are you being treated for?"

Chuck looked over each shoulder and smiled. "I don't see any HIPAA officials around, so it is probably OK. I had a small stroke. If there is such a thing. Believe it or not, I was playing golf. I was on the back nine, sitting in the cart, waiting for the group in front of us to tee off. Weird feeling. Just felt cloudy all of a sudden, like my brain was stuck in the mud. I had no idea what was happening until the left side of my body went limp from the waist down. I think I said 'stroke' to my friend, who was pounding a Rolling Rock in the driver's seat. I can't be sure because I don't really remember. Whatever I said, it got the point across. Or maybe it was the way I said it. Apparently, it came out slurred, and everyone knew I hadn't been drinking."

"That must have been pretty scary," Bill said.

Taking a gulp of coffee, he said, "Maybe for the group around me. I thought maybe I was having a heart attack, which, in retrospect, makes no sense. I just never saw myself as the type to have a stroke. Anyway, I spent a few days in the hospital while they stabilized and monitored my condition, and then I came here." He spread his left arm out as if to emphasize the point. "With the team here, I have regained some of my strength in the left leg. Funny thing is that I think it is now better than my right leg." He put his cup in the holder on his chair and rolled up his right pant leg. His knee was pocked with small scars that circled his kneecap. A large, faded, raised scar ran down the middle of the cap. It was clear he had surgery a long time ago.

Bill had seen his share of scar tissue from knee surgery. At least half the people he knew had gone under the knife for a tear. What caught his attention were the pea-to-quarter-sized uneven indents that randomly patterned the outside of his leg. He had never seen anything like them, but despite his curiosity, in fear of overstepping his bounds, he chose not to ask.

"Damn knee still wakes me up sometimes at night. I swear a gremlin hides under my bed, waiting for me to get into a deep slumber before stabbing me with his little knife."

He reached down and rubbed the outside of his kneecap as if simply mentioning it had led the pain to resurface.

"I am sorry to hear that, but I am glad they are helping you here."

"Me too. Don't wanna be in this chair forever. I can live with a cane, but I feel like the chair is another level of decline. So, where you from?" Chuck asked, pulling his pant leg back down before retrieving his coffee for another sip.

"Originally?" Not waiting for clarification, Bill said, "Philadelphia, well, Horsham really, outside of the city. I grew up there. I got my undergraduate degree at the University of Pennsylvania and then went straight into graduate school in Miami. I lived in a couple of places between there and here, just brief stops for work."

"Where did you go in Miami for your PhD?"

"Actually, it's a PsyD."

"I will pretend that I know the difference," said Chuck, scratching his chin with his free hand.

Bill laughed. "It doesn't matter. I went to Gulf Southern University in Miami. If you say you've heard of it, I will know you're lying."

"Can't say I have."

"It wasn't my first choice, but despite the lack of pay, long hours, and mentally draining work, believe it or not, it is tough to get into a doctorate program for clinical psychology."

"Really? Seems like we could use a lot more of them than we've got." He paused before continuing the thought. "And a lot less of the lawyers."

They both chuckled. Bill gulped the last of his coffee. Chuck followed suit.

The mystery of the scar on his hand gained stature after seeing the damage to his knee. Bill was itching to ask about his military service, as he imagined it would answer many of his questions. He glanced at his phone and thought it was better to leave those questions for another day. It was almost time to go. In truth, Bill was relieved to have the respite, as he was unsure how to approach the topic.

CHAPTER 14

SINCE THEIR FIRST meeting several weeks before, Bill and Chuck had rarely missed one of their lunch dates. Summer had unapologetically elbowed spring out of the way. As was increasingly the case, to both men, changes in seasons were but a flip of the page in a book.

Chuck slowly made his way to the pond. He rested his arms on the deck's railing and gazed at the circling fish. He tossed a handful of the color-enhancing pellets into the water. Were it not for the fishy smell, they could easily have been mistaken for grape nuts cereal. As the offering hit the water's surface, there was a fury of activity. Koi appeared from every direction, concentrating into a mass that seemingly left no water visible between them. The fish on the surface were abruptly pushed out of the water by rapidly surfacing koi from below, resulting in some fish lying on the backs of others. This inevitably created a panic as the fish flopped every which way to find their way back to the safety of the water. When Chuck began spending time at the pond, he thought the fish were underfed and hungry. Within days, he learned they were just gluttons whose appetite could never be satiated. They were programmed to eat, unconcerned by their visual display of desperation. Chuck did not judge them, as he knew all too well what that felt like.

Bill approached, handing a coffee to his friend.

"I changed to iced coffee, given how damn hot it is today. Do you drink iced coffee?"

"I do now," said Chuck, smiling with his eyes. He took a big sip from the straw. "Wow, I never knew what I was missing. That is good!"

"Glad you like it."

Chuck set his coffee on the banister of the deck and tossed the koi one more offering before closing the bag and placing it at his feet. Drops of condensation from the heat had already begun to run slowly down the coffee cup. He grabbed it to take another long sip. As was typical, Chuck wore a thick blue rubber band on his left wrist, the opposite hand of the one that bore the jagged scar. After weeks of their twice-weekly meetings, Bill considered Chuck a friend. He hoped his new friend felt the same way, making it safe to finally seek to satisfy his curiosity. The rubber band would make an excellent segue to what he wanted to know.

Bill dove in headfirst. "Why do you always have a rubber band on your wrist? When I first saw it, I thought it was one of those bracelets for a charity, you know, like for autism awareness."

"Can't say I am all that aware about autism." He pulled the band over his hand and stretched it between his fingers. He alternated between twisting the band and wrapping it around different digits. His playing with the rubber band like an instrument was almost mesmerizing. "I'm guessing you've seen how my hands shake when they're at rest."

"Not really," Bill said, though he had.

"Well, it ain't Parkinson's or anything like that. I have had it ever since I got back from the war. It has gotten worse over the years, and playing with the band keeps the shaking at bay, or at least keeps me from noticing it. You know, like they say about chewing gum while walking."

The mention of war was not surprising. While he often wore his John Deere or Boston Red Sox cap with the classic red pair of socks on the front, he would appear with his US Marines cap on rare occasions.

"Were you in the marines? I, uh, noticed you wear the hat sometimes."

"Yup, joined a few years after the end of World War II. I would have joined for the Big War, but my parents begged me to finish my degree. As soon as I graduated, I joined the military as a lieutenant in the marines. I think it shocked them. I guess they figured I would lose the itch once the war ended and be ready to use my newly earned business degree. They tried to talk me out of it initially but didn't harass me. They realized they couldn't protect me forever and knew how guilty I felt about not joining the Big War. Guilt that they were partially responsible for. Knowing that we were in peacetime, it must have seemed like it was not worth the fight."

"Is uh . . ." Bill paused.

Seeing that he was uncomfortable, Chuck made clear eye contact with Bill.

"Go ahead, ask your questions. I am an open book."

He took another sip of his coffee.

"What war was it? Sorry, like most people who work in social services, I am piss-poor with math. I know I should be able to figure that out from your age."

Chuck laughed.

"Korea."

"Oh, OK. I know that was in the '50s."

"You got it. Do you want to try the bonus round?"

Bill flashed him a sheepish smile.

"Is that how you got the scar?"

"What scar?" Chuck sounded incredulous.

"Um . . . the uh."

"Does it make me a bad person if I enjoy watching you crush the eggshells beneath your feet? I'm just messin' with you."

He rolled the rubber band back over the left wrist. He turned his other hand over to reveal the palm and traced the jagged line that cut across the surface using his index finger. He flipped his hand again and continued tracing to its end point almost midway across the back.

"That's what happens when you grab a machete by the blade. Slices through flesh like butter. Lots of nerves in the hand. Felt like I was holding the sun in the palm of my hand. Not at first, mind you. I was too filled with adrenaline, just trying to stay alive. I changed the angle just enough to keep it from plunging into my stomach. If not for my foxhole buddy, he might have made the second effort count. He hit the Chinese soldier in the side of his head with the edge of a trench shovel. Went down like a sack of potatoes. You could barely make out the left side of his face. It was hard to see where his left eye and nose ended and his lips began. It was like a kid's messy finger painting."

He had the full attention of Bill, who was lost in his words as if transported to a faraway place.

"Funny thing is, not even half an hour before that, we were cursing how damn useless those shovels were against the frozen earth. After that, you can be sure I had nothing but love for that thing."

"That is unbelievable," Bill said.

He suddenly felt small, and the man he had considered a peer only fifteen minutes before seemed to live in rarefied air.

"You said Chinese? Did you mean North Koreans? I thought it was a war between North and South Korea to stop the spread of Communism."

Chuck chuckled. "No, I meant Chinese. Don't worry about it. As it turns out, even the great General MacArthur made the same mistake. Only in his case, it cost many lives."

"I don't follow," Bill said.

"The North Koreans drove well into South Korean territory, well past the thirty-eighth parallel. My battalion and the army were called in to stop their progress. After surprising them with an unexpected water landing at Inchon, we managed to push them back from Seoul with little trouble. They were running scared. It was too easy. I sometimes wonder if things might have been different had they put up a better fight."

He paused to take another few sips of his iced coffee before the ice melted.

"MacArthur could do no wrong after his exploits in WW2. He cast a vast shadow. I never met the man, but I understand he could be intimidating. Anyway, he convinced Truman and the chiefs of staff that we should keep the momentum going and push the North Koreans back to the Yalu River near the Chinese border. Ever heard of the famous phrase from MacArthur that all the GIs would be home by Christmas?"

He could see that his friend had never heard such a phrase. In fairness, it didn't have the same place in history as his famous "I shall return" during the Philippines campaign in the Second World War.

"No . . . well, doesn't matter." Chuck continued. "He convinced everyone that we would reunite North and South Korea. He even held a ceremony declaring victory, handing out medals and doing *Life* magazine interviews while we hiked north toward the Chosin Reservoir on our way to the Yalu River and inevitable victory. There was some concern that Mao and the Chinese might enter the conflict if they believed we threatened to unify the peninsula or, worse yet, continue into Manchuria. Of course, as grunts, we had no idea either way. Most of us doubted it would be as easy as some commanders made it sound. Whatever concerns there were couldn't compete with the arrogance of the decision-makers who were many miles away from the fight. I am lucky that this is but an unwanted souvenir." He glanced at the palm of his hand again.

"Does it still haunt you, I mean, the memories?" Bill asked.

"I suppose I may have had some PTSD, or whatever they called it at the time, but I never got any treatment. After the war, I mostly put one foot in front of the other until I took enough steps to put some distance between the things that happened and the raw emotions that followed. Others weren't so lucky. Some carried it like the sixty-pound rucksack they hauled through the freezing winter marches."

"I can't imagine what that must be like. I mean, as a psychologist, I know all about PTSD treatment, cognitive behavioral therapy, medications, and group therapy. Still, I would be lying if I didn't admit to having some doubt about how that could make a difference against such horror."

"Guess it's easy to see the physical consequences—a missing arm, a mangled eye—but what ruins a fella is the trauma nobody else can see. Worse yet, those who can see can't relate to it, and why should they? War is unnatural, and so are the following rationalizations and conversations. Don't get me wrong, I still have some moments that I believe they call night terrors. In the spirit of show and tell, I've got one more keepsake I can show you."

Chuck temporarily placed his now-empty coffee cup on the ground and began rolling up his right pant leg. He continued methodically until stopping a few inches above his kneecap.

"See there?" He drew an imaginary zigzag in the air from above the knee down the side of his leg and back calf. His leg was pocked with different-sized scars like the markings in a pimento loaf. Some grooves were deep and almost the size of a half-dollar; others were shallow and no more than the diameter of a pea. Some marks had defined edges, while others had no discernable shape or boundary. There was no rhyme or reason for the pattern itself. Despite having never seen a gun wound, Bill instinctively knew that whatever left those marks could not have come from bullets.

"Shrapnel, courtesy of an RGD-33 stick grenade. I managed to dive out of my foxhole, but not before it exploded into a mortar, sending fiery hot fragments into my leg. My unit held a position just west of the Chosin Lake. We had a couple hundred in our division. We took up a strategic position overlooking the lake midway up a mountainside. We dug in as best we could, using a mixture of natural nooks, sticks, small boulders, and snowpack. The ground was frozen solid. It was pitch black and eerily quiet except for the haunting snapping sounds of frozen tree branches that periodically fired deep in the dark woods around us. It was always multiple degrees below zero before factoring in the wind. Men lost toes to frostbite, and hot water froze faster than it could be used. After several nights, we heard some faint chatter down in the valley.

"When the Chinese finally made themselves known, they appeared out of thin air. I will never forget the blaring horns they'd blast as they made their charge. It was so unusual to announce your tactical maneuver that it caused the hair on my neck to stand up. Who is so confident, or worse, so crazy as to make themselves known to the enemy? Naturally, we mowed them down in great numbers, but they kept coming, thousands of Chinese, dressed in attire that was no more suited for the elements than for a quick run down the driveway to retrieve the paper before retreating into one's home. The well-equipped Chinese soldier mostly used an old Soviet Zhongzheng rifle, an antiquated weapon. Some soldiers carried only a tree branch fitted with a knife tied to its end to serve as a bayonet. Other soldiers appeared to have no weapon at all as if their only job was to run behind the line in front of them, ready to retrieve whatever arms they could from their doomed fallen comrades. We would learn later that they had deployed more than one hundred thousand troops into North Korea. In only hours, our offensive switched to a series of rescue missions and complicated retreats. During the day, the corsairs bought us a much-needed respite, allowing us to retrieve our wounded and resupply. But at night, it was just us, the stars above, and, somewhere in the vicinity, an unmovable force hell-bent on wiping us out to protect the perceived threat to their homeland. On the third night of fighting, as was typical, we took shifts watching the line. Like an alarm clock set to an unpredictable time, most of us slept lightly, anticipating the bugle that would mean another seemingly endless push from the enemy. We were surprised by a small group, a reconnaissance team or maybe just some lost soldiers."

Chuck looked down at his feet and took a deep breath.

"Are you OK?" Bill asked. "Maybe we should pick this up again later. I'm not here to stir up bad memories." Bill now felt guilty for having probed in the first place.

"It's OK. Really. I just needed a minute. Sometimes, I swear I can still smell the burning of artillery and the bodies left in its wake." Chuck removed his cap to wipe the sweat from his brow before continuing.

"Unfortunately, a couple of lookouts drifted to sleep, allowing them access to our line from the west. I woke to guttural screams. We desperately scanned into the darkness as if on demand our eyes would rise to the threat, giving us the extraordinary ability to see what could not be seen. Following the direction of the screams on the wind, I could barely make out the shadows moving in the snow. To my horror, in a motion resembling someone trying to dig a fence post, arms rose toward the starless sky before plunging to the earth below. They were bayoneting marines as they slept in their sleeping bags. They must have known it was a suicide mission, as a vengeful mob quickly quieted them.

"That's the thing about combat: it is entirely random. I would not be here if I had been one hundred yards farther west. I think that is where the survivor's guilt comes from. You didn't think much about it till you got home from the war. It took me a long time to be grateful for the miracle of life when so many of my brothers were marked for death."

He took another deep breath and gazed at the koi in the pond.

"I have learned to appreciate the beauty of things, like these guys, but for years, I only saw the darkness in everything."

CHAPTER 15

AS SUMMER TURNED to fall, the two friends managed to fill in most of the essential details that brought them to their current destination. Bill shared his troubled—yet what he thought of as typical—upbringing: the fights between his father and older brother that dominated his teen years, his sibling's struggle with alcohol, and the dents to his brother's self-worth from an endless stream of bullying in school. He never looked for sympathy, knowing that if he threw a rock, he would surely hit someone who had suffered a similar fate. He was cognizant that his tribulations paled compared to his new friend's.

"Are you married? Any children?" Chuck noticed he wasn't wearing a ring but asked anyway.

"No, not even a pet."

"I see. Don't you get lonely?"

Bill smiled. "I never said I didn't have girlfriends along the way. I guess I haven't met the right person, or maybe I'm not the right person. Sometimes, I think working in my field has made me gunshy—not consciously, but I don't know. You see nothing but broken marriages, struggling children, and loss. Maybe I'll get married someday, but when it comes to children, I'm not so sure. I imagine years of watching my parents' marriage hanging on by a thread also didn't help. They were never on the same page after my brother ran into trouble. My father came from a cold upbringing, where staying between the lines was not only expected but demanded. When my brother struggled, my dad reacted harshly, the only way he knew how. On the other hand, my mother coddled him. The more he struggled, the more she hovered. It must have been confusing for my brother to have two completely opposing messages.

"I get it," said Chuck. "In some way, we are all products of our environment. It can take years to see that and even longer to do something about it." He felt sad for his friend. Life without someone to share it with was less rich, or at least it was from his experience.

"What about you? Did you ever tie the knot?" Bill asked.

"Me? Yes, I was married." Chuck gave no indication that he would elaborate.

"And?"

Chuck returned to the combat zone, a place seemingly as poor a fit for romance as anywhere. He rubbed his aching knee as he shared how he met the love of his life.

It was during the war. She was a nurse. While being treated for shrapnel wounds on his leg, he watched her with great interest. Every day, he hoped she would be assigned to his care. Instead, he was teased, only able to watch her attend to his brothers on the opposite side of the room.

She was tall, maybe even taller than him. Her chestnut brown hair was tightly tied in a bun under her nursing hat. She had high cheekbones, a petite nose, and dark, hazel-brown eyes beneath neatly groomed eyebrows. She appeared to wear little to no makeup save for her light red lipstick. Adding makeup would have been a disservice to her natural, beautiful olive complexion. Having little to think about as he waited for his body to heal, he observed her and imagined what she was like and what it would feel like to hold her.

On occasion, she would catch him in mid-gaze. Embarrassed, he would quickly avert his eyes but could never do so before making eye contact. He was sure some gravitational pull made him slow and dumb in her presence. When she entered the room, the ache and sting of his damaged leg disappeared as though she were an analgesic every bit as potent as the morphine he periodically received. The pain would become real again when she left, almost as if on cue.

After a couple of weeks of watching her come and go from his life, he assessed how the nurses were assigned to patients, and it became clear they would never come into contact through natural means. One morning, after having his leg cleaned and the dressing replaced, he leaned over to the nurse and handed her a note folded in a perfect, tight triangle. He nodded toward the target of his affection across the room as she worked on administering an IV.

"Could you please give this to . . . um." He paused, not knowing the name of the object of his affection.

"Katherine?" whispered the nurse.

"Yes, Katherine."

She tucked the note into the front pocket of her uniform. "Are we back in primary school, soldier, passing notes?" She smiled, making it obvious she was only teasing.

"But hopefully, this time, it will work." He smiled back.

"I will put in a good word for you. At least I can tell her how brave you have been in managing your pain."

"I would appreciate it; anything that can throw the balance in my favor."

After finishing the dressing, the nurse moved on to another patient in what had become a never-ending rotation of the wounded.

Chuck paused the story and turned his head, trying to locate a rehabilitation worker. He noticed one of the physical therapists walking from one building to another.

"Excuse me, Eva?"

"Yes, Chuck." Eva stopped and made her way over to Chuck.

"Can you please do me a big favor?"

"That depends on what it is, I guess."

"I have a brown leather bag about the size of a binder on top of my dresser. Would you be so kind as to get it for me?"

Eva looked at her smartphone. "I guess I have a few minutes before my next appointment."

"That's why you're my favorite," Chuck said playfully.

"Sure, Chuck. Until someone else does you a favor."

"How could you say that after all we've been through?" Chuck loved teasing the staff.

"Just imagine our bond if you were actually one of my patients." Eva laughed, walking away.

After several minutes, Eva returned. Chuck unzipped the bag and produced a weathered, slightly yellowed note folded neatly. Bill instantly knew what it was.

"May I?" Bill reached out his hand.

Without saying a word, Chuck handed him his precious possession. If there was any doubt about the level of their relationship, it was no longer a question. Bill carefully unfolded the note. The top section was short and to the point.

I know you don't know me. Just another in an endless parade of the wounded. Normally, I would not seek your attention in such an infantile way, but in my defense, I can't very well walk over to introduce myself to you. With my situation improving, I fear that if I do not take a chance now, I may regret it for the rest of my life. Fighting in a war, wondering if each day will be my last, I have found no patience for the fears and reservations that used to hinder me. I don't know you, but I have watched you from afar and know enough to warrant wanting to know more. I hope you don't mind, but I stuck to the juvenile approach and wrote you a poem. I hope you like it; if not, you can at least laugh with your colleagues at my expense.

How Would I Love?
What would happen if it were true for me?
If I could not hear, touch, nor see
Without my eyes, I could not share
Your beautiful skin and flowing hair
No smile to brighten my day
Fill me with joy upon my stay
And what of these lips if they could not kiss
No hands to run the curve of your hips
No sense of the physical measure
No tickle, no touch, no pleasure
Were my hearing the next to go
There'd be no comforting voice
To help me make a difficult choice
No words of nurture for a dream to mold
No lyrical thought to hold
What would happen if it rang true for me?
I could not hear, touch, nor see
What would remain for love to show
To grasp, define, and help it grow?
And then I recall what was once proclaimed to me
Without one's eyes, it is easier to see
What connects us is something divine
Beyond our space and time
Our hands and hearts exist to show
What, through God, we already know
A bond remains between you and me
One that we can't touch, hear, or see.

Bill refolded the note and handed it back to Chuck. "So, you are a poet too? I feel inadequate. Clearly, it must have worked."

Chuck looked up toward the sky. "It planted the seed. It got me an introduction. In the end, that's all I would need."

Bill's admiration for his friend continued to grow.

"Thanks for sharing that with me."

"It was the beginning of many years of a blessed life. We married a few years after the war and wasted no time starting a family. We had a wonderful daughter. She was smart as a whip, a bit sarcastic like her father, and had an admirable air of confidence. She was always comfortable with following her own path."

An audible sigh escaped from Chuck. "So many great memories until we lost her way too early. What they say about how unnatural it is to outlive your children is true. It is the reverse of nature's commandment. You raise your children trying everything you can to teach them to be a better version of yourself. By sharing your wisdom, you hope to spare them from the same mistakes you made. I think my wife and I did a very respectable job of that. I do. What you cannot do is protect them from things out of your control, just like you cannot avoid your fate when your number is up on the battlefield. I had come to terms with my mortality in the war but could never accept the unjust end to a life that was only beginning."

Bill put his hand on the older man's shoulder.

Chuck leaked a slight smile, appreciating the gesture.

"It happened quickly, or at least that is what we were told. They were killed in a head-on accident. The only survivor was my granddaughter, Cassandra."

As her name left his lips, his eyes swelled, and his hand, still clutching the note he shared, began to shake slightly. The mention of her name took him to another place. It was as if he had entered a dissociative state, temporarily oblivious to the world around him.

The words of Bill brought him back.

"Do you still see her?"

"Who?"

"Your granddaughter?"

"Oh, yes. She visits when she can."

"My friend, I better get back to the office. See you next week?"

"You got it."

CHAPTER 16

WHEN CASSIE WAS a teenager, she learned a painful lesson: inconsequential moments, meaningless footnotes in time, suddenly, without warning, could become incredibly consequential. Something that one minute was destined to become part of overwritten storage would soon become a permanent stain on Cassie's amygdala. This moment for Cassie arrived on a beautiful day in early October. The sun's rays wrapped the earth in a warm blanket at just the right temperature. Leaves offered only subtle hints that they would soon be changing.

The slight fading of green was only notable to a true naturalist. The black-eyed Susans showed no signs of fading, and those who purchased their mums early had only a few weeks of waiting before being rewarded. The warm days were followed by crisp nights, the kind that made your nose cold to the touch. The sound of the PA announcers and half-time bands from the Friday night football games across the valley competed with the din from the last gasps of the summer cicadas. It was a grand time of year. The weather was gorgeous, the apple cider was crisp, and the sunsets were picturesque.

Cassie couldn't say why, but she awoke in a bit of a mood that Saturday. As a typical teenager, her emotions were often a mystery, not only to her parents but also to herself. Being fifteen, she figured it must have been part of puberty. At least, that's how it was explained in her embarrassing middle school health class. Being naturally stubborn, she did not like thinking she was a puppet to her hormones like everyone else her age. She avoided being predictable at all costs. She was the type of person to take the unpopular side of arguments in a school debate or research paper. As a freshman, when they had a model UN in her social studies class, she asked to play the role of North Korea, a country that was not even listed as an option. It was not because she sympathized with their position on the world stage. She simply wanted the challenge of representing the hermit kingdom. The teacher knew better than to argue with her, figuring she would only further dig in her heels.

Her parents would often advise her against always taking the most arduous path. Sometimes, just go for the easy A, they would say. At the same time, like many of her teachers, her parents respected her passion for learning and her willingness to overturn not only small rocks but those that required much greater effort to unearth what lay beneath. To Cassie, tiny details mattered, each deserving attention as part of the larger story. Her papers were meticulously cited, always well beyond the required citations to support an argument. She stacked facts one upon another like the bricks of a fortress wall, impenetrable by opposing theories.

"Are you ready to go?" her father shouted from the bottom of the stairs.

Cassie was not. She had said to give her five minutes—fifteen minutes ago. She was up but sitting at the edge of her bed, scrolling through Facebook, her brain barely processing any of the information that flew by with each stroke of her finger.

"Gimme one minute!" Cassie shouted back.

"Come on, Cassie, you said that like half an hour ago. What's taking so long?"

What was taking so long was that she was in no mood for "FFF"—forced family fun. It had nothing to do with having an adversarial relationship with her parents. They were all remarkably close, never having fallen into the stereotypical separation and resentment that seemed a rite of passage for parent-child relationships during the child's teen years. She was not the type of kid to be embarrassed about being seen in the mall with her parents or feel like a loser that they still had Thursday night family movie nights. Being an only child, her interests at an early age morphed quickly to match the sophisticated ones of her parents.

While most kids would go to the circus or *Disney on Ice*, Cassie was busy with more esoteric ventures. She spent countless hours gazing into her microscope, watching paramecium taken from the pond in the woods behind her house. Her father sat beside her with a book to help identify the mysteries that unfolded in just a few drops of water under a slide. She would recite each finding as she methodically zoomed in and out, moving the slide back and forth, left and right. Her father documented the results in her journal. Rarely, Cassie had her father take a second look to validate what she saw.

Cassie pocketed her phone and descended the stairs. She grabbed her coat from the railing and followed her parents out the garage door.

"You wanna stop by Chick-fil-A on the way?" her mom asked from the front passenger seat.

"Whatever," Cassie said, staring out the window.

"What's the matter, Cassie? Is something bothering you?" her mother asked.

Cassie hated the question because there *was* often something bothering her and because, much of the time, she couldn't identify what it was. There didn't always need to be a reason, she thought, returning to her phone, a habit that served as a placeholder in the same way people would say "um" while making a speech to fill moments of silence.

"Nothing." It was partially true. There was something the matter, but nothing that could be cited, like one of the facts in her research papers. "I guess I am not in the mood to go pumpkin picking. Don't you think I'm a bit old to be still doing that?"

Her mom and dad glanced at one another. She was right, but for them it was less about the activity than just spending time together. She would still be at home for a few more years, but they knew how fast that time would pass, and they wanted to cram as many memories into their mental scrapbook as possible.

"You're probably right. We don't need to go," her father said, trying not to sound dejected.

"We can just grab a bite at the drive-thru."

"OK," Cassie said so quietly that it was unclear if she was talking to herself or replying to her dad.

The Chick-fil-A had only opened six months ago. They went there almost weekly despite it being about twenty minutes from their home.

They ordered the usual three orders of the four-count chicken mini biscuits, a coffee with extra creamers, bottled water, and a lemonade for Cassie. As they exited the parking lot onto the main road, her father looked in the rearview mirror.

"You sure you don't want to go?"

"I'm sure," Cassie said.

Her father turned left back toward home instead of making the right, which led to the farm several miles down the road.

Cassie nibbled at one of her nuggets as she returned to gazing out the window. She felt terrible about disappointing her parents. Only the night before, she was quite agreeable, even if not overly excited, to go to the pumpkin patch.

They pulled back onto Route 82, a four-lane road, two lanes on each side moving in opposite directions. The road was dominated by several traffic lights, with a football-field length between them. Cars simultaneously exited the main street into several strip malls to do their Saturday shopping. The traffic was thickening as the late risers were finally starting their day.

After a few miles, the traffic lights became scattered as the shopping centers were replaced with nondescript warehouses and the occasional sprawling farm dominated with yellow cornstalks as far as the eye could see. The sun was halfway up its arc toward its midday peak. Her father flipped down the visor to block some of the glare and switched on the radio to break the silence. He pushed a few preset buttons before stopping on 103.7 "The Mix." Annie Lennox's "Walking on Broken Glass" played. Having finished his chicken biscuits, her dad tapped his index fingers on the steering wheel, his hands in the standard three and ten position.

They passed by a sign notifying drivers that the right lane was ending and to merge left, the speed limit moving from thirty-five to fifty-five miles per hour. Her father slowly added pressure to the pedal, the four-cylinder Toyota arguing briefly before responding to the command. The single lane entered a period of rolling hills. The pattern created alternating moments of being shielded by the sun's glare to staring straight into it as the vehicle approached each peak. The maple and poplar trees, which sporadically lined the shoulder of the road, flew by, appearing and disappearing out of Cassie's view through the side window. The road's dotted center line, which allowed for passing each way, turned solid in response to the obstructed view from the rolling hills.

It happened as they crested the fourth and final of the hills and began their descent. Unexpectedly, a pickup truck crossed the solid line only a hundred feet in front of their car. Her father instinctively swerved toward the right shoulder, trying to create the required space to distinguish between a near miss and a catastrophic collision.

Technically, his quick response avoided a head-on collision, but only in the official description of the incident. Metal met metal as the front of the F150 truck struck the Toyota where the side of the car meets the front. The front light was obliterated into many pieces; its only remnants were tiny shards that spotted the asphalt like gems as they reflected the sun's rays. The cabin collapsed over her father, pushing the front seat into the back such that there ceased to be a front and back at all. The car spun, doing a complete rotation from the impact until finally coming to a rest. It faced straight ahead as if it could continue driving down the road had it not been a pile of steel, plastic, wires, and foam, with shredded paper from the Chick-fil-A bags sticking out. The front airbags were deployed immediately. As always, they were all wearing their seatbelts. It would not matter. The force of the crash caved in the entire steering column and all but about a foot of the front passenger side. Both Cassie's parents died instantly. They were pinned in the wreckage.

Sirens blared from both directions as ambulances, fire engines, and the local police department raced to the scene. The blue F150 spun two hundred degrees before reversing across the road into a ditch on the opposite side. What was left of the front of the truck pitched up toward the sky as its bottom half sat deep in the ditch. The truck was the raised variety with extra clearance from the large tires and shocks, a modification that would later be credited for saving the driver's life. He would never walk again but would live to replay the accident and his role in it. His guilt was compounded by his careless decision to scan the radio dial while driving, hoping to track the bet he placed between 'Bama and LSU. It was a foolish action that would end two lives and forever alter two others. In a meaningless form of karma, he would lose the two-hundred-dollar wager.

Cassie remembered waking to the presence of stark white lighting. Looking around, she noticed an old TV held to the wall by a mechanical brace. There was a small desk at the foot of her bed with what appeared to be a couple of books whose titles she could not decipher. The corner of her eye revealed a colorful print of the Philadelphia Zoo and a table full of presents, cards, and flowers. Is it my birthday? she thought, trying to make sense of her surroundings. Where are my friends? Where is my family? she wondered, more confused than anything else. She shifted in her bed to adjust for pressure on her arm. Then, she noticed an IV running from her wrist up and over the top of the bed. The contents dripped slowly, and she felt her bewilderment quickly replaced by fear.

"Cassandra, sweetie, you're up. I will . . . uh . . .wait here, honey," said the shift nurse, quickly vacating the room.

Wait here. I'm hooked up to a machine, Cassie thought. Where the hell would I be going?

She still felt groggy from what she assumed were drugs in her system but did not fail to notice the nurse's apprehension and quick about-face. For a moment, Cassie closed her eyes and took a deep breath, half hoping that upon reopening them, she would take hold of this dream and steer it to calmer waters. Her moment of distraction was interrupted by a deep voice that she could not place. Opening her eyes provided no additional clues.

"Cassandra, Cassandra," said the man dressed in a dark suit and dark blue tie with a fleur-de-lis pattern. "Cassie," he repeated this time in a fading voice, as if he were a teacher on the first day of school trying to remember the names of his pupils.

"I . . . uh . . ." He paused and looked up at the nurse as if looking for guidance. There was none offered.

Cassie put a temporary end to his struggles. "Who are you?"

Seemingly relieved to be able to address something more concrete, simpler, he replied, "Cassandra, I am your Uncle Davis. You may not recognize me. You haven't seen me since you were probably five years old, when your mom and dad came to Ithaca to see me."

Thinking back, she had no memory of her uncle. She was hospitalized. How could she be expected to remember? Judging from the cast on her left arm and bandages on her right, something had gone terribly wrong.

And then, at once, the question was on the table. There would be no more reprieves. The intersection and moment that would change everyone's lives in the room had come down upon them like heavy snow.

"What happened? Where's my mom?" Cassie asked, eager to get past the odd situation in which she found herself.

"Cassie, you were in an accident."

While this was obvious, judging from her injuries, it was upon hearing the word *accident* that she felt a rush of adrenaline run straight to her heart, bringing with it a nervous anticipation of dread. Somehow, in the milliseconds between his words and the announcement that would alter her existence forever, she put it all together. Her estranged uncle, her injuries, the hospital bed, the "birthday" presents and flowers.

"They're dead; they died in the accident, a car accident," her uncle said in what sounded cold in tone. But how could such news be presented in any other way?

She entered the world in the same hospital where her parents would exit. She, too, left some things behind—not just the bloody bandages and empty IVs but a specter that would permeate the halls like the potent smell of disinfectants.

Cassie alternated between gazing out the car window and closing her eyes in hopes that somehow upon opening them she would find it had all been a dream. She watched familiar downtown landmarks come into view before retreating in the car's wake. Each edifice they passed brought a sharp pain deep beneath her sternum. Here was the playhouse where, as a seven-year-old, she played one of the wicked stepsisters, a performance that brought her usually reserved father to shed tears of pride on the car ride home. Then, the small art studio where she took private pottery classes with her mother. The corner café where she would order a stack of blueberry pancakes, which she never managed to finish. The endearing memories she had assumed would be immovable, permanent pages in the story of her childhood, now brought her a deep and unfamiliar pain that seemed inaccessible, lodged deep in her heart. She closed her eyes tightly to fight back tears and to spare her additional suffering from watching her former life fade into the rearview mirror.

They had been driving for a little less than two hours when they approached a steep hill in the countryside. On both sides, farms dotted the rolling landscape. Endless fields of dried cornstalks dominated the scene. Distant farmhouses settled in the valleys, accessible only by winding dirt roads.

In the distance, a farmer was tending to a burning pile of debris, occasionally stabbing it with a pitchfork to keep the flames alive. As they crested the zenith, the road rolled in a series of long, gradual slopes to the valley below. A substantial home was perched on top of an upslope near the bottom of the valley. The property demanded attention as it grew in stature with each passing second of the descent.

"We're home," he said, pointing a hundred yards ahead to the property. If his home in Ithaca had been this grand, she would have remembered it. It was the only structure within a quarter mile.

Cassie counted no fewer than two dozen windows. A massive wooden front door sat beneath an overhang that was made to appear as if it were being supported by matching sculptures of God-like muscular men adorning long beards and loin clothes. There was a long, semi-circular driveway made of light gray-blue paver stones. In the middle was a twenty-foot-tall fountain. There were two layers. The top consisted of a porcelain ornate bowl with deep grooves on the edges. Water bubbled up from a pillar in the top and rolled down into the bowl before escaping through the grooves into the much larger copper bowl below, which, upon overflowing, would collect in a square pool encased by black marble walls. The sun reflected off the copper structure, creating intricate light patterns in the grass and mum-filled flowerbed surrounding it. Each window had ornate iron baskets filled with what appeared to be dead dahlias. Watering them alone looked like it would have been a part-time job. There was a detached garage big enough for three or four cars. Its gray stone veneer matched the larger abode. The shutters were a faded burgundy red. Even the mailbox at the beginning of the driveway was elaborate, encased in a stone structure the size of a small shed. The mailbox lay inside the middle of the frame. Two synchronous cutouts on each side of the mailbox lay behind iron bars, as if they were small jail cells. Inside of each was a gas-powered flame. Dried clematis vines climbed up the sides and across the top. The still-green grass on the five-acre property was almost too perfect, making it difficult to determine if it was real from a distance. There was not a single burned-out patch to be found.

"That's Jackson, er, at least I think that's his name," he said, pointing to a short man in Dickies work clothes sweeping the front steps. "He comes by a few days a week to tend to the property."

Cassie was unsure whether that was his first or last name, but doubted she would remember it in ten minutes anyway.

"There are ten bedrooms upstairs and a master downstairs. Pick whichever you want. Many of them are empty of furniture. Not many people go upstairs. I generally entertain visitors in the ballroom downstairs."

Did he say ballroom? Cassie wondered. Her parents' four-bedroom house seemed plenty big enough, and she wondered why such a place was needed for anyone, let alone a bachelor.

"OK, thank you," Cassie said in a quiet, fading voice.

As he parked the car inside one of the garage bays, he turned to face Cassie, who had decided to ride in the back, having made the excuse she was tired and wanted the option to lie down. She thought it would make it less likely she would have to talk to her uncle. While the tan leather seats of the Jaguar were comfortable, she remained upright with her head resting against the window for most of the journey.

"I can't imagine what you are feeling right now," her uncle said. "I wish that I, uh, you know, could say something or do something to make it better. Whatever you need, just ask, OK?"

Cassie stared at her shoes and nodded without making eye contact.

"OK, then. Let's give you a quick tour of the place."

The inside of the home was ornate, each room painted in shades of mostly French blues, pale greens, and subtle yellows. There was scarcely a wall that was not covered with original art. Cassie, who knew her way around an art museum and had art history in school, thought most were Impressionist works. A couple of pieces looked like Renoirs, and given her uncle's money, she wondered if they might be originals.

Several rooms had floor-to-ceiling built-in bookshelves with a ladder that could be rolled across the front to reach the highest shelves. There were few paperbacks and nothing that would be found at the local bookstore. These books were old, perhaps as old as some of the art and sculpture scattered throughout the home. She imagined the housekeepers spent more time dusting the ancient tomes than anyone ever spent reading them. Four double doors led into the massive ballroom, which was the size of two basketball courts. Functionality clearly took a back seat to making an impression. Her uncle's visitors praised his collections, fueling his ego, while the multiple furnaces fueled the distant and unused rooms.

"There are six bathrooms . . . well, maybe five and a half," her uncle said, scratching his chin as if trying to tap into the virtual map in his head. He opened the door to one of the bathrooms on the second floor. It was huge. Cassie figured it was twice the size of her parents' master bedroom at home. The waterfall shower was big enough to park an SUV with still enough room for a VW Beetle. The bathtub was vast and deep with ornate clawed feet.

"The tile floor heats up in most bathrooms." He found the switch on the wall. "Ah, yes, here it is. Just flick this on, and it should be nice and toasty within a few minutes. Just remember to turn it off when you are done to keep the electric bill down."

Cassie found it strange that he had concerns about energy costs, given that he had enough unused rooms to house a small college's entire fraternity population.

After showing her the remaining bedrooms and massive kitchen, he pulled back the window drapes in one of the upstairs bedrooms, revealing a sizeable endless pool.

"It's heated. It also has a current you can adjust and swim against. There are built-in shelves around the edge if you want to sit in the water jets and relax."

Cassie wondered how she ended up in this parallel universe. Only about a week ago, she was doing homework in her room, surrounded by her Clash, the Who, and Doors posters, which had now been swapped out for the finest art.

She selected the bedroom at the far end of the second floor. It was smaller than the others. If her uncle had not thought it strange, she would have chosen the walk-in closet. She unpacked what she had in her suitcase, filling a few of the mahogany armoire's drawers.

The rest of her things would be brought by movers hired by her uncle. He rightly guessed that Cassie did not want to set foot in her own home. Understandably, she could not bring herself to care about getting back any of her things. They were all tainted. If it were up to her, she would forever stay in the clothes she was wearing now.

Sitting on her plush bed, she grabbed the super-soft blanket and clenched it in her fists, hoping the texture would somehow soothe her. She lay back in the bed without bothering to take off her shoes. She imagined herself becoming just another part of the bed. In the days and weeks that followed, she would spend much of the time in the closet with a pillow and soft blanket. She liked the darkness, only the light from her iPhone illuminating the space.

An image would replay constantly. She fantasized about boarding up the closet, nailing it shut, and cutting herself off from the world. People would search for her in earnest before deciding that perhaps she never existed in the first place. She would be free from expectations. The world would stop. There would be no therapy sessions, no homework, and no faking a smile to ease the awkwardness she imagined everyone around her wished desperately to escape.

Initially, her uncle would tuck her in at night. He attempted to comfort her with words, but he tried too hard, and it came across as insincere. The moment he left, she would return to the closet. In what seemed like unnecessary cruelty, Cassie would wake many mornings momentarily unaware of her surroundings, giving her a brief respite from reality, only to quickly become conscious that it all was real.

Once again, Cassie pictured herself in the back seat behind her mother. She could just have easily sat behind her father. Her choice of where to sit was always random. Sometimes, the choice was dictated by what junk might be on the seat. There was no clutter to speak of on this fateful day. It was simply luck that she chose the only seat in the cabin that remained intact. At least, others would report it that way. The newspapers correctly called it a tragedy and called Cassie's survival a miracle. Cassie did not and would not see it in the same light. How could a miracle be a curse? What good was it to be alive when all you could think about was the embrace of death?

In the years to follow, Cassie would reflect on the seemingly trivial moments of that day. What if she didn't take so long to get ready in the morning? What if she hadn't wasted time numbingly scrolling through Facebook? On some level, no matter how distant in her mind, she understood that those were just random chains of events for which she could not be held responsible. After all, she was a girl born of science, steered by reason and cause and effect. The one thing she could not rationalize or forgive herself for was her moodiness that day.

She replayed the decision to change her mind about going pumpkin picking over and over again. Remembering the disappointment and rejection in her father's eyes caused her heart to feel as if it stopped pumping. Was she mean or just moody? Was he sad? Had she hurt her parents' feelings? She searched the depths of her mind for details that would relieve her guilt. There was nobody left who could help her remember or help her to forget. She was alone in ways that went well beyond being a sole survivor. There were levels of loneliness and emptiness that before the accident she had not known existed. She had never known that pain could be so deep that it had a taste, a bitterness that seemed to linger in her mouth.

CHAPTER 17

THROUGHOUT THE SUMMER and fall, Chuck and Bill rarely went a week without seeing one another. Impacted by some of his war injuries, Chuck's rehabilitation was taking longer than expected. However, he had made enough progress to warrant being transitioned to step-down skilled care. Weekends in the valley were now dominated by typical soggy, raw November weather. The cold did not bother them, especially Chuck, who, after being exposed to frostbite from treacherous winters during the Korean War, seemed incapable of feeling a chill anymore. Neither of them liked being forced to sit in the rain under the gazebo, where they would seldom have any privacy. Their time together had become precious, an open confessional between two men of different generations who shared the bond of repeated loss, whether on a battlefield or due to the slow march toward the death of the many addicted and depressed patients at Maybrook. While the books to be written would have vastly different content, they belonged in the same section of the library.

As the calendar approached mid-November, they were treated to an unusually warm, sunny weekend. Bill was excited to see his friend again. He had come to depend on their meetings as his own, free of cost, talk therapy. The more he listened to Chuck, the less alone he felt.

Chuck sat on a bench under a gorgeous dawn redwood, one of the few conifers that shed its needles for the winter. The needles were the color of Gulden's mustard, revealing a beautiful transformation that would be gone in another few days. The tree could reach a height that, while not on par with its cousin, the coastal sequoia, likely made it the tallest tree in the county.

Bill handed him his coffee and a Boston cream donut and sat beside him.

Chuck gazed up to the heavens.

"Beautiful, isn't it?"

Bill followed his eyes upward.

"Sure is. I can't believe I never noticed it before. Guess I would make a poor naturalist." He smiled.

"I can't be sure, but I think I saw them in Korea. I remember the giant trees because their yellow needles scattered far and wide on the snow. During the warmer months, their broad limbs provided valuable shade and cover from the enemy. I feel a special bond with this tree. Maybe it's watching over me like it was so many years ago. Stupid, I know."

"Not at all. It's hard to look at it and not see the divine."

Bill took a sip of his coffee and stared off into the distance at nothing in particular. He appeared to be asleep with his eyes open. He stayed this way for several seconds before being brought back by Chuck.

"You OK?"

"What . . . oh yeah, I am fine," he said unconvincingly.

"I think I know you well enough by now to detect bullshit. Are you going to make an old man dig—one who, might I remind you, recently had a stroke?"

"Sorry, um, it's just . . ." His eyes glistened a bit, but he was not shedding any tears. "It's just that . . ." He momentarily paused, searching for how to string the words together that would make sense to Chuck and himself. "We lost someone last Tuesday."

"Someone ran from the facility again?"

Bill had shared stories of mental health technicians grabbing walkie-talkies and flashlights before heading out into woods and farmlands in search of committed patients who ran for it while on a smoke break or walking back from the cafeteria.

"Not exactly."

"Oh." Chuck knew that could only mean one thing.

Their eyes met, and Bill knew he did not need to speak the word.

"I hope you know it's not your fault," Chuck said.

"I know. Been doing this long enough to know that the forces of suffering, addiction, and trauma are not easily overcome despite our best intentions. I can't imagine how his parents are dealing with this. They were an amazing support system. They showered him with love and turned over every rock but could never find the answers."

"I don't know what to say. I am not so stupid to think there are any words."

Chuck looked into Bill's eyes and saw how vulnerable he had made himself. It was a level of trust he had not experienced since being in the trenches with his brothers in arms. As much as he liked Bill, he was now sure he loved him. He looked at him as the grandson he never had. He wanted to protect him while, at the same time, knowing he was brave and strong enough not to need it.

"How much time do you have today? I mean, before you have to head back."

Bill glanced at his phone and checked his calendar in Outlook.

"I can stay longer. I don't have anything until 2:00 p.m. today."

"OK, good. I want to tell you something—something I have never told anyone before."

Bill looked puzzled but felt comfort in knowing that he had made himself vulnerable, and rather than judging him, Chuck was about to reciprocate. Bill was amazed at how strong their bond had become. What was once a stranger across the pond had become family.

"You know, the worst part of war is killing someone. Ending the life of someone you don't even know, someone who never wronged you. Innocent people meeting their end because they carry the wrong flag and appear across from you in some field that neither of you has any affinity for. You don't know the story behind those you kill, but in a way, that makes it worse. Try as you might to build your own background story, one where they were cruel to animals or violent criminals, the likely scenario always resurfaced. Coming to terms with the fact that you killed someone who was a good listener, a friend to someone in need, someone's child, was," he paused for a moment, "no, *is* almost impossible."

One of the nurses appeared across the pond at the side door of the facility.

"Chuck, are you going to eat lunch?"

"OK if I take it in my room later? I am talking to my friend."

She smiled, knowing how much their friendship had grown since Bill first appeared in the spring.

"Sure, no worries."

What Chuck said next shocked Bill. It did not fit the man he thought he had pegged.

"There is only one person I ever killed that I have never lost sleep over." He took a deep breath and stared into the distance. "It wasn't in the war."

It took a few extra seconds for those five words to sink in.

Bill's mind quickly filled the open space with images of an old man shooting an intruder or maybe even stopping a robbery.

"You know, when someone hurts somebody you love—and I mean really hurts—you will do anything to protect them, especially when they can't protect themselves."

"I'm not following."

Chuck had not said too much, not yet. It was not too late to pull back and say nothing more.

Fuck it, he thought. I am old. I have had a stroke. No telling when I could have the next one. The one that keeps me from being able to get this off my chest.

Bill thought of stopping him from sharing something he probably did not want to know—not only because it might forever change how he viewed his friend but because it might force him to report it to the police. He felt he had no right to stop him. They had come this far. They had both shared things that they entrusted to no one else. What message would it send if, after opening his soul about the suicide, he would shut down and silence his friend who had been holding in something that was eating him from the inside?

"Remember I told you how my daughter and her husband were killed in an accident?"

"Yes."

"And that my granddaughter survived?"

"How could I forget?"

"Well, her legal guardian was Cassandra's uncle, her father's brother, a big shot real estate investor, Davis Ripley. Ever heard of him? He was on TV a lot."

"Can't say that I have, no."

"Anyway, it's not important. He was a bit of a local celebrity, filthy rich, and considered a pillar of the community. I recall only meeting him once at a graduation party. I was simply happy that he could be a model of success for Cassie and would be able to provide for her financially."

He paused to wet his dry throat by gulping his now lukewarm coffee. Bill sat anxiously, anticipating an inevitable dark turn in the narrative. There was a "but" coming. What lay on the other side was a mystery, but he was confident it would reveal a line in the sand and the potential end to the bond he had hoped would never be compromised. Given Chuck's age and state of health, he knew that the relationship was destined to end painfully, in the same way you adopted man's best friend knowing you were committing to the guarantee of future heartbreak.

"Of course, I spoke to Cassie often. She was always guarded like she had never been before the accident. I chalked it up to the overwhelming circumstances she was dealing with. Understandably, she was very depressed, anxious, and withdrawn. I only cared about her getting better one day at a time. I just wanted her to know I was always one call away. Even when she told me she was missing school, I figured it was because she was too emotionally unstable to go.

It wasn't until she asked, spur of the moment, to sleep over that same evening. I couldn't put my finger on it. It just seemed off. What changed everything for me was when I saw the bruises. She swore they were related to gym class, falling off her skateboard, or even getting in a scuffle at school with a bully. She had many excuses, all ready to go at a moment's notice. I started to line up the dates when she missed school—she often called me when she was home—and the bruises. I'm sure now that calling me when home from school, asking to sleep over with little notice, and not hiding the bruises were calls for help. I'm ashamed to say it took longer for me to put all the pieces together, but her uncle had no history of abuse, and, in fact, he was painted as a hero in the media for taking in his niece."

He made eye contact with Bill and could see he was laser-focused on every word. Chuck paused to take another sip of coffee. The sun had crossed its high point in the sky and peeked through the dawn redwood, creating long shadows across the sidewalk.

"Anyway, I finally confronted her the next time she came over. She denied it, at first. She was pretty stubborn. I pressed pretty hard, maybe more than I had a right to. I knew the only way to get her to open up was to summon her parents' memory. I told her it was my duty to protect her and that her parents would suffer had they known something was happening and nobody was stepping in to do what they couldn't do. There was a flood of tears and wailing so deep that I swore she might be the first-ever casualty from sorrow. Even as I say it now, I can feel the rage boiling inside me. Motherfucker!"

Bill could see him clenching his free hand and shaking his feet anxiously as if forced to move to relieve some of the pressure.

"I knew he had to go, and I had nothing to lose. After ending so many lives that didn't deserve it, I would finally end one that did, and, well, after some careful planning, I did. I was so careful, a benefit of disciplined planning from my time in the service, that I made it look like an accident. My granddaughter lived with me until she went away to school. Funny, I still have nightmares from the war, seeing the faces of the fallen frozen in time, their last expressions before I pulled the trigger, or of my brothers being pulled back into foxholes with fewer parts than when they had left it only moments before. I can't say I have ever been awakened from what I did to her uncle. If that were my only transgression, I would sleep like a baby."

Later, as Bill pulled into his reserved parking spot at the hospital, it occurred to him that he had no recollection of the drive from the rehabilitation center. He remembered giving his friend the customary hug before departing but could not recall exchanging words. He'd validated Chuck's feelings about his granddaughter's suffering at the hands of her uncle. Did he condone his behavior and the actions he took? He hoped not. He became angry. Why did he have to share that with him? Abusive or not, he had committed a heinous act. It was inexcusable.

Upon entering the Maybrook facility, feeling nauseous, he made a beeline for the bathroom and flipped the exhaust fan on. He struggled to process how the man he admired was maybe someone he never actually knew. The queasiness quickly passed, but for the remainder of his shift, he went through the motions, managing to get through the day. A minor storm was rolling through the valley, causing Bill to leave the office later than usual, when the rain began to fall more sporadically and the setting sun poked through a few of the breaks in the clouds. The waterlogged road was already drying, the steam rising from whence it came. Within minutes of exiting the country road to hop on the two-lane highway, traffic slowed. A fallen tree from the passing storm blocked the left lane ahead.

The sun had returned to dominate the sky, even if only briefly, as it lowered behind the horizon—only the occasional puddle provided evidence of the downpour that had passed through. The traffic crawled, leading Bill to glance at drivers who momentarily appeared alongside him. Many of his fellow commuters made eye contact before awkwardly returning to face the front. In his transit of stops and starts, he had a strange thought. If he could have been so wrong about his old friend, if he could so badly misjudge what others were capable of, how could he be sure about anyone?

How many people had he encountered over the years, whether words were spoken or not? By the law of averages, a few must have committed a crime that remained beneath the surface. How could he be sure the person waiting behind him to order bagels hadn't sexually assaulted someone? Was it impossible that the person in the left lane with whom he just made eye contact got away with a murder some twenty years ago? He had learned enough statistics in graduate school to know that the probability he crossed paths with someone—whether in a laundromat, an elevator, or at a sporting event—who had taken a life was all but a certainty. As he finally made it past the road blockage, he watched a worker dividing the tree with a chainsaw and wondered what part of his life he was hiding. Later that night, when Bill turned out his light, he felt less sure about the world and his place in it.

CHAPTER 18

THE MONTHS THAT followed Cassie's accident were memorable not so much from specific events but rather from a familiar feeling that permeated each day. She was beginning to adjust to living with her uncle, but the house did not feel like home, and she held out little hope that it ever would. Her emotions lay buried somewhere beneath the frost line. While it protected her from the worst of the pain, it did so by entrapping her feelings in her own frozen tundra. Her uncle, friends, and grief therapist would tell her that time would heal the wounds, that she would never forget but would be able to find happiness again.

After months of therapy and a steady regimen of Zoloft and Ativan, she had only managed to be able to put one leg in front of the other. The best that could be said was that she was functional. She weighed the possibility that that might have to be enough. Like watching the sun disappear behind the clouds, she could only stare into the sky for so long, waiting for it to come out the other side before inevitably losing interest.

Despite her uncle living only a few hours away as a child, she rarely saw him. He divorced when she was only a toddler, had never remarried, and had no children. Aside from his failed marriage, by all other accounts, he was a success. Her father used to say he was a master at knowing how to take everything right to the edge without ever going over. As a child, he was able to manipulate his friends, convincing them that his ideas were their own and allowing him to dictate what games they would play. He usually got his way and did so without alienating others around him. Being one step ahead of most of his peers in school and, in fact, many of the teachers, he was always seen as someone to watch.

His magic touch followed him to college. His string of B's and A's belied that he barely needed to hit the books. He excelled at finding the shortest and easiest path to whatever prize he sought. Upon graduation, he watched his friends follow the age-old tradition of taking their rejection letters from job applications to the local bar in exchange for fifty percent off a beer. By contrast, her uncle always seemed to know someone who knew someone, bypassing the anonymity that plagued those around him looking to make a way in the world. It seemed he was just luckier than most, but those who knew him best knew better. He cultivated relationships and said the right things at the right time to the right people.

His charm would later turn into change. Energy was never wasted; every move had a purpose. From the outside, what seemed to be dumb luck and good fortune was, in truth, the sum of careful calculations and a natural grasp of probabilities. He had some detractors along the way, but they were usually people who saw themselves as victims, the type who were convinced that scratching off a lottery ticket would somehow reveal that they owed one hundred dollars.

While Cassie's father found success by outworking those to his left and right, his brother achieved even more with considerably less sweat. Her father was risk-averse, whereas his brother seemed only to see value in things that could bite him in the ass should they go off the rails. Her father admired that about his brother, and despite the uncertainty, he never bet against him to achieve great things.

After only a few years of punching the clock in a nine-to-five job as a junior financial analyst for Fidelity, Uncle Davis was able to move on to helping manage the real estate investment trust portfolio.

It was there that he learned about real estate. More importantly, he found something he was genuinely passionate about for the first time in his life. He became a star and began making rounds at various financial outlets. His charisma, confidence, and above-average looks made him a preferred guest on shows like CNBC's *Squawk Box*. He even had a catchphrase: "Numbers always tell a story." Many analysts viewed investments from the prism of 10-Ks, financials, technical charts, and cash flow. Her uncle saw the market as one part psychology and one part geometry.

He had become a one-man EF Hutton. "When he spoke, people listened." Having him as a pundit meant ratings for the financial networks and publishers. Though he remained on the payroll of Fidelity, he became only a figurehead they occasionally leveraged to reinforce their brand. Much of his time was spent buying commercial real estate. While he missed on occasion, a significant amount of the time, he struck gold. He became wealthy enough to live off his investments and parlay his brand into high-paying public speaking engagements and regular TV appearances. Being a financial wiz was a means to an end.

What got him out of bed in the morning was the praise and admiration from his peers and his adoring followers, who mistakenly thought they could turn his seminars and speeches into riches. In truth, her uncle's advice, while enticing, was mostly information already known by market insiders and investment banks and, therefore, had limited value for the small investor. While he was on the inside, despite their efforts, his *Wall Street Journal* reading, seminar-attending flock remained firmly positioned on the periphery. He knew that people could not turn anything he said into real dollars but believed that the excitement he generated was satisfactory.

In the following years, he amassed a net worth of almost half a billion dollars. He attended many significant political gatherings on

K Street and frequented the most exclusive real estate and chamber of commerce events. He had become a fixture among the elite. In this crowd, he discovered that getting a seat at the table was easier than keeping it. He was not the only entrepreneur with the Midas touch.

He made significant contributions to public projects to stay relevant and quiet his critics, who called him self-serving and a talking head. This included a $7 million donation to build a new cancer ward for children. While it made him feel warm inside, he had to admit it was not easy to decipher whether it was done as a selfless act or because he enjoyed seeing his name carved in marble above the entryway. He followed this up with a $4 million gift to his alma mater to build new locker rooms and a state-of-the-art training facility for its football program. In time, the gesture would help the team move from a periodic contender to a winner of multiple NCAA championships. Carved in stone and recorded in history books, his legacy was now all but assured.

While he loved his brother, they barely saw each other in the decade leading up to the accident. Like many families who were busy with the mundane activities of daily life, their relationship had been reduced to the simple exchange of Christmas cards. Cassie smiling with Mom and Dad behind her, one hand on each of her shoulders, all dressed in the same cheesy Christmas pajamas. Her uncle's card, by contrast, showed him in some exotic location, usually an island that Cassie and her parents had never even heard of. The only sign that it was a Christmas card was that it said, "Merry Christmas." Even though she had only ever seen him twice in her life and could not even remember those meetings, she liked getting his card, if only to look up his whereabouts on the antique globe in her room.

CHAPTER 19

ALMOST A YEAR before taking in Cassie, during a chamber of commerce event, leaders in the community, eager to ride the wave of Davis's success, asked him to consider running for an open seat in the state legislature. He rejected the suggestion. The political "machine" was not worried. Their political analysts and former campaign managers had been there before. His resistance was a wall that could easily be scaled. They knew all it would take to move this man of immense pride was a steady diet of ass-kissing and relentlessly appealing to his ego. After all, this man liked to put his name on things.

While some influential people liked to make anonymous donations and keep their names out of the press, the same was not true for Davis. He leaked his charitable contributions to the media. Having state senator by his name would be something to add to his legacy. He would be a success in the two worlds of business and politics.

As was often the case, he grew impatient with the familiar. Now in his late forties, his ambition had become a parasite of the mind, feeding continually on his ego and requiring him to replenish it endlessly.

With no shortage of disciples to add lighter fluid to his ambitious nature, he finally agreed to run for the vacancy in the state senate. It became another means to stay on top and remain relevant. He figured an added benefit was that he could help pass or squash legislation that would impact his real estate investments and tax bracket. Following a couple of months of polling, the committee reported that they could only find a single weakness in his ability to win in a general election. He was divorced and had no children. There was concern this would make him unfavorable to a certain percentage of constituents who could not relate to a non-family man.

In perhaps the most remarkable example of his lifelong ability to be in the right place at the right time, in a twist of tragic irony, his brother, who had always erred on the side of caution, had died along with his wife in an accident, leaving him with a solution to the gap in his resume. He was Cassie's godfather. What was once an impossible scenario on paper had become a reality. When the press got wind of how he'd recently jumped in to care for a wounded and suffering teenager, what once was a significant weakness in his electability suddenly had the potential to be his greatest strength.

After securing the Republican nomination in the primary, the campaign took stock of what worked and what might need to be tweaked to ensure a favorable outcome in the general election. The consensus was that if the strategy wasn't broken, don't try to fix it. The approach remained largely the same. His opponent from the Democratic Party, Walter Copeland, was the opposite of Davis. He represented the third generation of a political family that could only be described as a juggernaut along the lines of the Bushes. The Copelands had a former governor and US senator as part of their legacy. The newest Copeland to enter the fold was a gifted orator, having been schooled in debate from an early age. It was always assumed he would add another chapter to his family's Camelot story.

The campaign strategies for both parties were predictable. Walter's team took shots at Davis's lack of experience in government, repeatedly pointing out that to get things done, you had to know the nuances of how to work across the aisle. "What makes you a business success can be the very thing that means failure in government," was a well-repeated line in Copeland's stump speeches. He emphasized that Davis would spend more time learning the ropes than helping the people. Walter continued to drive the need to be able to negotiate and compromise across political parties. The government was more about knowing how to influence others over whom you may have no direct authority. He argued that Davis's position at the top of his kingdom meant he had control over everything: the purse strings, the strategy, and the people beneath him.

Davis countered with a steady diet of pointing out Walter's "silver spoon" upbringing, one where he even had the donkey lapel pin on his onesies. He emphasized that Walter's only employment was as a member of his father's political team, or other jobs earned through his family's political network. "If we look in a dictionary for the meaning of an insider, we will see your picture," Davis would say. "How can we be sure you can ride a bike yourself once we take off the training wheels?" was an oft-repeated line during Davis's campaign fundraisers as it emphasized Copeland's guarded and gifted life. After a few debates and months of ads on heavy rotation of each man attacking their opponent's shortcomings, the polling remained within the margin of error.

What had been a strength for Davis in the primary was now looking to be a weakness. He was an outsider and, therefore, a risk. A further concern was his apparent lack of likeability compared to his competition. It became clear that the undecided would crown the winner, either adding to Davis's résumé of triumph or delivering the first absolute failure of his life on a very public stage.

As Davis sat with his campaign team following a meeting with supporters in the Four Seasons hotel in downtown New York City, a bold strategy was brought to the table.

"We need Cassie if we are going to win this election," said Syd Amos, his lead campaign strategist. Everyone referred to him as "Amos."

"I have already worked the story into countless speeches and events. We need some fresh ideas."

"No, I mean, we need to *see* Cassie. She needs to become tangible to the voters. They need to see her smile and laugh. They need to see her affection for the man who rescued her."

Davis said, "I hardly rescued her. She barely talks to me. It's hard enough to get her to leave the closet sometimes."

"They don't need to know that. We can coach her. She doesn't need to do much. Seeing her is different from hearing about her. Voters need to see what's in your heart."

"No, absolutely not. Cassie has been through a lot. I can't ask her to do it. It has barely been six months since the accident." Despite his objections, his only genuine concern was putting the fate of his campaign in his niece's hands.

"Look, do you trust me? I mean, do you believe I know what I am doing?"

"Of course I do, it's just—"

Amos interrupted. "Then let me do my job. Just a few appearances, that's all."

Davis stared out the floor-to-ceiling window of the hotel suite, watching the endless traffic lights reflecting off the puddles, and crossed his arms. His team fell silent, anticipating the result of the calculations that were processing through his mind. He scratched his chin and watched the drops roll down the window, one after another.

What other options were left? There must be some other paths to victory that didn't involve Cassie. Despite searching the depths of his mind, no solution could be found. A pang of guilt quickly passed through him as he pictured his brother, knowing he would not have approved of what he was about to do. As a business executive, he had learned the art of stuffing negative feelings deep inside, starving them of the light they needed to grow. He turned to face his team. Amos had his hands in his pockets. His fidgety hands betrayed his effort to look casual as he played with his keys. Davis's eyes met Amos's. The message conveyed was one of vulnerability. It was a position he was unaccustomed to and, all things being equal, hoped to avoid in the future.

"OK. OK."

A team member handed him a glass of scotch as Davis sat in one of the room's ornate, high-backed chairs.

"So, what's next?" Davis asked.

"Leave that to me," Amos said, crossing his arms. "You've had a long day; just sit back and leave it to me."

Davis eased further into the chair, taking a generous gulp from his drink. He welcomed the physical burn as a preferable alternative to the doubts swimming in his head.

A couple of days later, Cassie thought she heard the doorbell but couldn't be sure. She stopped what she was doing and listened intently. The house was big enough that, at times, she couldn't locate the source of a sound or was left to consider that they were only inventions of her mind. The familiar "ding-dong" faintly repeated from downstairs. Cassie took her time descending the stairs. She knew it couldn't be a suitor or even a friend, for that matter. Outside her occasional sleepovers with her childhood confidant, Kayla, her home might as well have been on Easter Island, her only company the ancient moai gazing out to sea. When she opened the door, she was surprised to see a tall, dark-haired, brown-eyed, slender man. He had one of those long dress coats and carried a small leather briefcase. Figuring he was selling something, she was about to turn him away when he extended his hand.

"Syd Amos. Nice to meet you, Cassandra. I am your father's—excuse me, I mean uncle's campaign manager." For someone trained and well-practiced at saying the right thing at the right time, his first impression left much to be desired. Cassie had never seen him before but felt confident he was being truthful. She extended her hand in return.

"I'm sorry, but he's not here right now. He went to Home Depot."

She began to shut the door, expecting him to make his exit. Instead, in a nonthreatening way, he put his hand against the door, stopping its motion.

"Actually, Cassie—is it OK if I call you Cassie? I am here to talk to you about your uncle. I know it is a Saturday afternoon, and a girl like you probably has a full dance card. I promise to get out of your hair quickly. I was hoping to get a few minutes of your time."

"OK, I've heard my uncle speak of you a few times, but do you have some ID?" She realized it was a pointless exercise since, at this point, there was nothing to stop him if he wanted to barge in.

"Of course, where are my manners?"

Syd Amos pulled out his money clip, which was full of ten- and twenty-dollar notes, an Amex card, a Chase Visa card, a US Healthcare ID, and his driver's license.

"Here you go."

Cassie scanned the ID.

"People always say they hate their ID, but I don't think it's half bad." His tone suggested he was not looking for any confirmation and none was given.

"OK. Come on in."

Cassie took him to the kitchen and sat at the table.

"Can I get you a drink? Water, Diet Coke?"

"Nothing, thanks."

He took a seat opposite Cassie at the table.

"So, what's this all about?"

"Of course, let me get to the point."

"Your uncle, well, he's slightly behind in the polls, and there isn't much time to make up ground before people make their choice."

Cassie listened intently, wondering where this was headed.

"Look, I am going to be straight with you. Your uncle needs help—more specifically, your help. He's not comfortable asking for it. That's why I'm here."

He paused for a moment to let the point sink in.

"Cassie, do you know what a campaign manager does?"

"I assume you manage the campaign," she responded sarcastically, but not in an ill-spirited way.

Syd Amos sat back in his chair and smiled. "Yes. I guess the title is a bit of a giveaway. But, more precisely, it's my job to turn over every stone to try and get your uncle elected."

"But what does that have to do with me?"

"Would you say that your uncle has provided for you?"

Cassie knew he was referring to her uncle taking over guardianship following the accident.

"Of course."

"Well, I believe in reciprocity. It's what turns the world's gears. Without it, there is no community, nothing to bind us together."

"Look, you don't need to butter me up. What are you asking exactly?"

"Your uncle did tell me you are sharp as a tack and not shy about sharing your thoughts. That's great! In fact, it's what we need. We need you to have a bigger role in the campaign and to be more visible at some public events."

Amos looked for any signs from her facial expression and posture. He thought about immediately following up with the real ask, speaking publicly about the accident and the role her uncle played in the immediate aftermath. He decided on first building a solid foundation, one brick at a time, before diving into the deep end.

"Sure. If you think it will help."

"Great! Thanks, Cassie. Your uncle probably won't be too happy with me that I went behind his back to ask. But I'm here to help him win, and if pissing him off is needed to make that happen, well . . ." He didn't finish his thought.

Later that afternoon, as Syd Amos sat across from her uncle at their campaign headquarters, they joined glasses of scotch in a toast. Their plan was a success.

CHAPTER 20

EVEN AFTER BEING on the trail for a few months, Cassie felt out of place. She began to second-guess her decision to help the campaign. She was younger than everyone, apolitical, and shared little of their interests. Most of her time was spent sitting in the corner, endlessly browsing the internet on her phone. Occasionally, she would be asked to stand next to her uncle for a photo shoot or media event.

When her parents were still alive, on rare occasions, she would be invited to a school party. Inevitably, she would find herself at some suburban home of a schoolmate whose parents were conveniently out of town. Red solo cups were everywhere, filled with beer, wine coolers, or cheap vodka. What wasn't anywhere to be found was anything without alcohol. Cassie would fill her cup with the first thing she could get her hands on, as she had no intention of consuming it. Often, the one or two classmates she came with would wander off to socialize with other kids, leaving her alone. Few things were worse than the feeling of holding up the wall, taking imaginary sips from a half-filled cup. She hated the sense that everyone was staring at her, wondering why she was standing all alone or, worse, why she was invited in the first place. This was preferable to the truth that nobody was looking at her. She was a specter, irrelevant and invisible. Her attendance was neither required nor prohibited.

It was much the same at her uncle's political gatherings; she felt slightly better knowing she was usually the youngest there and being alone was less a symbol of her lack of popularity and simply the product of her being in the wrong age group. This changed when she met Passion. Being a teenager and therefore a little judgmental, Cassie pegged her as pretentious or snobby when they were first introduced. How could she not be given that name?

"Hi, Cassie. Nice to meet you. I'm Passion." She extended her hand, which was covered with an assortment of rings and a dangling bracelet that noisily shifted down her wrist. She was beautiful, with long, wavy red hair, hazel eyes, and dimples that appeared when she smiled.

"Same here," Cassie said as she shook her hand.

"Being at these things must bore you to tears. I can't think of a worse place to be for a non-political junky, especially a teenager."

"It's not too bad," Cassie said, making no attempt to be convincing.

"I was going for a coffee run down the street. Want to join me?"

Cassie looked around the room and figured it was better than the alternative.

"Sure," Cassie said with a slight smile.

"Great, let's go."

Passion's car, an eggplant-colored Mercedes, was as odd as her name. It was clearly old and had a massive chrome grill with the classic Mercedes hood ornament. It had subtle tail fins and the body of an old-style yellow cab. Cassie quickly realized Passion could not be easily typecast. It made Cassie want to get to know her. As they pulled out of the parking lot, the engine roared much louder than would be expected for the speed they were traveling. As if reading Cassie's mind, Passion said, "Sounds powerful, but it's all bark and no bite. It's from the late sixties. It has no power. I am not ashamed to admit that eighteen-wheelers have passed me more than once when climbing hills on the interstate. But what it lacks in power, it makes up for in personality, and I never have issues finding my car at the airport."

Cassie laughed. "I love it. It's exactly the type of car I would like."

"Do you have your license?"

"Yeah, but I don't have my own car yet. My uncle has talked about getting me a used one. I think he would have bought one by now if there wasn't a bus to take me to school."

They pulled into a small coffee shop called the Farmhouse. The menu was all in chalk on a large blackboard behind the baristas.

"Get what you want, I'm buying," Passion said.

Cassie's order rolled off her tongue despite its complexity—half this, half that.

"Geeze, what happened to black coffee or a cappuccino?" Passion laughed. With the back of her hand, Passion tapped her on the shoulder. "I'm just kidding."

They took a seat in the nearly empty café. "So, you're a strategist for my uncle's campaign?" Cassie wasn't sure if that was the correct term.

Passion nodded. "Basically. My job is to look beyond the surface. I don't just look at the polls; I scrutinize them. I deconstruct them to find opportunities, like what issues are likely to sway votes with a certain demographic. It's my job to know who is providing lip service and who will back my candidate."

"And you like that?"

"I don't just like it. I love it. It combines all my favorite things: history, communications, and psychology. You use all those things to solve a puzzle on who, what, when, and where to focus in order to win." She took a deep sip of her black coffee. "Funny thing is, I am not political. The enigma wrapped inside a puzzle gets me up in the morning."

"It must be nice being so sure of yourself," said Cassie.

"Let's not go that far. Let's just say my love life, or lack thereof, makes up for it."

Passion asked Cassie many questions in a genuine way. She was an active listener, as evidenced by her follow-up queries. Cassie talked a bit about herself, something she scarcely did. She felt comfortable with Passion as she sensed the goodness in her.

"Look, you seem like a nice kid, Cassandra."

"Call me Cassie."

"Between you and me, just be careful. This is not my first rodeo. I've been on a few campaigns since graduating from Syracuse."

"What do you mean?"

"Look, politics can be messy. There is always a reason behind every choice and every action. I would love to give your uncle the benefit of the doubt that he had you tag along because you were interested in politics. But knowing your tragic history, I think it is far more self-serving than that."

Cassie ran her finger around the edge of her cup. "You're good. That's exactly why I am here."

"Oh, so they told you."

"His chief advisor, Amos, said he wasn't polling well in terms of likeability. I think the plan is to change that using my story."

"From a political strategy viewpoint, it is sound. From an ethical perspective, I'm not so sure. How do you feel about it?"

"Not great, but I figure he took me in and provides for me. Anyway, it is only for a couple of months."

"OK, but I am going to be looking out for you. There are a lot of sharks in this business."

"Yeah, and you're like a dolphin."

"If you say so." Passion could not follow the metaphor.

"You know, like how dolphins scare off sharks by spearing them from below with their beaks."

"You're pretty smart, aren't you? Let's head out."

As they approached the car, Passion walked to the passenger side.

"What are you doing?"

Passion tossed Cassie the keys. Unprepared, she dropped them.

"You're driving. I've had too much to drink."

"Too much coffee?"

"Don't want another DWC. You know, driving while caffeinated."

Cassie smiled and shook her head. "Terrible play on words."

As they returned to the campaign office, Cassie couldn't be certain but was reasonably sure she had just made a friend over coffee. Usually, it took her months of trial and error and starts and stops. She thought, maybe this campaign thing wouldn't be so bad.

Over the next few weeks, Passion made good on her promise to keep an eye on her. They enjoyed each other's company, and going for coffee became a regular event. They even continued to split driving duties. Mostly, Cassie had little to do. At times, she wondered why they bothered to ask for her help. Her job was to be seen, not heard. She was a moon orbiting the gravitational pull of her uncle, kept close for media events. She would smile for the cameras before returning to the shadows to do schoolwork. Her role in the play couldn't have been more straightforward. She had no lines to memorize. The ultimate supporting character or extra on a movie set, she began to wonder if there was merit to Passion's warning. Perhaps the sea of politics was infested with sharks, but, to this point, she was only ever asked to dip a toe in the water. Her relationship with Passion was just what she needed. Passion was the proverbial older sister she never had, old enough to offer her wisdom but not so old as to be unable to relate to what it was like to be in high school.

After another campaign stop, this time in Oswego, New York, Amos, who usually rode in another car, opened the door to the backseat of the town car and slid in next to Cassie.

"Off to Rochester. Exciting, isn't it?"

Cassie couldn't read if he was being facetious.

"I guess." Cassie barely made eye contact before returning to her book, *Native Son.*

"Mind putting down the book for a moment?"

"Sure."

Cassie folded the corner of the page and set the book on her lap.

"Just wanted to tell you how grateful we are to have your support during these last couple of months. It has made a difference."

Given the minimal movement in the polls, she knew this was only lip service.

"That said . . ." Amos paused. "We think it is time to give you a more prominent role. We think you're ready. It's a win-win situation. You can help your uncle while building your resume for college at the same time. Speaking in front of the cameras at your age shows a lot of confidence that most kids can't claim."

"OK, but what do you want me to talk about?"

Suspecting this day was coming for some time, Cassie already knew the answer. It was time to bring out the secret weapon, the surprise witness to win the case. She knew she was not being asked to discuss taxes, jobs, or increased crime in the major cities.

"We can talk more about that when we get to Rochester. The best news is that there is no prep needed. No teleprompter or memorization."

Amos put on his headphones as he scrolled through prior footage of her uncle's speeches. Cassie had more questions but returned to her book.

CHAPTER 21

AFTER CHECKING INTO the Hyatt, Davis handed Cassie her room key.

"We'll be up in about thirty minutes to walk through tomorrow. It's a big day. I know you will do great."

Cassie headed to the elevators across the lobby.

"Hey," Davis shouted across the room. Cassie turned around, her bag in tow.

"Yes?" Cassie's voice sounded both irritated and exhausted.

"Nothing. Nothing. I was going to say, order room service, whatever you want, OK?"

"Sure, thanks." Cassie squeezed into an elevator a jovial woman held for her. She would have preferred to wait and ride alone but did not want to be rude. The bellhop wheeled their bags away as Amos and Davis headed to the lobby bar for a drink.

Cassie fell backward on the bed, letting her bag slide off her shoulder to the floor. She took a deep breath, exhaling out loud. The more time she spent around her uncle, the less honorable she felt about supporting his run for office. His behavior became more problematic with each city they put in the rearview. Her only solace was that she sincerely doubted her ability to move the needle one way or the other.

Most notably, Cassie became acutely aware on the trail of how he treated the opposite sex. What initially appeared to be an anomaly had become a well-established pattern. Her uncle was always available to grant an exclusive and even last-minute interview for someone with the proper credentials, meaning the correct measurements. Many more established and older journalists found getting time on his "busy" calendar more challenging. There was even one time that her uncle emerged from an exclusive interview in his hotel suite with his fly down. Several minutes later, a young, blonde reporter exited. It could have been nothing, but Cassie knew where to put her chips if she were a betting girl.

Cassie had noticed a pattern in how he talked to the women versus the men who worked for his campaign. While he would offer constructive criticism or suggestions to his male staff, he would have only insults for the women. More than once, Cassie walked in on a staffer in the bathroom cleaning off tear-streaked eyeliner following one of her uncle's character assassinations. To the less informed, it would be easy to ask why a woman would put up with such harassment. Cassie knew better. For a poli-sci major or someone looking to build political acumen, holding even a low-level position in the campaign was a stepping stone to realizing a greater career goal. She was sure her uncle knew that, giving him leeway to push the boundaries.

Only a week ago, Cassie saw the worst of his cruelty. She was prepping in the hotel's bedroom suite when she heard him dressing down a twenty-something staffer in the other room. She might have doubted what she heard if it were not for one of his campaign advisors intervening and pulling her uncle aside to let him know he had crossed the line. It had something to do with a revision to the speech that would be fed into the teleprompter later that evening. Apparently, the staffer or someone else had inadvertently cut out an entire paragraph of material.

Her uncle responded with heavily layered sarcasm and vitriol. "Are you stupid? Looks alone ain't gonna get you anywhere, honey. You need to have something between the ears. Looks don't last forever. If you have nothing else to bring to the table, it won't be hard for your husband to find what he needs somewhere else in this town."

Cassie, dumbfounded, dropped her blush on the bathroom sink and raced into the other room in just enough time to see the poor girl exiting. A staff member was on his hands and knees, compiling the papers tossed across the floor. Her uncle turned his back and gazed out the window at the sun setting over the Manhattan skyline.

The election was only a couple of months away. The pressure was enough to bring even the most balanced person to their breaking point. So much work had been put into something without a guarantee of a reward. It was like filling out a thousand-page application for admission to a college, but in this case, it was the only college the person applied to. The brand her uncle had built over years of financial success and celebrity would come down to a binary decision. The prospect of a public failure for all to see was incongruent with how he had built his sense of self. In this case, failure was indeed not an option. He had greased the right palms. He had feigned interest in the right things and disavowed people, places, and things that were unpopular in the circles that made up his constituency. He did what he was told. He said what he was told to say. He even tugged on the heartstrings by introducing Cassie to the public. In short, he had done everything that was asked of him. It infuriated him that a vote was required. He deserved it. They owed this to him. It shouldn't be left to the masses, most of whom he looked down upon. In his estimation, not one voter deserved to cast a decision on his fate, yet he knew he had no control over their collective voice. Win or lose, this was about him. It was about his legacy, not theirs. He owed them nothing.

After putting back a few drinks, Amos and Davis brought Cassie into the main hotel suite to review the plan.

"OK, Cassie, let's walk through the itinerary for tomorrow. Your uncle will be speaking on the steps outside the mayor's office. We expect a couple hundred people in the audience, and almost all of them should be supportive. Inevitably, a few members of the opposition will be there, holding posters and maybe even heckling."

Cassie did her best to listen but felt she was doing her part just by being present. She closed her eyes for a moment as if hoping that upon reopening them, she would find herself in the safety of the closet in her uncle's mansion.

"His speech will run for about ten minutes. No new content. Your uncle will cover the same themes that got him this far. Repetition is key at this point. Don't worry about the media asking you questions about policy. If, for some reason, they do, answer that you believe in your uncle and his character to be able to lead. We expect, and in fact have ensured through friendly media, that you will get some questions about how you came to live with your uncle. What we need you to do—"

"I got it," Cassie interrupted him. "It's the pathos part of the presentation. I know all about it from studying Martin Luther King's speech in school." Her tone suggested she did not want to be talked down to.

Amos was surprised. "Um, yes, that is exactly what we need. But just in case, let's make sure we are on the same page. I know it is difficult and uncomfortable, but we want you to reference losing your parents in an accident."

Again, Cassie jumped in. "And how my uncle swooped in to save the day."

Amos looked over at her uncle, leaning against the wall with his arms crossed. His expression was one of concern. Could Cassie be trusted to say the right thing? Her uncle took a step forward, placing his hand on her shoulder. Cassie was surprised by his firm grip. It was not painful, but neither was it gentle. It was a message to Cassie that failure would not be accepted once the cameras stopped rolling and they were back home behind closed doors.

"Cassie, I know this is hard, but it is important for us. You are a smart girl. I know I can count on you to give it your all."

Cassie, feeling cornered, nodded. "I got it. No problem."

"Good. Good." He gestured to Amos to proceed.

Amos picked up where he left off. "So, all you need to do is reference how difficult that period of your life was and how instrumental your uncle has been in helping you rebuild your life."

Was difficult? Cassie thought. His choice of past tense by itself was very dismissive, as if it were a distant chapter in her memoir.

"I don't want to put words in your mouth. It will be far more genuine if the words come from your heart. The race is close, Cassie. Putting heart, or as you say, pathos, into the home stretch could be the difference."

Following the event the next day, they returned to the hotel suite, where local business leaders and key campaign team members greeted them. Judging from her uncle's mood afterward, Cassie played her part to perfection. Everyone rushed to heap their praises on the rising star. Their secret weapon delivered, hopefully laying to waste the enemy whose name sat less than an inch away on the ballot but was miles from the party's values.

The spread of food was impressive both in variety and presentation. Cassie filled her plate and retreated to her adjoining room, shutting and locking the door between them. She looked at her puffy eyes in the bathroom mirror and felt disgusted. She felt used. No, she *was* used, and she had allowed it. The real Cassie lay beneath layers of makeup and teased hair. She feared whether she would still recognize herself even after it was all removed. The tears shed were real but cheapened by political theater. Her emotions and grief, which were her own, had become a matter of public record. She found herself in the car's back seat again, where her pain had become secondary to her uncle's heroism. Powerless, she was only a passenger, forced to watch as things inevitably would barrel toward another crash.

Cassie went up and down the hotel hallway, bobbing in and out of rooms, desperately wanting to talk to Passion about what she was feeling. When she couldn't find her, she assumed she was sick or maybe in the field consuming more data. There hadn't been a single day since they first met that she did not see her at the campaign office. Just a few days before, she'd offered to review Cassie's school paper on the pros and cons of the Reagan administration. They exchanged cell phone numbers and texted almost daily, even over weekends. She approached her uncle's chief advisor as he exited the buffet line.

"Where has Passion been? Is she sick?"

"Oh, Passion. Nobody told you?"

"Told me what?"

"She quit."

"What?"

"I don't know, something about wanting to go in a different direction with her career."

Cassie looked to be in shock.

"I'm sorry, Cassie. I know you got along well, but it's the nature of politics. It's common for people to get burned out. There's a lot of pressure and long hours."

Cassie texted Passion.

"Where are you? I heard you quit. Can we talk?"

A day passed, then another, and a third, with no response. Cassie could see that she had read the texts. Why wasn't she replying? Cassie scrolled back through her memory. Did they have an argument? Did she say something to offend her? It was possible; she seemed to have a knack for doing that without trying. The more she reflected on it, the less she believed that she had quit. It made no sense. Passion was passionate about political science. It brought the nerd out in her, just as nature did for Cassie. So many people Cassie had met seemed out of touch with their inner nerd, or worse, had buried it so far beneath the desire to be popular, to represent an Instagram version of themselves, that they no longer had any awareness of it. Passion was not one of those people. She was the genuine article. She could be taken at face value. It was one of the things Cassie loved about her. She never had to spend time trying to interpret her angle or underlying motivation. There was little mystery, allowing their conversations to be authentic and warm. She always gave Cassie the answer key ahead of the test.

Even her uncle was in touch with his inner nerd, though he would push back hard on that terminology. His inner fire was not about politics, real estate, or finance. It was about attention. He craved it. He fed it through appearances on CNBC, public charity events, award ceremonies, newspaper interviews, and now through political theater. Cassie knew there was more to Passion's disappearance and aimed to find out.

CHAPTER 22

A FEW DAYS AFTER her speech, Cassie was reading a book when she heard her phone buzz on the nightstand. She hoped it was Passion finally coming up for air. Instead, Kayla's name and photo appeared on the screen.

"Hey, Kayla."

"Hey Cass. Are you OK?"

"I'm fine. What's up?"

"I barely recognized you on TV this week," Kayla said.

"Why is that?" Cassie asked.

"I dunno, you looked . . ." Kayla paused, trying to find the right words, "older and well . . ." She paused again.

"Well, what?"

"It just seems like they are trying to make you eye candy. For someone who used to hide their curves by wearing boy's T-shirts, I guess I'm not used to all the makeup and high fashion."

Cassie had recently given up fighting to do her own makeup. She despised the thirty-plus minutes she spent getting her hair and makeup done before each appearance but never considered it an overt plan to sexualize her.

"Jesus," Cassie said. "Do you think that is what they are doing?"

"I'm not sure, Cassie. But I know it's not you, and I wouldn't put it past your uncle. I don't like that he pulled you into all of this after everything you have gone through. I guess I don't trust him. He seems like a bit of a scumbag. No offense."

"None taken. It's only a few more weeks until the election. Thank God."

"You're probably right." Kayla did not sound convinced.

"Call you in a few days?" Cassie asked.

"Sounds good."

Cassie slid the phone into her back pocket as she peeked at her reflection in the mirror. While she never considered herself a beauty queen, she preferred her natural visage to the doll she became on the campaign trail. She thought, *Just a few more weeks,* as she climbed into bed and pulled the covers over her head.

About a week after her talk with Kayla, things began to change. As she walked the halls and sat in class, like a cool draft, she could feel eyes upon her. She didn't like it. She watched as classmates whispered to one another as she passed by. Was she imagining things? Was she being judged? Her father used to tell her, when she was feeling self-conscious or embarrassed, that nobody cared that much about her and her life.

She tried to remember this as she sat alone in the back of the bus en route to her home. When she returned from school, as was typical, her uncle was nowhere to be found. She made herself a sandwich in the sprawling and sterile kitchen, pulled up a stool at the counter, and logged onto her laptop. Between checking her assignments on PowerSchool, she took bites of her PB&J. Her phone buzzed on the countertop. She flipped it over and saw that someone posted a comment on one of her uncle's Facebook posts. It was a photo of him on stage with her smiling, pointing at someone offstage. She noticed an unexpected amount of likes and comments on the picture. As she scrolled down, her heart sank. She dropped her sandwich on the plate. Her finger swiped down as if its free will controlled it. All the comments seemed to be about her.

Not sure why she is always on camera. She's not even that pretty. Well, she does have a nice pair of hooters.

What a pathetic attempt to gain sympathy votes.
Like she's the only one who ever lost someone.
Boy, must be tough having a multimillionaire uncle take you in.
Boo-Hoo.

Cassie couldn't stop scrolling despite the damage inflicted by each arrow shot her way. Much like her scrolling finger, tears began to flow on autopilot. She had heard of cyberbullying but had never had the misfortune of experiencing it, mainly because of her lay-low strategy on social media. Her social media accounts were private, but her uncle's were not. She now understood why Kayla had been concerned. Her father was usually spot-on with his words of wisdom but could not have been more wrong in this case. People were not focused on their own lives. They seemed to have made a point of destroying hers for reasons she could not understand. Rebuttals and encouraging comments were quickly snuffed out by the insatiable desire to tear her down.

Almost two hours passed, and Cassie's sandwich remained in the same place on her plate; the white bread had already begun to stale in the open air. She bounced from one local news site to another as if wishing to torture herself. A similar, if not as extreme, pattern emerged. Those online news outlets that allowed commentary were full of positive and negative thoughts about her uncle, but that was not all.

Cassandra is hot! I would do her.
She's OK. Wouldn't kick her out of bed.
Wouldn't mind being part of her campaign.
Seems like she suffers from RBF.

She knew that meant "resting bitch face." She sat at the counter for so long that the sun had begun to set, and the room was almost entirely dark, sans the light that remained on in the living room. She heard the familiar sound of her uncle's Jaguar pulling into the four-car garage. The garage door was still going down when he entered the mudroom.

Cassie did her best to compose herself and wipe the tears away. He was startled when he turned the corner in the kitchen.

"Cassie. Jesus, you scared me. What are you doing sitting in the dark?"

He flicked the light on. Cassie felt like a cockroach, wishing she could scatter under a doorframe, away from the light and her uncle's gaze. Resting bitch face or not, she was never very good at hiding her emotions.

"What's wrong? Did something happen?"

He put down a stack of folders he had under his arm and pulled up a stool next to her. Cassie, afraid to speak for fear of losing it, unlocked her phone and showed him some comments on his social media page.

"Oh, fuck. Those fuckers! What kind of person says that? Fuckin' cowards hiding behind their keyboards. I'm going to see if we can trace these and bury those assholes."

Cassie felt relief, even if only a little. Maybe he shared her disgust. Maybe her uncle had the capacity to care, at least when he was sober.

"I thought I was just paranoid that people were talking behind my back at school. Now I know that they were. I never asked for their opinion. Who are they to judge me? They don't know me. They don't know my family. They don't know the guilt!" She was crying so heavily now that she could barely get the words out between breaths. "I wish they could feel what it's like. I wish I could give them my pain. Let them carry it. Motherfuckers!"

"OK, OK, take a breath. Take a breath."

She hadn't felt this out of control since waking up an orphan in the hospital.

"I can't do this anymore. I can't do this anymore. I can't do this anymore." Cassie repeated the words as if the more she said it, the more it would come to pass.

"OK, Cassie. OK. It's going to be OK."

He put his hand on her shoulder and squeezed. It was not unlike the contact she had felt before when he had sent a subtle message demanding compliance. He seemed robotic. His responses, both verbal and physical, were as if he were following an owner's manual for assembling furniture. Cassie went to sleep broken but relieved that she would no longer need to appear in public.

The following day, Cassie woke to the welcoming smell of coffee brewing in the kitchen. She slept through the night, the emotional exhaustion outweighing the hurtful comments that had now taken residence in her mind. Her hair was disheveled as if caught in a wind tunnel. Her well-worn pajamas had several holes.

"Hey, there," her uncle said, entering the kitchen. "Sleep, OK?" he asked as he filed through some papers that appeared to be a copy of a speech.

"I guess," Cassie said, pouring herself a cup of coffee.

Just as quickly, her uncle left the room. A minute later, his campaign manager walked in.

"There she is," he said as he refilled his mug. "You better get ready, Cassie. We are in the home stretch now."

"Excuse me?" Cassie said.

"We have one appearance this evening in Elmira. Did you forget?"

"No. Didn't my uncle tell you? I am done. Didn't he tell you what happened?"

"Yes. Yes, he did, Cassie. It is horrible. There are a lot of jerks out there. But if you are going to be in politics, you need to learn to let it roll off your back."

"I guess it's good that I am not in politics then," Cassie said, fully intending the sarcasm, her anger rising.

Her uncle walked back into the room. His eye contact told her everything she needed to know.

"No. No!" Cassie said as she hurled her mug against the kitchen island, causing it to break into two and splash coffee across the counter and floor. "But you promised! You promised."

"I did no such thing, Cassie," her uncle said in a soft but firm voice.

"How could you ask? After what I showed you? After everything they said about your niece?"

"Cassie, this is too important to stop now. We need you."

"I won't do it. You are a self-centered prick for asking. Do you have no feelings at all?"

"Cassie." Amos attempted to intervene.

She pointed at him. "No. I don't want to hear anything from you, you fucking lackey. I can't believe my chicken-shit uncle tried to have you do his dirty work."

The campaign manager looked down at his feet, recognizing the issue was beyond him now.

Her uncle jumped in. "Cassie, people said some terrible things, but you need to be strong. To succeed in life, you have to be able to show strength during these moments."

"I won't do it. Find yourself another pawn. My father would never make me do this."

"That is why your father could never achieve his full potential. He was smart—probably smarter than me—but he could not push himself beyond his comfort level. He was too soft, too concerned about what the world around him wanted. If you're not careful, you will turn out just like him."

The campaign manager shifted his feet uncomfortably. He looked at Davis, expecting to see immediate regret on his face. To his amazement, there was none. An invisible line had been drawn between Cassie and her uncle, his aspirations on one side and her well-being on the other. It was a threshold he refused to cross.

It had been almost two weeks and there was still no word from Passion. Desperate to talk, Cassie texted her one last time.

Where are you?

Why won't you respond?

I thought you cared about me.

I thought you were different.

Amazed, Cassie watched the three dots appear on her phone. Passion was replying. The dots would repeatedly appear, only to disappear once again a moment later.

Please, reply, Cassie thought. You don't need to craft the perfect sentence. I just need to know you are there, that you care.

Cassie, I am SO SO SO VERY SORRY.

Can we meet? I can explain. I mean, I want to explain.

Can you stop by the house after school tomorrow?

No. I would rather not.

You take the bus home from school, right?

Yes.

How 'bout I pick you up out front of the school.

Sure.

CUL8R.

Cassie responded with a thumbs-up emoji.

The next day, Passion pulled up in the familiar purple Mercedes. Cassie tossed her bag at her feet and jumped into the front passenger seat. Passion surprised her by reaching over and giving her a tight hug. Cassie hugged her back, her anger and confusion about Passion's disappearance melting away.

"Let's go somewhere we can talk. Is there anywhere around here?"

"We could park at the baseball fields across the street. It's offseason, so nobody will be there."

"Perfect."

Passion pulled into the small but empty parking lot. The line of pine trees in front of them swayed aggressively in the wind. There were bleachers along the third-base line, but given the cold wind, they decided to stay in the car.

Cassie looked over at Passion. Passion's usual confident demeanor had given way to a look of fear and uncertainty.

"So, you want to tell me what's going on? Did I do something wrong?" Cassie began to tear up. Her voice gave way slightly.

"No. God, no! Please don't think that," Passion said, gripping the steering wheel tighter.

"Look . . . I . . ." Passion couldn't finish her sentence. The tears fell hard. Her attempts to wipe them away were futile.

"Oh my god." Cassie pulled her right hand off the wheel and covered it with her own.

"Please, tell me what's wrong."

"I don't think I can. I mean, I don't think I should, but I don't know how else to explain why I left so abruptly. I had no choice. I never meant to hurt you. I'm still in touch with one of the campaign staffers. She told me you have been relentlessly bullied since your speech. At the time you needed me most, I abandoned you. I couldn't think straight. I never wanted to hurt you."

"I believe you. I just want to help."

Passion retrieved her right hand to wipe away the tears.

"It's your uncle."

"My uncle? I see the way he treats people. I understand if you don't want to deal with him anymore. I wish I didn't have to."

"I wish that were it, Cassie. I wish I trusted my instincts and left earlier, but I wanted to protect you. I care a lot about you, Cassie." The tears started again. "In the end, I couldn't even protect myself."

"I don't understand."

Passion looked out the driver's side window, avoiding eye contact.

"He assaulted me." She said it matter-of-factly, as if reporting it for the news, as if it had happened to someone else long ago and far away.

"Oh my god." Cassie sat stunned. She knew her uncle was misogynistic. She knew he generally disdained women. But she never believed he could be a predator.

"That motherfucker! We have to go to the police."

"No!"

"No? How can you say that? He needs to pay for what he did to you."

"What he did to *me*. It's me. It's my choice. You don't understand. He is powerful. He has the resources to make the story whatever he wants. He can ruin me. Nobody will believe me. Your uncle is surrounded by spin doctors and experts in character assassination. Before they are done with me, I will be painted incompetent, a hanger-on, or, worse, a single-white-female type."

"OK, OK," Cassie reassured her that she would not do anything without her blessing. "But," Cassie paused, "we have to do something."

"I appreciate your friendship, Cassie, I do. It's not that I am afraid to go public. I would love the chance to destroy him."

Cassie stared out the passenger window, picking at a loose thread on the seatbelt. They sat in silence for what felt like a few minutes before Cassie turned toward Passion, her eyes wide as if she had finally figured out a geometrical proof.

"I am scheduled to speak again on Tuesday night. It's a stump speech in the middle of bumble-fuck New York. I am trying to remember the name. I know it ends in 'burgh,' but that is pretty much every other town in this state. I will expose him for how poorly he treats women. I don't even have to mention you. I have seen other instances of him verbally abusing female staffers."

"No! Promise me you won't do that."

"Why not? It's true."

Passion appreciated Cassie's sense of justice and bravery but knew such a tactic would put her at significant risk.

"He sexually assaulted me. He has demonstrated that he is verbally and emotionally abusive. I am certain he has physical violence in this toolbox. It's too dangerous. Promise me you won't do that." The thought of seeing Cassie victimized brought tears to her eyes.

"Fuck! We have to do something. Anything."

Passion tilted the rearview mirror toward herself. She wiped away some lingering moisture around her puffy eyes. "I look like shit. Man, I am an ugly crier." She smiled. Cassie remained stoic, frozen by her inability to accept such a brazen injustice. "Look, Cassie. There may be a way to use his celebrity against him. The always effective, if not particularly creative, leak to the media."

"I love it. Like that guy Snowden."

"Maybe, but instead of trying to expose an entire system, we are just trying to disarm one man."

"So, how does one leak something?" Cassie asked, her academic thirst for knowledge revealing itself once again.

"I have a friend in the media. He is someone I trust."

"You mean there is someone in the media with morals?"

"I know, right?"

Passion pulled a pen and an envelope out of her purse. It was an electric bill. She ripped it open and put the invoice back in her bag. Flipping over the envelope, she wrote down a name and cell phone number. Isaac Rubenstein, it read.

"He is AP, Associated Press."

"So . . . umm . . . how does this work? Do I ask him to meet me in a dark alley somewhere?"

Passion could tell by her facial expression that Cassie was not being facetious.

"Afraid not. This is not *All the President's Men*."

"*All the President's Men?*" Cassie failed to get the reference.

"Nothing. Just, that's not really how it works. But neither will an anonymous report. Isaac will want a way to ensure there is some level of credibility to the accusations."

"Fine. Why don't I get a burner phone? I can call him on that and then ditch it after we talk."

"Geez, you need to stop watching all those crime shows," Passion said, her witty comment not matching her stone expression. "You will have to identify yourself to Isaac. Ultimately, he may want to meet you somewhere. Not in some parking garage but maybe a café outside of town. Can you get a car?

"I will ask Kayla."

"Kayla, your friend?"

"Yes."

"I suppose that's OK so long as you don't tell her what this is about. The less she knows, the better."

"You're probably right."

Cassie felt terrible about lying to Passion, but she had no intention of hiding the truth from Kayla. She had a right to know and decide how much to get involved if she wanted to get involved at all. Since the day they first played in the creek in Kayla's backyard, they had one another's back. There were no secrets between them, and she was not about to start keeping them now.

"So, now the important part. What are you going to say to Isaac? You can tell him how Davis has continued to make you campaign despite the harassment you have received. Maybe tell him how he treats women in his campaign, especially compared to how he deals with men."

"Do you think that will be enough? I mean, there are lots of men in positions of power who openly flaunt their sexism. It hardly seems to matter. Sometimes, even women vote them in based on what their husbands tell them to do. They must be getting some support from women voting against their interests. At least when those interests don't match that of the men in their life."

"You don't paint a very good picture of our gender," Passion said, sighing.

"Am I wrong?" Cassie asked.

Passion thought for a moment. As much as she wanted to contradict her assessment, she knew she was mostly right. "No, unfortunately."

"Look, I know that you don't want—"

Passion stopped her midsentence. "Don't go there. Don't even suggest it. This is not some Lifetime movie or an Erin Brockovich moment. Sorry to disappoint you, Cassie, but that's not me."

Cassie put her hand on her shoulder.

"I'm sorry, Passion. You could never disappoint me." She leaned over and hugged her tightly as Passion began to sob heavily.

"I'm so sorry. I'm so sorry." Cassie felt a pang of naïveté and guilt. She knew that in her anger and desire to bring down her uncle for what he did, she disregarded the fear and pain it would bring to Passion. She would leak what she had to the reporter, hoping it would be enough to reverse the momentum of her uncle's campaign.

"I wish I was as strong as you, Cassie. Everything you have been through. You lost your parents and have to live with a predator. I used to think I was strong. I saw myself as an independent woman, in control of my destiny, but then . . ." Passion paused, trying unsuccessfully to resist the next wave of tears.

"Passion, you are independent. You are strong. You remind me of my mother. If you think I am strong, it is because of my mom, and nobody reminds me of her more than you. Being around you gives me hope. It gives me confidence. That's why I was so scared when you disappeared."

Passion looked outside the driver's side window. It had begun to rain, the kind of precipitation that made it difficult to tell whether to turn on the wipers.

"He drugged me."

"He drugged you?"

"Your uncle. He put something in my drink. He asked me to review the most recent polling numbers and to interpret some of the data. It was around one in the morning when I arrived at his suite at the Sofitel. He had several binders of charts from recent polling on the coffee table. As soon as I entered, I sensed something wasn't right. Amos was always part of our meetings. He was a data junkie, and your uncle always wanted him to have the latest information firsthand. Amos was nowhere to be found, and nobody else was in the suite."

Now, looking directly at Cassie, she continued.

"I . . . I guess I didn't want to give him the satisfaction that I was intimidated. I saw how, piece by piece, he tore down the self-esteem of others. He had never been able to do that to me. I wasn't about to let him do it now. I sat in a chair directly across from him and the coffee table, ensuring I was closer to the door. I was ready to bolt at a moment's notice. Given his lack of respect for the female mind, I was sure he was oblivious to my strategy. I felt very much in control." Her eyes now moved down to her lap. "He had two glasses and a bottle of wine. He must have already had something in my glass. Before I knew it, I awoke to him on top of me. I thought it was a dream, a nightmare. When it dawned on me that it was real, I attempted to push him off of me. My arms and legs felt like Jell-O. I willed them to resist, but they betrayed me. That fucker looked me in the eyes, saying some shit about how he knows I have wanted this since I first laid eyes on him and how I was so lucky to be fucking a future state senator of the great state of New York."

Tears filled Cassie's eyes. Hearing that she was assaulted was horrible enough, but the details took root in the soil of her mind and grew like a weed, like in the first warm, sunny days of spring. What was a blank slate, free from the burden of details, was now a mosaic of suffering and the loss of her friend's sense of self. Cassie said nothing. She wanted to give Passion her full attention, listening to every word; her mind did not wander for even one second.

"You know what the worst part is?" Passion's nose was red from the salty mix of tears and mucous. "When he finished, he wanted to go over the numbers like nothing had happened. Like I had imagined everything. First, he raped my body. Then he tried to mindfuck me. I hate myself for letting him get the better of me. He outsmarted me. I thought I had it all figured out. I am fucking pathetic."

Cassie reassured her with the usual and factual retort that she was not to blame, that she was, in fact, brilliant and had no control over what had happened to her. She knew the words would fall away as they moved from her ears to the part of the mind that would interpret them. No words or actions could undo the damage. It was not a rational process; its only remedy was gradually learning to find self-love again through therapy, medication, support, and a spiritual healing journey. For the first time, Cassie wanted to kill her uncle. She felt the sunshine was wasted on him and should be forfeited to Passion. He only deserved the night.

Cassie and Passion alternated between talking and hugging for a long time, so long that by the time they were done, the automated parking lot lights had flicked on, casting a shadow out to the pitcher's mound. Cassie offered to drive home. Passion exited the driver's seat without responding and walked to the passenger side. Cassie slid over on the bench-style seat and turned the key. The ride was silent and seemed longer than it was. Cassie pulled up to the curb a few doors down from her house, shifted the car into park, and exited the vehicle. Passion robotically moved to the driver's side. She rolled down the window.

"Bye," Passion said, with a smile that could not hide all the pain underneath.

Cassie leaned over and kissed her on the forehead.

"Don't worry, Passion. You will get through this. I am not going anywhere." Cassie's eyes suggested a determination that Passion had never seen before. "I will ruin him."

After Passion drove away, Cassie decided to walk around the block before entering the house. She was half hoping her uncle was there so she could stab him with a kitchen knife and half hoping he would never come home at all.

CHAPTER 23

IT HAD BEEN a whole week since Chuck last saw his friend. He had sent Bill five unanswered texts, all but the last one read. Chuck recognized that sharing was a risk, not because Bill might turn him in if he hadn't already done so. He did not fear incarceration at his advanced age. What worried him was that his new friendship was forever shattered. Chuck could count his remaining friends on the fingers of a single hand, and when weighing the depth of those friendships, he had to admit that some of those fingers only extended to the knuckle.

While Bill could focus during work, which came as a welcome distraction, his nights were marked by interrupted sleep. The cognitive dissonance was worsening. He had just managed to fall asleep when a heavy downpour suddenly woke him. The raindrops created a din of sound as they relentlessly bounced off the shingles above his head. He rolled over to check his phone. It was 3:45 a.m. He was relieved that it was Saturday morning, and he need not be concerned about another fragmented night of sleep resulting in the slow grind through another day of work. Having not yet been in a deep sleep, his elastic mind generated his first clear and hopeful thought since hearing his friend's confession.

What if Chuck was lying? Lying might be too strong a word. He didn't seem like the type, and being a psychologist, he knew his instincts were correct far more often than they weren't. Chuck was old; surprisingly, he did not know exactly how old, as it either never came up in their discussions or, just as likely, Bill could not recall his exact age. He'd just had a stroke. Perhaps it affected his memory, or maybe there was senility. For all he knew, it was conceivable that Chuck didn't even have a granddaughter. He never shared a photo of her, and Bill had never crossed paths with her during visiting hours. Bill felt great relief at the thought of the story being too fantastical to be accurate. He took a deep, fulfilling breath, releasing the tension that had built up over the past several days.

A few hours later, Bill rolled out of bed, uncharacteristically early for a weekend. On this particular Saturday, he had a purpose, something important to attend to. Being a man of science, he was eager to prove his hypothesis that his friend's tale was an unconscious fabrication. He quickly showered and made a cup of donut blend coffee in the Keurig machine. He toasted a couple of whole-grain blueberry waffles and wolfed them down without putting them on a plate. After filling his Colorado State thermos—he no longer remembered how it had come into his possession—he sat in front of his laptop, ready to begin the journey. If there had been an incident, he figured he could find it in the news. He knew the name of the victim and the town. He even knew his friend's granddaughter's name should it be needed.

Bill started with some keyword searches.

He put in "Murder" and the name of the victim in the browser. It returned several results, but they had little to do with murder or the target of his inquiry. He feared his search would not bear any fruit before remembering that it was made to look like an accident, even if it had been a murder. He changed the search terms to what everyone thought had happened.

This time, he first tried the victim's name, followed by the word "accident." Garbage results, like abstracts from seemingly unrelated research papers, came up. One of the results was about baseball. How the algorithm produced that, he could not say. At the bottom of the page, a promising headline caught his eye. "Prominent Community Leader Running for Office, Dead." He clicked on the link.

The publication was the *Village View*. The paper identified the county where the event occurred, and the date, November 15th, was close to the general election date.

He was anxious, unsure what he would find, hoping it would be nothing and that his friend's only crime was losing his faculties. As he scanned the digitized article, he found it interesting to see the old advertisements. He was surprised by how many larger businesses from a decade ago no longer existed. He was sure that HHGregg was a thing of the past, probably done in by the 2008 subprime mortgage debacle and subsequent crash in equities.

It was a particular image that first caught his eye. The picture was of the unmistakable yellow tape that separated a curious public from a possible crime scene. The photo appeared to have been taken from the front of the house. An investigator was frozen in time, pointing to an upstairs window.

"Davis Ripley, 48, community leader, TV personality, and wealthy bachelor, was found dead in his foyer when authorities executed a welfare check requested by a campaign team member after being unable to reach Mr. Ripley for several days. He failed to show up for a couple of meetings, including an agreed-upon post-election interview with a New York Times *reporter.*

The cause of death remains uncertain, but authorities believe he may have taken a serious fall inside the residence. The time of death has not been provided, citing the ongoing investigation."

Having found his first breadcrumb, Bill felt what could only be described as excitement. Being analytical by trade, he briefly wondered if that made him a bad person. Regardless, his curiosity as an investigator outweighed any reservations about continuing.

With new confidence, he proceeded. There were subsequent updates on almost a daily basis. Several local publications picked up the story but mostly regurgitated previously reported facts. Even the *Wall Street Journal* published a small article on the death, given his celebrity status and prominence in the real estate market. Nine days later, some additional details were released courtesy of a leak.

"New details have surfaced in the ongoing investigation into the death of Davis Ripley, former Republican candidate for the NY State Senate. An unnamed source familiar with the investigation confirmed that the victim died from a serious fall down a flight of stairs."

So far, there had been no discussion or consideration of foul play, but it was always possible that the authorities were holding that close to their vest. He continued to work meticulously through the search results before getting to the next breadcrumb that seemingly drew a conclusion.

"In a press conference today, the District Attorney of Anson County announced that the death of Davis Ripley was officially classified as an accident. Per the DA, 'Sometime on the evening of November 15th, Mr. Davis lost his balance, descending the stairs on the second floor, resulting in his falling down more than twenty steps. He died from blunt force trauma to his head and neck. Toxicology reports showed his blood alcohol was two-and-a-half times the legal limit. As a matter of procedure, his granddaughter, the only person living in the house at the time, was interviewed about her whereabouts. She reported that she had spent the night at her grandfather's house. This was confirmed by her grandfather and two neighbors, who reported seeing a blue Toyota sedan in her grandfather's driveway when they left for work in the morning. They were familiar with the vehicle and knew his granddaughter sometimes used it. Her name has been redacted given her status as a minor."

The article reported that the DA abruptly stepped away from the podium and was replaced by a department talking head, who was peppered with questions about the details of the incident. The spokesperson only parroted what the DA had already said, and the remainder of his responses were dominated by the words "No comment" and "We cannot comment at this time."

Bill leaned back in his office chair, trying to take in everything he had learned. His lower back responded with a short jolt of pain, a reminder that he had been sitting in the same spot for several hours while failing to pay ergonomics any mind.

A few days later, after another long day at work, Bill crashed on his faux leather couch and flicked on the TV. There was nothing on, but it did not matter. For Bill, it was just white noise, a way for his brain to decompress as if coming to the surface slowly to avoid the bends. He stopped on HGTV, always reliable for safe, inane programming devoid of controversy. He craved predictability, something to contrast the lack of control in his chosen profession. It was why he repeatedly found himself watching the same movie. Knowing the ending was not always a bad thing.

He opened a bottle of Blue Moon and took a few swigs while he waited for his Lean Cuisine to finish microwaving. His thoughts returned to his old friend. It had been two weeks since they chatted in person or via text. Knowing his granddaughter's name, he decided to look her up on Instagram and Facebook. Until then, finding it creepy, he'd managed to avoid the temptation. Did searching her social media make him a stalker? It seemed the opposite of what a psychologist should be doing.

After grabbing his angel hair pasta with zucchini from the microwave, he entered his study, or more accurately, his second bedroom, and logged onto his computer. He left the TV running on *Love It or List It*, a show he was reasonably sure he had seen every episode of and yet could not remember a single one.

He figured she had to be about thirty years old now and that she lived about two hours away. He searched for her name on Facebook. He had a few hits on people who shared her name, but they all appeared to be much younger. Switching to Instagram, he repeated the search. While some teenagers appeared in the results, one image midway down looked promising. He clicked on it. As luck would have it, the account was public. He clicked on some of the photos. A few of her were in what appeared to be a coffee bar or small concert venue. He scrolled down before stopping when catching a name on the wall behind the barista station. There was a woman, possibly a college student, behind the bar. She was smiling, her hand outstretched to the cameraman, unsuccessfully requesting not to have her picture taken.

The name Crescent Café was on a giant chalkboard on the brick wall. It had the names and prices for the full drinks menu—cappuccinos, lattes, and smoothies. There was a small offering of creative food listings, like pulled pork quesadillas and honey, pineapple, and avocado flatbread.

He bookmarked the establishment's web page and saved the address on his phone. Scrolling back through the photos, he took a couple of screenshots on his phone. Satisfied, he parked in front of the TV and changed the channel to a college baseball game on ESPN Classic. Nothing put him to sleep better than baseball. It was as likely he would wake on the couch as in his bed down the hall. It depended on his level of tiredness. Generally, the closer it was to the end of the week, the more likely he was to wake in the morning curled up on the coach. It was Friday night.

CHAPTER 24

SITTING IN THE driver's seat, with the engine idling, Bill adjusted the rearview mirror to take a quick look at himself. A myriad of thoughts swirled through his mind.

He hoped the few pictures he had would be enough to identify her. Cassie posted infrequently. Either this was not her primary method of participating in the digital world, or she dipped her toe in the water only to conclude that the whole exercise lacked meaning or purpose.

Bill had no presence on social networks. He did not want to deal with denying requests from former patients and coworkers. Furthermore, for Bill, the internet was a place of extremes, where one shared trivial details of life that nobody cared about or hyperbolic opinions that had little purpose other than to elicit a negative response from strangers. Seeing so many adolescents victimized by social media only further ensconced his belief that it was a boundaryless wasteland. The anonymity of the internet gave rise to a new, weaker brand of bullies—kids who, in the light of day, would never think of saying hurtful things and casting aspersions without the cover offered by the safety of firewalls and untraceable accounts.

He took a glance at her photo. Her wavy, dirty blonde locks sat just below the shoulders. In the front, her face was hugged by two blue strands of hair, both terminating just below her chin. She was wearing a white Rolling Stones T-shirt, the iconic red lips jutting from the middle of her chest. Her eyes were dark, appearing almost black. Her slight smile failed to hide her dimples even if they were not on full display. Outside of the obvious dye job on her bangs, she appeared not to be wearing any makeup. She had full lips, high cheekbones, and a neatly upturned button nose that fit the rest of her features like a glove. Bill found himself daydreaming, temporarily losing himself in her beautiful, soft, slightly pale skin. A leaf collection truck passing on the street behind him finally snapped him out of the reverie. He tucked his phone into the pocket of his jeans and punched the café's address into his GPS. It was sixty-four miles, an estimated one-hour-and-twenty-one-minute drive.

After stopping for gas and a breakfast sandwich, he pulled onto 22 South, the road that would make up a significant portion of his journey before ending in a series of left and right turns for the last few miles. There were two lanes on each side of the road. Traffic was light and Bill made excellent time.

Bill found beauty in the rolling mountains and hills that dotted both sides of the route. It was late autumn; some trees held onto the last of their leaves, but most were bare. A sign indicated he was within the city limits. The road had a string of car dealerships, an Applebee's, a Panera, and a couple of strip malls. His GPS matched the roadway signs that pointed left or right at intersections, indicating the way downtown.

The name on the strip mall's sign caught his eye before the navigation system announced he was approaching his destination. He clicked cancel on the car's interface and pulled into the sizable parking lot. It was just after 11:00 a.m. He pulled through a parking space so that he could pull forward when it was time to leave. He could see some movement in the establishment. Now that he had found the place, he realized he had no solid plan for what to do next.

Assuming he could identify Cassie, if she even still worked there, what would be his next move? Asking if she was abused by her uncle or aware that her grandfather was responsible for his untimely death was not in the cards.

Inside the walls of mental health facilities, broaching such sensitive topics was familiar. The table was already set, leaving little mystery about why people were there. Time was not a luxury in the treatment center. Each patient's insurance clock started ticking before being shown to their room. Getting to the graphic and personal details was done with the same caution as asking someone about their favorite color. The complications of his plan began to surface. Bill, logical and fact-oriented by nature, realized that the emotion generated by the unfolding mystery had dulled his typical, methodical approach to things. What if she wasn't even working today? How would he find out her schedule? What if she looked nothing like the picture on his phone? Would he be able to recognize her as the same person? Assuming employees didn't wear name tags, which was highly likely, how would he identify her with certainty? He supposed he could ask for her name if she were to take his order. *Thank you, and your name is? Well, thanks again, Cassandra.* It would be awkward but not entirely uncouth. It could just be seen as someone being polite.

Prepared to order a coffee, he walked past a couple of large wagon wheels out front and entered the café. He was surprised that the old country farmhouse motif continued throughout the interior. There were beautiful, large wooden beams, complete with natural grooves and knots. The walls were mostly plaster, painted a pale, soft yellow. The bar was J-shaped. Several barstools were tucked under the straight part of the bar. The curved section held the register where orders were placed. An "Order Here Sign" marked with a down arrow hung from the ceiling, eliminating any doubt on where the line started. Surprised, he saw a beer tap centered on the bar over the stools. There were some microbrews he had never heard of and some staples like Guinness and Shock Top. He recognized the familiar, if not edited, listing of drinks and meals on the back wall with the chalkboard. On the opposite wall was a dry-erase board listing the singer-songwriter schedule for the next several weekends. Bill realized it was a café by day and a small club at night. The café was closed on weeknights outside of Thursday and Friday nights when they held open mic nights.

Scanning the place, he saw typical patrons, students working on a project, seniors playing cards, old friends catching up, and the ever-present next great author working on a manuscript. What he didn't see was anyone who resembled the purpose of his journey. Two people were behind the bar. One prepped food while the other was busy preparing a latte for a customer, who waited compliantly in the "Wait Here" area opposite the register.

He could hear someone in the back turning on and off a faucet, accompanied by the clatter of pots striking one another. He ordered a drink while waiting for the dishwasher to reveal him- or herself. After placing his order, he found a table with two seats and parked himself facing the bar.

He played with his phone, reading the news as he patiently waited. About fifteen minutes later, a tall male with earlobes stretched from plugs surfaced from the back as he pulled off a pair of dishwashing gloves and tossed them on a cart in the back of the bar. It was clear Cassie was not there. While not surprised, he sighed out of frustration and took a sip of his coffee. He glanced around the barista area, hoping they might have a photo board of the workers or a schedule lying around. There was nothing. Patience, he thought. A good investigator does not find the answers they seek on a fixed schedule. He decided to walk around the town, surveying the many mom-and-pop shops before stopping somewhere for lunch, after which he would stop back in the café. He stuck around as he figured it was conceivable that Cassie would be part of the change in shift as the café transitioned to a nightclub.

The town was quaint. While some stores had the typical country crafts from local potterers and folksy signs, a few had unique stuff. There was a stained-glass shop with gorgeous offerings meant to hang in windows. The large floor-to-ceiling windows out front were perfect for leveraging the sun's rays, maximizing the beautiful handiwork within. Bill wished it wasn't so cloudy. In the back of the room, you could watch artisans, glass blowers, and carpenters in the act of creation. A sign indicated that full stained-glass windows could be custom built and installed in place of regular windows. Bill thought that would be amazing but realized it would not be permitted by the townhouse homeowners association and, even if it were, would be out of place. Plenty of older farmhouses in the area would be perfect candidates. He made a note to remember this place should he ever buy a single home and want to take advantage of such fantastic craftsmanship. After grabbing a club sandwich at Annie's, a small, fifties-style diner on the opposite street corner, he returned to the café. As it had now switched to the nightclub, he ordered a twelve-ounce draft of Elmira's Black Bunny Pale Ale and sat at the bar.

One of the workers from earlier was rearranging the tables to face the small concert stage. Three new people were behind the bar, wiping down freshly washed mugs. None of them looked like Cassie. He milked his beer and then another over the next few hours. He glanced at his watch. It read 7:14 p.m. A woman with a vintage orange sweater and long cream skirt that appeared to be from the '70s had begun tuning her acoustic guitar, pausing to adjust the mic to match her height as she sat on a high stool. Bill was tired. As much as he wanted to hear some music, he decided it was time to get back on the road.

If he wanted to see Cassie, he would need to make a return visit. He flicked on the headlights of his car and pulled out of the lot. The rural route back home was dark, the only illumination coming from his car's low beams and the occasional truck passing the other way. The mountains could no longer be seen in the autumn sky. As the miles passed behind him, he felt overcome by a sense of loss—not like that of separation from a loved one but rather from a disconnection from himself. He had driven more than an hour to find a woman he did not know, following breadcrumbs laid before him by someone he had only met a few months ago. Was it any different from how he'd come to be a therapist? How could he be sure he was not being steered by the invisible hand of his past? Was his drive for success all these years from within or only a way to ensure he lived up to his father's expectation that he "not be a problem"? Were his accolades borne from an inner desire separate from the drive to ensure he did not end up like his brother? Was his choice of profession simply his subconscious search for an answer as to how what started as a loving family with the best intentions ended up so fractured? Had he not found the "one" to settle down with out of fear of recreating the dynamic of his youth?

CHAPTER 25

BILL DID HIS best to leave the friendship with Chuck behind and allow the man's tale to fade with his eventual passing. He was successful for a few weeks, but his civic duty and the innate desire to discover the truth, like a squatter, took residence in his mind. He decided on a compromise. He would make one, and only one, more trip to the café. He would let fate decide. He finished his last group of the day and was out the door in near record time. It was a Thursday, meaning open mic night.

It was early December, and the first real bite of freezing air had entered the region. He was surprised to see a thin sheen of ice forming on his car window. Being ill-prepared, he had no scraper in the car; he wasn't sure if he even owned one. Fortunately, the defroster made quick work of the window, and he was on his way. The night sky was mainly black, allowing a full display of the cosmos. He searched for the big dipper and, upon locating it, decided he was ready to go. The occasional headlights in both directions illuminated the night, though, for long stretches, his car was the only one on the horizon. He flicked on the high beams, revealing tree lines at the edge of his peripheral vision. It was desolate, but he did not feel lonely. Deciding to hand things over to fate was freeing. While he hoped he would get the answers he sought and that this chapter of his life would end satisfactorily, the process would provide the sustenance needed to move on regardless of the outcome.

He made it to the café in record time. Surprisingly, there was less traffic on a Thursday night than on his venture from the weekend. As he pulled into a parking spot, he noticed more cars than usual, all parked near the café. Open mic night was a bigger draw than he had imagined. He caught himself looking at his hair and teeth in his rearview, ensuring he was presentable as if he anticipated meeting someone.

The tables had been arranged in front of the stage. Each table had a small white candle flickering in the unfelt breeze. Most were already occupied. People chatted over pints of beer in frozen glasses with a sheen similar to his car window only a couple of hours prior. Some chose red or white wine over what was on tap. The crowd was mostly older, complemented by the occasional twenty-something. The way people exchanged hugs and laughs gave Bill the impression that many knew each other. He sat alone at a table for two against the back wall, farthest from the stage. He did not recognize any workers behind the bar but felt sure none could be Cassie. A woman hustled back and forth between the back room and the soundboard. She had an impressive nose ring, and her ears were almost completely covered with bling. Her hair was dyed deep black, and she wore what appeared to be black lipstick. Her bright smile and cheerful eyes belied the message from her chosen wardrobe.

It was then that he noticed her. A woman walked through the door carrying a guitar case. She nodded to the nose ring girl and headed straight for the stage. She pulled a stool closer to the microphone stand. The quickness with which she adjusted the height suggested she had done it a million times before. The spotlight came on as she pulled her Fender acoustic guitar from the case and put the strap over her shoulder. Bill could not believe it. He pulled up the screenshots from his phone and compared them to the unnamed musician. He was confident it was her. It had to be her. Not only did the hairstyle match but she was also of similar height and physique.

What sold him was her beautiful pale skin under the glare of the soft white light. She tuned her instrument and looked out at the crowd, her small dimples displaying a genuine and welcoming smile. It matched what she emoted in the photo, her features combining to form a one-of-a-kind image, not unlike a fingerprint. Bill felt his heart racing. He had to stop himself from running to the stage to ask for her name like some crazed groupie. He took a swig of his beer to break the tension. The lights in the café flickered, indicating the show was about to begin. Another artist entered carrying an instrument and sat in the back corner.

The singer opened with "Under the Milky Way" by the Church, a song that took him back to college, sitting in a basement bar with ragtag furniture and sticky floors. The nostalgia made him smile inside. As the first lyrics echoed through the sound system, he could barely believe what he heard. Her voice was slightly raspy, as if she'd just woken up, yet it was extremely powerful and clear. She had full command of her range, never over-singing notes. She knew how to use silence and the beat between notes to accent her talents, leaving the audience waiting and anticipating the next lyric. Bill was mesmerized. He was no longer at home or a club but somewhere in between, the glorious limbo rarely discovered amongst a cacophony of noise that saturated daily life. She followed with "Smiling," a deep cut from Alanis Morissette. She put her twist on it, leveraging her distinct voice. There were a couple more songs that Bill liked but were unfamiliar. She closed her set with "Closer to Fine" by the Indigo Girls. She received applause that seemed far more voluminous than what the size of the crowd could conjure. Bill found himself clapping hard as if trying to outdo the rest of the audience.

In a stroke of luck, as she put away her instrument and stopped to reset her hair tie, he heard the confirmation he was seeking.

"Great job, Cassie. Thanks for playing 'Closer to Fine.' I know you get lots of requests."

"Anything for you, Sam. You know that," Cassie said.

A few other people, who appeared to be regulars, approached the stage to shake her hand and exchange pleasantries. He couldn't quite make out some words of encouragement that seemed to be related to an unwell pet. Bill took his place at the back of the haphazard line. He wondered why he was so nervous. When he approached and looked into her eyes, he could swear it was minutes before he found any words. In truth, it was only a brief pause.

"Hi, uh, just wanted to say you have an amazing voice."

"Thank you. You're very kind," Cassie said with an appreciative smile. All the words he'd rehearsed tripped over one another until he could no longer form a lucid thought. By the time he corralled the words back into place, the moment, his opportunity had passed. After a brief meeting with a few more people in the crowd, Cassie put her guitar away, moved behind the bar, and leaned the case against the wall.

On this particular night, she opened her shift with a brief concert for the patrons. As she poured a few beers for customers from the tap, the next musician set up. Bill hoped this was not his first time behind a microphone, especially after following the previous act. He decided to stick around through part of the set. While the musician was not as good as Cassie, he held his own. Unlike Cassie's set, Bill could not identify any of the songs. He wondered if they might be his own. Bill had no musical ability that he was aware of, but even if he had, he could not fathom putting himself in such a vulnerable position. Bill had acted admirably in countless situations the rest of the world would never consider putting themselves in. He once spent an entire summer working the 911 dispatch for a psychiatric crisis center. Despite facing matters of life and death, he followed his training, a script of what to say and what not to say. By contrast, a musician walked a tightrope that was uniquely their own, their creativity on display for the world to accept or reject. In a word, it was personal.

Having finished his single beer long ago, Bill decided it was time to depart. Before doing so, he took a final gaze at Cassie as she was wiping down the bar. He would have preferred it if it weren't the case. Still, there was no denying he was attracted to her: the way she moved, her radiant smile, and how her voice brought life to what only hours before was a one-dimensional photo, the possible subject in a tragic story.

It was 10:15 p.m. when he pulled out of the lot. His turn signal clicked as he waited for traffic to pass. He glanced in his rearview and thought, What have you gotten yourself into?

CHAPTER 26

NOW THAT HE HAD located Cassie, he felt obligated to determine the veracity of her grandfather's admission. He knew he could not walk up to the register, order a drink, and ask, "Do you have half-and-half, and did your grandfather murder your uncle?" Such a sentence had never been spoken on earth and would remain that way. He understood his only play was to get to know her. He figured it would not form as organically as the relationship with her grandfather. The challenge both excited and frightened him.

Bill made the trip three out of the next four weeks. Of the two nights he found Cassie working, she only performed once at open mic night. He tried to order food or drinks when she took the orders or worked the register. No words were exchanged other than the typical banter made during an exchange of money and goods. However, he knew she had seen him enough now that she could point him out of a lineup. In his mind, he had achieved his first goal, even if it was the easiest. He would need some reason for talking to her, a topic, preferably something he could identify with, a possible common interest.

He returned to her Instagram page, and the shameful feeling of spying returned. He pushed it away, thinking there was no other way. She had barely posted anything since he'd last looked. There was some reference to the school she was attending, but there would be no reason he would bring that up in a conversation short of saying, "Hey, I was stalking your Instagram account the other day and noticed . . ."

It was then that he remembered the tattoo. When Cassie took off her flannel during her last show, there was an arrangement of Japanese characters wrapped around the bicep of her right arm. It wasn't much, but it would have to do. He would ask her what it meant. Undoubtedly, it was a question she had fielded a million times before from both the purely curious and those looking to flirt. However, Bill's motive was unique. He was trying to solve a possible murder.

Two weeks later, he made the return trip. He arrived later than usual. It was just past 8:00 p.m. If she'd played that night, he may have missed the show. He took his usual spot along the back wall and turned on his laptop, happy that it provided a distraction and cover for why he would spend hours at the café. He patiently waited for her to move from making the drinks to taking orders or working the register. Frustratingly, neither happened. He had been there almost two hours. At one point, she made her way out to the tables with a spray bottle of disinfectant and a rag. As she wiped down the tables, she slowly made her way closer to his table. It was time to adapt and alter the plan. He mustered the courage and waited until she was wiping down the adjacent table.

"Excuse me." He was embarrassed. His voice was too quiet. She didn't hear him over the dishwasher unloading and the patrons' chatter. He tried again, this time louder. "Excuse me."

She turned to face him, bottle in one hand and the now wet rag in the other.

"Yes?" She made direct eye contact. Again, he was taken aback by her beauty. Focus, he thought. You are here for a reason. A man has admitted to a murder. The truth must be uncovered, regardless of how you may have felt about the old man when you met.

"Sorry if this is a bit weird, and I'm sure you have been asked this by a ton of people." He was drawing this out and felt a sense of panic.

His phrasing sounded like he was gearing up to hit on her or ask for a date outright. She seemed to pick up on his mental gymnastics.

"My shift ends in an hour," she said, acknowledging the delay. A genuine smile quickly followed. "Just kidding. I work in a café and concert venue with alcohol; I doubt there is much you can ask that I haven't heard."

"Well, I was just curious about the tattoo on your arm."

"Oh, that?" She began tracing the writing with her index finger. She laughed. "Tell you what. I know you are here most Saturdays, as am I. You tell me what you think it means next time you're here. Guess right, and I'll give you a drink of your choice on the house." She reached out her hand. "Deal?"

Her handshake was as welcoming as her disposition. Given her guitar playing, her hand was softer than he would have imagined.

He sat for another fifteen minutes or so before leaving, thus avoiding the appearance that he was only there to ask a question and, having met his objective, was ready to go. As he drove home, embraced by the dark winter sky, he felt alive, barely noticing the chill that lay upon the valley. It took him almost no time to realize he would have no way of guessing what the tattoo meant. He could not remember the characters and, even if he did, knew no way of typing them into a search engine. It hardly mattered. He would find some proverb or spiritual quote online. The important thing was that he had a reason to continue the conversation. He allowed himself to feel proud that he was closer, even if only fractionally, to understanding what Chuck may have done, and he could hardly wait until the following weekend.

CHAPTER 27

TWO WEEKS LATER, Bill pulled into the café. It was 8:30 p.m., well after the usual start of open mic night. The parking lot was surprisingly sparse. The forecast had called for a slight chance of snow, but it was hardly the type of thing that would register with the inhabitants of upstate New York. Puzzled, Bill glanced in the front window and saw that the lights were on, and he could make out at least one patron at the bar.

There was nobody on the stage. Besides the string of clear white LED bulbs across the ceiling, it was mostly hidden in shadows. It was evident that nobody had answered the call to summon the courage to perform in front of an audience. If there was ever a night to do so, this was it. There would only have been an audience of two, not including Bill.

He was relieved to see Cassie on autopilot behind the bar. The slow night could work to his advantage. He may have more time to talk to her. Would she remember him? Of course she would. He chided himself for being so childish. It wasn't long before he received confirmation.

"Hey, stranger, so, whatcha come up with?"

Bill feigned confusion, trying to play it cool by pretending not to know what she was talking about.

"The tattoo," she said.

"Oh yeah, that." He was sure she saw right through his shenanigans.

"I have no idea. Is it something like 'Peace is found within?'"

She laughed. "Wow, that's not very inventive. It just says, 'The before and after.'"

"Wasn't even close," Bill said.

"So, what does it mean?"

She respectfully pushed back. "Now that I cannot tell you. That's just for me."

"Got it. I can respect that."

"Tell you what, I'm gonna give you that free drink even though you didn't guess right. It's not like it will help turn a profit tonight." She nodded toward the empty tables.

Bill pulled up a stool at the bar. It felt odd being the only one.

"What'll be, sailor?" Cassie asked with a sheepish grin.

"Coors Light, I guess."

"You really live on the edge, don'tcha? You know we have some good local microbrews."

"OK, surprise me."

She grabbed an ice-glazed mug and poured him a pint of Switchback IPA.

Bill was not a fan of hops and generally avoided IPAs. He said nothing as he graciously took the beer and took a gulp.

"Really good. Good call."

"Right?" Cassie said, proud of her self-proclaimed beer snob status.

"So why is it so dead tonight?"

"Every so often, nobody shows up to sing. This is especially strange because, if they had, there would also be nobody to sing to."

After wiping down the bar, she set down the rag and leaned back against the dishwasher behind her.

"So, what's your story? You live around here?"

He thought about lying, as it would no doubt seem strange that he would drive well over an hour to go to a café by himself most Saturday nights. Never being much of a liar, he decided to tell a tale based on a true story.

"No, actually, I live in the Maybrook area."

Cassie looked surprised. He knew what was coming next.

"And you come all the way down here? Maybrook has a college nearby, albeit a small one. And where there are students, there is no shortage of places to get a coffee or a drink."

Bill attempted to avoid the question by asking her another question in response.

"Do you know it?" He already knew the answer.

"Oddly enough, I do. My grandfather is in rehab up there. He had a stroke."

"I'm sorry." Bill clasped both hands around his mug and avoided eye contact.

"It's OK. He is doing quite well. I visit him fairly often, but at weird times, given my schedule with school and work."

"That's good. So, I take it you are pretty close then?"

"You could say that. He has been a lifesaver for me. He was the only person I could depend on during tough times."

Bill took another drink. "Sounds like a special guy."

A slight feeling of shame began to rise within him before he quickly pushed it back down. Of course, he could not come right out with the question about her grandfather's extraordinary claim, but he could probe more to validate his story around the edges.

"Do you have any other family, brothers or sisters?"

"Nope, only child. Can't you tell by how self-absorbed I am?" Bill guessed she was kidding, but her facial expression left the question open-ended.

"Are your parents local?" He felt like a jerk asking that question, knowing it would likely cause her some pain.

She looked into the distance and curtly responded, "No, not really."

Bill was annoyed with himself. She was a little upset, and he didn't get the confirmation he sought. He felt foolish for thinking she would reveal a family tragedy to a practical stranger.

"Anyway," Cassie said, putting her elbows on the bar opposite him and resting her chin on her clasped hands. "You never answered my question."

"You mean, why I come here?"

A small piece of Bill wanted to tell her the truth, that he was there to see her. Since meeting her gaze that first time, he had thought of little else. He had enough sense to shove that down in the same place where he quarantined his shame.

"I work at the Maybrook facility. I'm a psychologist. I mainly work with adolescents and adults with co-morbid diagnoses. The common thread is that they all have some addiction: alcohol, drugs, especially opiates, even the occasional gambling or sex addiction."

"I guess you already see the irony in that." She nodded at the drink in front of him.

He appreciated her wit.

"I guess that is part of the reason I come here. It's not uncommon to run into a former patient at a watering hole in town only weeks after discharge. No matter how many times it happens, it is always super awkward. Most of the time, we pretend not to recognize one another." Bill laughed a little. "Although, believe it or not, sometimes, they will come right up to me, drink in hand, and chat like we are two old buddies from college. I'm not sure if that is admirable or frightening."

"Probably both." Cassie rolled her eyes as if to say, *What a crazy world.*

The only other worker at the café that night was a chubby twenty-something kid in a Grateful Dead shirt. He even sported a beard as if trying to emulate Jerry Garcia. He was beginning to flip chairs on top of the tables.

Bill took out his wallet, preparing to pay for his one beer. He slid a ten note toward her. He was caught off guard when she put her hand on top of his and gently pushed it back. He instantly felt a warmth that was not unlike the comfort felt from hot chocolate after shoveling snow in the bitter cold. Her lips moved, but he was in a trance and couldn't be sure what she said. He assumed it had to do with rejecting his offering.

Something told Bill it was the right time to take a chance. "I know you are closing, but I was wondering if you would like to get a cup of coffee with me sometime."

"Really? I work at a bar that serves beer and coffee. You think that is the most desirable place to go on a date?"

A date? Did she think that was his intention? Was that his intention? Bill was no longer sure himself. He reminded himself again that a man's life had been snuffed out. If she viewed it as a date, that was on her. He would oblige, but only to see that justice was served.

"I guess that's pretty stupid."

"Relax." Cassie smiled. "I would love to."

Bill extended his hand for a shake as if closing a business deal.

She shook his hand gently. Her eyes met his. He knew how utterly ridiculous it was to shake on it but was happy she let it slide. Cassie asked Bill for his number and texted him so he would have hers. They tentatively agreed to meet somewhere the following Sunday afternoon.

CHAPTER 28

CASSIE'S RINGTONE, currently on the pinging radar setting, snapped her out of a daydream she could not recall. Her grandfather's face, sporting an Orvis fishing cap, popped up on her phone. It was a little unusual to hear from him in the evenings, as he had morphed from a night owl to a morning person sometime after the stroke. Whether this was due to cause and effect or simply a random correlation, she could not say.

Her grandfather was hardly diminutive. Despite his advanced age, there was still some evidence of the brawn he carried as a younger man. Over the years, his shoulders bore accumulated weight many others could not carry. Cassie attributed much of this to his ability to compartmentalize. While he never had the luxury of choosing which battles to fight during the war, he had the gift in the civilian world of knowing when to dig in and when to let things roll off his back. The scars of war may have marked his body, but like an old oak tree, it only seemed to make him more imposing.

"Hey, G," Cassie said, using the nickname she'd given him, one that favored brevity over creativity.

"Hey, Cass," her grandfather said.

"What's up?" Cassie asked.

"Um, not much, I guess."

She knew her grandfather would not readily divulge whatever was on his mind. He was old-school in that he felt it was always his job to advise the younger generation, never the other way around—especially when it came to family.

"It's late. There must be something up."

"It's just . . . I dunno . . . it's kind of dumb."

"Come on, that's never stopped you in the past," Cassie teased.

"OK. I'm not sure if I ever told you, but I made a friend at the hospital."

"That's cool. Is it your roommate?"

"Fred? The guy who blasts the TV and only watches game shows? No, the friend is not a patient and doesn't work here either."

"You've piqued my curiosity. Who is it?"

"He's a doctor—no affiliation with the hospital. We sort of developed a friendship. It kind of just happened. You know the place where we usually meet by the koi pond?"

"Yeah."

"He showed up one day sitting on one of the pond's benches. He was reading a book. I thought he was there to see a family member, but after thirty minutes, he would leave having never talked to anyone."

Cassie listened intently.

"After he continued showing up every few days, I started a conversation. I expected to discuss the weather or something stupid, and that would be the end of it. You still there?"

"Yes, I'm just listening."

Cassie always found such a question a sad indictment of a world dominated by sound bites and social media. If she gave someone her full attention, she often found herself needing to confirm she was still on the other end of the line. Having to throw in the occasional "uh huh" annoyed her.

"It turns out we had a lot in common despite the age difference. He's been through a lot. He would visit regularly, always bringing me a coffee. I told him about my life. He did the same. It gave me something to look forward to."

"What am I, chopped liver?" Cassie said, her tone making it clear she was not genuinely hurt.

"Cassie, I love your visits, but I know it's hard for you to get up here with your school and work, and I am not exactly free to travel now."

"I know," Cassie said. "So, then, what's the problem?"

"He stopped coming. Just like that."

Cassie thought it strange but went to her Rolodex of excuses, hoping to ease his anxiety. "You said he was a doctor. I am sure he is swamped. Maybe he's traveling or on vacation."

"Maybe." Chuck was unconvinced.

"Maybe his schedule changed and doesn't line up anymore."

Chuck's silence spoke volumes. "He has my number. I texted him a few times. Nothing."

Cassie was not used to hearing her grandfather be this vulnerable. He'd bonded with this person, and his usually impenetrable ego was wounded.

"I'm sorry, Grandpa. It sounds like the creep ghosted you."

"Ghosted me?" He was unfamiliar with the vernacular.

"I mean, he just dropped out of your life like an apparition. What a fucker! Screw him. You are better off without people like that in your life."

"You're probably right. It's just that sometimes it can get lonely. Getting old. Being a widower. Just never wanted to be one of those guys who show up at McDonald's when it opens and stays for several hours nursing a cup of coffee while reading the newspaper cover to cover."

"Do people still do that?"

"Probably not. But I am afraid to find out."

Having responded with pure emotion, Cassie returned to more logical explanations.

"Did you have a fight? Did you offend him or something? You've never really been politically correct, G."

The long pause before responding was noteworthy.

"No, no fight. I . . . uh . . . I don't know. Maybe it was something I said."

Cassie could tell he was holding something back but did not want to press.

"Tell you what. Why don't I come to see you on Saturday during visiting hours?"

"You don't need to do that, Cassie."

"I'm coming—end of discussion. I'll even bring you some coffee. Some of the good stuff from my café in a thermos."

Cassie clicked the end button on her phone and set it on her kitchen counter. She felt a pang of guilt. While she saw her grandfather every three weeks or so, she knew it could and should be more. As much as she tried to convince herself that she had a full dance card, the reality was that, much like working out, she could do better if she carved it out as a priority. It wasn't like her free time was constructive. She didn't go out much with her coworkers and hadn't bonded with anyone at school, mostly because her classes were remote. Binge-watching Netflix could hardly be called a prior commitment.

The next morning, Cassie texted Dr. Taggart. She had not heard from him about their date, but it had not even been a week since they exchanged numbers.

Won't be working this Saturday. Family commitment. Wanted to let you know in case you were coming this weekend.

She watched the three dots appear, indicating a response was forthcoming. They appeared and disappeared just as quickly. This happened several times before she put the phone down while he crafted the "perfect" response. When her phone pinged a few minutes later, she chuckled when all it said was *OK*. So eloquent, she thought. She wondered what his initial responses had said.

A few minutes later, he added, *No worries. I look forward to seeing you. How does the following Sunday sound?*

Cassie provided a terse response.

Sounds good.

As a performer, Cassie appreciated how he had made himself vulnerable by asking her out. She also had to admit that he was handsome, even if she pegged him as a few years her senior.

CHAPTER 29

BILL FELT A nervous trickle in his stomach and heart. Was his anxiety attributable to his undercover operation and the possibility of being discovered, or was it due to his undeniable attraction to Cassie? He pushed the hangers aside in his narrow closet. After taking out a button-down dress shirt, he decided it was too formal. It was cold enough for a sweater, but they made him feel puffy, like a snowman or a schoolboy at church. He would rather be cool in case his nerves triggered unwelcome perspiration. He decided on a burnt sienna long-sleeve polo shirt from Ralph Lauren. Casual yet still classy, he told himself. He grabbed his favorite gray dress pants from Banana Republic and sat on the bed to tie his brown Ecco shoes.

He stopped in the bathroom for some last-minute grooming. There was no choice to be made regarding cologne. He hadn't worn any since high school. A swig and spit of mouthwash, a quick check of his hair, an extra pass of deodorant, and he was ready. He grabbed his winter coat and headed down the stairs to his car, parked fortuitously in a spot in front of his place. Usually, someone else got to it, and he was forced to park a couple of aisles away. He sighed upon approaching the vehicle. A thin layer of frost covered it. The kind of frost that mocked you when you applied the scraper, always leaving behind alternating clear and patchy lines of ice. It was cold outside, and he had never bothered to buy a pair of gloves, so he sat in the car waiting patiently for the defroster to make its slow march up the window. It was a quarter of seven. He would still be on time.

He connected his Bluetooth and flipped on his '80s hair metal playlist. A highly educated academic and self-accepting nerd, he had never outgrown his love of bands like Skid Row, White Lion, and Cinderella. Regardless of what people thought of the oversaturated glam of the time, he always appreciated the songwriting and musical talent of the musicians before Nirvana buried them in a time capsule. He cranked "Wasted Time" by Skid Row, tapping his fingers on the steering wheel as he turned out of his community. The GPS was set to Cassie's home address, 156 Cowpath Road, an unfitting name given that the nearest cow was miles outside town. He rolled down the main street, passing the café on his left. The blizzard from a week before was still evident, even more so than in Maybrook.

Piles of snow, mostly a dirty mix of brown, black, and white, were stacked high at the edge of sidewalks and parking lots. There were not enough places to put it all. The streets had a soggy mix of slush and ice from the continuous cycle of freezing and thawing. The storm drains did their best but could not keep up with the erratic conditions. Pools of water splashed under Bill's car as he steered to avoid the worst of it. Before arriving at the Willow Tree community, he passed a couple of pizza places, a deli, and a Speedway gas station. He pulled into her lot and glanced up at the connected condominiums.

He scanned the many windows and wondered which was hers and if she was looking out at him. Don't be stupid, he thought. She is not some sad puppy waiting for its owner to come home. He followed the sign to 200–299. Her place was number 248. As he climbed the stairs, he had trouble discerning whether he was just nervous or embarrassingly out of shape. Taking one last deep breath, he knocked on her door.

"One sec!"

A few seconds later, he was eye to eye with a stunning Cassie. Her light blue sweater had a subtle pattern of white stars around the collar. Alternating darker blue and white stripes popped against the lighter blue. He was glad he chose not to wear a sweater. In who wore it better, there would be no contest. Her jeans hugged her hips and legs perfectly, not ungodly tight as seemed to be the style of the day. They were complemented by high-heeled black boots with fluffy grey wool around the cuff. Her lips had lightly applied red lipstick. Cassie's hair flowed down lightly, brushing her shoulders.

He wished it weren't the case, but Bill was enamored with her. This was not part of the plan. As an expert in human behavior, he reminded himself that he was well-versed in identifying and maintaining healthy boundaries. He had always been able to compartmentalize, whether it was blocking out the acrimonious moments from his childhood or leaving the tribulations of his patients at the door. There was nothing wrong with two consenting adults enjoying one another's company. Still, he knew the boundary between his feelings about Chuck's reprehensible actions and his attraction to Cassie was hard to see, much like faded lines on roads that all but disappeared at night during a rain shower. It could be navigated but would require caution and a clear mind.

"You look nice. I love the sweater." Bill wondered if he was as awkward as he felt.

"Thanks, so do you." Cassie smiled and grabbed her coat and Coccinelle brown leather bag.

"Ready?"

"Yup, my Bentley is out front."

"Being a psychologist pays better than I thought." She seamlessly got the joke and carried it forward. It was a small thing, but it gave him hope that the rest of the date would be as free-flowing.

"What do you have in mind? I know we were going to play it by ear," Cassie said.

"It's a surprise. It will either be the coolest idea ever or a complete bust."

"At least you don't put too much pressure on yourself," Cassie said.

Bill chuckled. "Sorry, it's been a while since I have been on a date; I guess I am a little nervous."

"That's OK, me too. We can walk on eggshells together."

Ten minutes later, they had left the small town in the rearview mirror. The road was windy. The CRV navigated with ease as it gripped the salt caking the street. For Cassie, the country roads always brought back memories of the accident, but the pain that used to accompany them had long since waned.

"You're not taking me into the wilderness to kill me, are you?" Cassie said with a smile.

They climbed steeply up a hill and, upon reaching the top, could see the dotted lights of the town in the valley below.

"We're here," Bill said.

At the nadir, Bill made a right down a country road.

"There," he pointed to several rows of cars parked with lights on.

It was then that Cassie saw the massive movie screen. It was cycling through advertisements of local real estate agents, restaurants, and various spas.

"A drive-in? Are you serious?"

"Sorry, we can do something else."

"Are you kidding me? This is amazing! I haven't been to one of these in I don't know how long and never in the winter. I didn't think these things still existed."

They paid the attendant at the booth. Two movies were listed: *It's a Wonderful Life* and *Frozen*. It was the second annual "Cinema in the Snow" weekend. While Christmas had passed, it was still the heart of the winter season, and both selections provided broad appeal for children and adults.

Bill pulled into a spot and tuned to the station to hear the movie. He reached over his shoulder into the back seat before he noted the surprise on Cassie's face. *Oh my gosh, she thought I was making a move.* Her look was not defensive but rather one of being caught off guard. Bill grabbed a thick comforter and a CVS bag full of mixed Halloween snack-sized candy bars, a pack of Twizzlers, and some Milk Duds. He revealed a thermos of hot chocolate and two cups.

"Diabetes for two," said Bill, feeling good about himself now that he knew she was impressed by his creative choice in entertainment.

As if on cue, Cassie said, "I am impressed. Really. How did you know about this place?"

I Googled "odd things to do, unique things to do, cool things to do" in the area, and this came up on one of the lists.

It's a Wonderful Life was starting. Car lights flicked off like lightning bugs realizing they were out of season. It was pitch dark minus the screen and a heavenly display of stars overhead. When Jimmy Stewart came on screen, Bill quickly noticed Cassie whispering the words on cue.

"I've seen it so many times. I love the black-and-white background. Somehow, it adds to the mood of the film."

She even parroted Jimmy Stewart's words on a few of the more famous lines, complete with his unique way of speaking.

"Not bad," said Bill.

"Thanks, it comes in handy during job interviews." She chuckled.

"I can imagine. I see you don't have a law degree, but you know, what the hell, you nailed that impression. We can use that kind of thing at the firm," Bill said.

While most of the cars left their engines running to keep the heat on and ensure the batteries did not die in the wintry night air, Bill spread the blanket across their laps to keep their legs warm.

Toward the movie's end, Cassie pulled on the generous com-forter, puffed it up around Bill, and laid her head on his shoulder. Bill smiled inside. Every part of his body tingled. He could no lon-ger deny it. If there was a perfect moment in life, this was it. This was enough for him—this moment. Under a cold, starlit sky, he knew the feeling of pure unbridled joy. He pulled his arm out from under the covers and wrapped it around her shoulder. She leaned in further. No words were exchanged. None were needed. As the movie credits rolled, Bill was aware that he had failed to garner a single piece of information about the mystery he was trying to solve.

When he dropped her off at the end of the night and walked her to her door, he wondered if he should lean in for a kiss. Was that still the way it was done? In the age of social media, had the rules changed? He wanted to make sure everything went smoothly after what, in his view, was a magical evening. Were the same thoughts swimming in her head? Fuck it! He was not a school kid anymore; it was time to grow some balls. She met him halfway as he leaned in for a kiss, throwing him a lifeline from any lingering doubt. Her kiss took him to another place, a visage he had forgotten existed. He reconnected with a feeling he had not realized was missing until then: the sense of hope, the right to expect more out of his life. Her lips were warm against his despite the cold that surrounded them.

Looking into her eyes, he felt like she was someone he had always known, perhaps in another life. There was something differ-ent. There was a sense of familiarity and security usually reserved for aged relationships born of shared experiences. Was this what people meant by love at first sight? Could he be so lucky? He thought of the signs he would see during a team's playoff run, saying, "Why not us?" Yes, why not us? The click of a door closing on the floor below broke the trance. As they separated, he couldn't remove the smile from his face.

"I . . . uh . . . just want to say I would like to see you again. I don't know if I am supposed to wait a day or two before saying that. I am trying to remember the rules. But to be honest, I don't care. I like being with you. Hope you can deal with that."

She smiled and rolled her eyes. "I think I can cope."

He gave her another quick kiss and headed downstairs to his car, suppressing the desire to skip all the way there.

The bitter cold invigorated his already racing heart. Why can't we always feel this happy? he wondered. Would there be any wars if everyone felt like this all the time? His thoughts regressed to those of a romantic child excited about their first childhood crush. It mattered not. If he could preserve the joy in a mason jar, he would. His shoes crunched against the icy parking lot. He looked up to the sky, which was full of stars. He took a deep breath, telling himself to hold onto the moment for as long as possible.

If Bill had any guilt about pursuing a relationship with Cassie and putting his moral disgust on the back burner, it had temporarily been starved of oxygen. Bill had an extra skip in his step at work in the following days. He felt like he was inside a protective bubble, like a character in a video game with temporary invincibility. Even his colleagues seemed to notice. Barbara jokingly asked if he was helping himself to the med drawer. Not ready to share the new development in his life, he would attribute it to getting more sleep.

His newfound energy even extended to his home life. He was eating out less, choosing to cook more. He started using the gym that was part of his townhouse community fees, even if only a couple of days a week. He felt pathetic that it took someone else to reignite his life's pilot light. More than that, he was a little scared that he hadn't even realized how languid his existence had become. On numerous occasions, sitting in his office, entering notes on his patients' care, he would realize he was clenching his jaw. This habit had become so commonplace that it would recur for prolonged periods before it surfaced in his consciousness. He wondered if he had been doing the same with his emotions, packing them tightly for so long that he was no longer aware of it. No matter, he figured, the cage had been unlocked, and he planned to make the most of it.

In the following weeks, Bill and Cassie explored all the town had to offer, which wasn't much. TripAdvisor only had four recommendations, one of which was an agricultural museum that was technically in an adjacent town. Another was a ghost tour of the historic downtown village. They joked that ghosts should've found more enticing places to haunt. None of it mattered. They were their very own Fodor's guidebook, with the only element of importance being that they were in the same place simultaneously. Spring was advancing in the valley. Forsythias were in full bloom.

On occasion, Bill would find himself trying to stitch together pieces of conversation that he missed, not from wandering thoughts but from her distracting beauty. Most of the time, he was successful. After all, he had years of experience from endless intake interviews, where he was generally not as present as he probably should have been. They scoured the countryside and every small town between Maybrook and Mount Allure. There was not a bookstore, coffee shop, or antique market they had not browsed. Neither of them ever acknowledged it, but if asked, they would admit it was not the destination but the journey they cherished. In route, they talked about everything from global warming to when they were obsessed with MTV's *Real World* during its height of popularity.

Bill usually could subvert his guilt, but there were still moments when it managed to surface. There were unexpected triggers, such as when he escorted patients to offsite twelve-step meetings. The steps were recited at the start of AA and NA meetings. He knew them by heart. But knowing them and living them were vastly different.

While he never suffered from addiction, he managed to follow and disregard the steps in equal measure.

Two steps in particular needled him, interrupting his peace of mind by filling the vacuum in quieter moments.

Step 9: Making direct amends to people harmed except when to do so would injure them or others. Had he harmed Cassie? He didn't think so. Not yet. But if he were to come clean, would that not injure her? They were falling in love. They were happy. There was an argument to be made for keeping silent. Cassie had done nothing wrong. Why should she be denied a shot at love because of something her grandfather may have done? Stepping forward with what he knew could harm Chuck, possibly marking the end of his freedom, but Bill remained unconvinced that would be such a bad thing.

Step 10: Taking personal inventory and, when wrong, promptly admitting it. This was the one that felt like a dagger to the heart every time a patient recited it. Not only was keeping the truth from Cassie wrong but it was a dereliction of his responsibilities.

Bill may not have been an addict, but that hardly meant he was completely sober. He, too, hid conveniently behind the warped reflections of his hall of mirrors. But like those in his care, he had to face the reality that the clarity of introspection demanded.

Would Cassie see him differently if she discovered his secret? Would it be the end of their relationship? Bill watched countless marriages dissolve after one or both partners got clean, revealing truths that their addictions had once obscured.

Bill grew more anxious by the day that Cassie would find out his secret. It wasn't out of the realm of possibility that his name could come up in one of her conversations with her grandfather. He'd created time and distance between himself and Chuck, but it gave him little comfort that it afforded him immunity from being discovered.

As his feelings for Cassie grew, so did his desire to procrastinate coming clean. I will tell her tomorrow, he would say to himself as his head hit the pillow. Inevitably, he found himself repeating the mantra in the nights that followed.

CHAPTER 30

SLEEPING TOGETHER FOR the first time was a completely natural progression. No words were spoken. There was no mystery as to how and when it would happen. Everything about their relationship was formed by letting it breathe. It had the benefit of spontaneity to keep things exciting while enjoying the comfort of security, knowing that they only had eyes for each other. After returning from seeing the play *You Can't Take It with You* at Mount Allure University, they stopped at Bill's home. Despite having been together for a few months, they had yet to stay over at one another's place. It had nothing to do with chastity or religion; it was more of an unspoken agreement to allow their courtship to grow slow and strong like the oaks that lined the entrance to his townhome community. They were not burdened by the need to proclaim that they were going steady or exclusive. She need not adorn his letterman's jacket to ward off would-be suitors.

As was customary, they dropped their coats on the loveseat, which was its only real purpose. Bill was reasonably sure that nobody had ever sat there, himself included. He flicked on the television as they parked on his sofa. They discussed the play, which Bill found more appealing than Cassie. Tired, Cassie kicked off her sneakers one heel at a time and pulled her legs up on the couch. She removed her sweater, and placing it against his shoulder, rested her head. A one-inch strand of hair escaped the tuck behind her ear and covered her right eye.

She looked up at Bill, her one eye locked into his while the other remained obscured. It made her appear flirtatious and triggered a shot of adrenaline that Bill had not felt in many years. His mind went offline, giving complete autonomy to his animal instincts. He put the palm of his hand against her cheek and gently stroked her exposed eyebrow with his thumb. He leaned in to kiss her. Their kisses increased in intensity, rising to a crescendo. She pulled back for a moment, removed her V-neck ribbed gray T-shirt, and tossed it along with her sweater on the loveseat, joining their coats.

Bill removed his button-down shirt in record time. They continued to kiss passionately. He placed kisses on her neck, alternating sides until reaching her collarbone. She giggled from the sensation. Her arms quickly filled with goosebumps, which made Bill smile in delight. As they disrobed, Bill glanced at the sliding-glass door leading to the balcony. Thank God, he thought as he saw that the blinds were closed. He was too excited to pause to secure their privacy from the homes across the courtyard. They explored every inch of one another's bodies, alternating between fingers and lips, touching and stroking, most of the time their eyes locked onto one another. Bill attempted to drag out the foreplay as long as possible. He knew there was no way he could last long, and he did not want to disappoint her.

She pulled him closer as she lay back on the couch, making it clear what she wanted. He obliged. Despite his best efforts, it was over faster than he had envisioned.

"Sorry . . . I'm sorry," he said.

"It's OK." With a serious gaze, she spoke the words he had hoped for but never let himself fully believe would ever be said. "I love you, Doctor."

His eyes filled with water. He was on the verge of crying tears of joy, something he thought happened only in movies or when soldiers returned home to their children after a tour of duty. Countless times, he felt the sting of tears from life's tragedies but never from pure euphoria.

Bill said, "I love you more," and smiled, realizing he sounded like some teenager refusing to get off the phone first in an endless contest to prove who loved whom more.

Driven by an overwhelming desire to ensure that this moment was stamped in their memories forever, Bill kissed her gently around her belly button and inner thighs until she finally directed him to eliminate the building tension.

It was a night of firsts. It was the first time they professed their love, spent the night together, made love, and let themselves believe they could find happiness in another. It was also the night Cassie told Bill about the car accident.

Pulling the covers over their naked bodies, Cassie turned on her side, facing Bill.

"Remember when you asked me about my parents? Whether they were local or not?"

"I do." Bill could picture himself fishing for answers at the bar that night.

"I didn't lie. They weren't . . . er . . . aren't local. But I left something out."

Bill anticipated what would be coming next.

"They died in an accident when I was only a teenager. I was the only survivor."

While he already knew what he had just been told, hearing it from her directly struck him differently, eliminating any chance his empathy would appear staged.

"My god, Cassie! I didn't know. I am so sorry."

"How could you? I don't like talking about it, but I thought I should tell you."

"I can't imagine how painful that must be."

"I still miss them every day, but the sting is largely gone. It's the years after that that are hard to . . ." Cassie's thought trailed off. "I had to go live with my uncle after that. It was a one-hundred-and-eighty-degree turn from my former life. He was wealthy, super wealthy, and incredibly successful in business. He ended up running for office. I was practically part of the campaign. It felt like I was on the trail more than in school."

Bill, knowing about the abuse, was unsure how to respond or contribute to the conversation.

"You'd think all of that means I, at least, fell into a fortunate situation." Cassie played with the comforter's tag. "You'd think, but you'd be wrong."

"What do you mean?" Bill felt a jolt of shame.

Cassie took his hand and looked him in the eyes.

"Let's not completely ruin a good night. I will tell you about it another time."

Bill was a little frustrated. He was eager to discover the merits of what her grandfather had told him and finally understand what may or may not have happened to her uncle and why.

He knew it was selfish, wanting to know more according to his schedule while his secret remained locked inside a vault. Bill felt a pang of guilt as discernable and somatic as the feeling of hunger. His heart commanded him, Say something. Come clean! His head countered that there would be a better, more appropriate moment to do so. As Cassie fell asleep in his arms that night, his fear of being found out was only lessened by the comparable weight of his guilt. He was disgusted by his cowardice. He was a hypocrite. He preached the importance of honesty in recovery to his patients as he kept the truth from the one person he loved beyond measure.

CHAPTER 31

A COUPLE OF weeks later, sitting at Cassie's kitchen table, Bill's patience was rewarded. "I want to show you something," Cassie said, pouring Bill a cup of Earl Grey tea before filling her own.

Cassie moved to the other room. Bill followed, taking a seat on the couch.

"I haven't shared this with anyone but my grandfather." Cassie retrieved a DVD from a cheap CD rack and slid it into the Blu-ray player. "I had it converted from VHS. I'm not sure why; it brings back some bad memories. I guess I thought I should have it in case it helps me reconcile something down the road. Probably sounds stupid." Cassie shrugged her shoulders as the machine swallowed the disc.

"Not at all. I think it is genius. That way, you would have it if you were ever ready to watch it, and if that day never came, no harm, no foul. I'm not sure there is such a thing as too much information when it comes to understanding who we are."

Cassie put the video on pause. "You know what? This is probably on YouTube or something. After all the backlash that came from it, there was no way I was going to check. Have you already seen it? You must have been curious."

"No, I haven't," Bill said, happy that he could tell the truth while conveniently failing to mention that he tried but was unsuccessful in finding it.

"I haven't watched it in forever. Not since . . ." Cassie paused for a moment. "Well, not in a very long time."

Cassie pushed play.

The estimated turnout was spot on with the campaign's prediction. As they stood at the podium, several dozen people gathered in front of the wide staircase. Many held the campaign signs they were handed when they'd arrived. They had them high for the TV cameras that scanned the audience. The mayor, a fellow Republican, introduced Davis. Cassie was positioned behind her uncle's left shoulder while his chief strategist stood over his right. Davis made his typical speech to the partisan crowd, emphasizing his position as an outsider and self-made success in business. If elected, in his version of Reaganomics, he promised the same fortunes would trickle down to every family across the great state of New York. By contrast, he cast his opponent as an insider, someone who would always view the world from an inside-out perspective and was, therefore, out of touch with the citizenry of the Empire State.

Davis's voice grew to a crescendo as he pointed to the crowd. "I am one of you. Let's look at how to fix this great state from the outside in."

Cassie watched the crowd cheer as Davis raised his fist into the air. He pointed to various people in the crowd, mouthing, "Thank you." Whether it was for show or he was addressing people he knew was hard to say. In politics, by design, it was not always possible to differentiate fact from fiction. Selling white lies was part of any campaign. Her uncle had made it an art. He took credit for whatever benefited him while skillfully shedding responsibility for failures.

Cassie edged toward the podium. Her uncle felt her presence and turned around. He bent down slightly as she spoke into his ear over the crowd's din. He smiled and stepped back, allowing Cassie to take his place at the microphone. The plan was executed to perfection. Amos smiled ear to ear, knowing his strategy was off to a great start. The media bought it. They had made Cassie's decision to speak seem spontaneous. She was moved and had to say something.

Cassie scanned the crowd. The lights of the cameras temporarily blinded her. The butterflies she felt while she waited now swarmed like a plague of locusts.

"Hello," her voice cracked. Not a great start. "My name is Cassandra. Davis is my uncle."

She looked over her shoulder, making eye contact with him. She wondered if her reservations were detectable to the audience. Judging from their applause, it wasn't.

"I know I am only a teenager and not very political, but, well, I think my uncle would represent our state well. He has always been a success. When he puts his mind to accomplishing something, it's like nothing can stop him. He has a no-excuses mentality when it comes to demonstrating results. If you are tired of the same old politics, stall tactics, and gridlock, consider a man of action when you go to the polls. I ask you to check the box for my uncle."

The crowd cheered and began chanting "Davis" repeatedly. Davis raised his hand and nodded to the crowd in appreciation. As was part of the plan, he and his campaign manager stayed in the background, allowing Cassie to get as much face time as possible. After about a minute, the din from the crowd began to die out.

A local Fox News affiliate reporter shouted to Cassie as if on cue.

"Cassandra, Cassandra, do you have time for a few questions?"

As planned, Amos approached the podium as if to intervene and deny the request. As coached, Cassie put out her hand, stopping his intervention.

"Sure, I have a few minutes."

The crowd laughed, appreciating how she positioned herself, tongue in cheek, as a political figure.

"Everyone knows your uncle's success in real estate and business.

But the public wants to hear more about him as a father figure. I know your uncle became your guardian a year or so ago after a tragic event. Can you share anything about what he has meant to you over such a challenging time?"

As the crowd filled in beneath her feet like lambs, Cassie took a deep breath and scanned the horizon. The border collie they believed would take them home was actually a wolf purposely tugging at their heartstrings. For Davis, it was like shooting fish in a barrel as the crowd became putty in his niece's hands. Amos stopped short of the podium but shook his head no as if to say, *You don't have to answer that question.*

Again, Cassie held out the palm of her hand and spoke into the microphone.

"It's OK. I am happy to answer your question. As some of you probably know, I was in an accident over a year ago. I survived."

She paused as she was unexpectedly overcome with genuine emotion. Her uncle's heart raced. It is working, he thought. It is working.

"My parents didn't." Cassie wiped away a few tears but managed to keep herself together. "I was alone. Scared and in shock. My uncle did not hesitate. He was there when I woke from the accident and immediately took me in. He has made sure I have everything I need as I try to rebuild my life. It hasn't been easy. There's a long way to go, but without him, I, well, I don't know where I would be."

She looked back at her uncle again. "Thank you, uncle."

Cassie pressed stop on the player and skipped back a few seconds. "See that?"

"What should I be seeing exactly?" Bill was perplexed.

She paused the DVD and put her index finger to her uncle's face on the screen. She pressed play again.

Her uncle nodded and smiled. As she returned to her spot, he gave her a tight hug.

"The only thing less genuine than the hug was the gesture that followed," Cassie said. Bill saw that her uncle appeared to be wiping away a tear with the back of his hand.

"I didn't think much of it at the time, or maybe I didn't notice it. But I can tell you today it was political theater. I never saw him cry. Not at his brother's funeral or the many nights I cried myself to sleep after losing my mom and dad."

"It's strange that he would put you in the middle of all that, especially after what you had been through," Bill said as he watched another staffer at the mic close down the event. "That's a ton of pressure for a teenager. If he could do that, it's not hard to believe he would fake his tears for political advantage."

"Yup," Cassie said as she ejected the DVD and retreated to the kitchen. She returned with a bowl of Tostitos and salsa, crunching a chip along the way. Smiling, Cassie quipped, "Tostitos and tea. Has a nice ring to it, but beyond that, I realize it's not the best combination."

She put the food on the coffee table, sat beside Bill, and, leaning over, kissed him on the forehead. "Dig in."

Cassie watched the blue-and-orange flames dance in the gas fireplace. With warmer weather on the horizon, she maximized whatever opportunities she had to use it. She missed her parents' wood fireplace, the sound of crackling wood and random embers flying like shooting stars in every direction, but the lack of prep work and cleanup was a fair tradeoff.

Cassie woke from her brief trance. "After that, things got steadily worse. I always had laser focus in the classroom, but after the accident, much of the time, I had some type of trauma-induced ADD." She paused, looked at Bill, and smirked. "Before you say anything, Doctor, I know that's not how ADD works."

Bill nodded, agreeing to keep his psychobabble to himself.

"I looked forward to weekends because I didn't have to put in the effort needed to engage in small talk or participate in class just enough to avoid scrutiny. I figured out pretty early on that my uncle had no interest in my life or lack thereof. Mostly, this was a good thing. Whenever he asked how I was doing, his busy hands and lack of eye contact made it clear that nothing I said would be absorbed. I learned it was easier to give trivial answers, many of which I had at the ready. The less reflective, the better. Stump speeches and dinners with donors had replaced my self-imposed weekend quarantine."

The mention of quarantine brought Bill back to how he had handled Kyle. He wondered if he had been too harsh in putting him on room restriction and whether he made the right decision with his discharge.

Cassie continued. "Like any teenager, I had no idea what I wanted to do for a living. But even back then, watching slimy, disingenuous politicians and businessmen feed at the trough helped me rule out my uncle's path."

"I don't blame you, but did telling your story end up helping your uncle's cause?"

"It seemed to. My uncle was gaining in the polls. He was within the margin of error." Cassie's expression made it clear that any correlation between them still troubled her. "I did my best to opt out of future events, arguing that I had done my part and that there shouldn't be much use for me anymore. My uncle disagreed. He said I was his personal rabbit's foot. Cassie's facial expression changed. Her tone went from self-assured and direct, as if she were reporting the news, to one more labored and reflective.

Cassie sighed as she shared the horrifying cyberbullying that followed her big speech. Reciting her uncle's disparaging remarks about her father's lack of success, Cassie tossed the balled paper towel she was still holding from the chips on the coffee table. "Do you know how cruel you have to be to say something like that?" Her voice cracked from a mixture of sadness and rage. "That was my dead dad he was talking about. It was his brother, for god's sake."

Bill grabbed Cassie's hand as her eyes swelled. He was saddened by what he was hearing and the impact sharing the memory had on her. He had seen too much in his years of practice to be surprised by bullying or selfish and calculated behavior. But this hit differently. While he tried to convince himself otherwise, he knew it was because, in this case, it was all done to someone he loved. Even so, caring so much about someone put him in touch with a level of empathy he had never known. Over the years, he had become adept at viewing the world logically. His family life showed him a line, and he understood that being on one side brought admiration while the other led to contempt and scorn. His world was driven by logic and reason. If a problem could be defined, there was always a resolution. He had become an excellent practitioner, one of the best, in formulating a diagnosis. Still, beyond the label he assigned to those in his care, he began to appreciate that identifying the source of someone's suffering was not the same as validating it.

CHAPTER 32

CASSIE AND BILL had run out of things to do not only within their towns but within a two-hour drive. While neither of them were big shoppers, they decided to make a road trip to the outlets outside of Rochester. On the way back from their day trip, Cassie asked Bill, "Have you ever heard the phrase, 'Anger is sadness turned inward?'" Bill replied with his mouth full, having just taken a bite from the granola bar he retrieved from his pocket. "I'm not sure that line even makes sense."

"Right? After the accident, I remember this one therapist telling me that. She loved saying it. It's a catchy line, to be sure, but hardly actionable. What was I supposed to do with that? Should I not have been sad that my parents were taken away from me? Should I not have had venom for the other driver, who placed a wager above my family's future?"

Sensing that the conversation was turning more serious, Bill put his snack down.

Cassie continued. "When I think about how I felt back then, I can't distinguish anger from sadness. I think it was a buy-one-get-one-free sort of deal. I'm not sure I ever felt one without the other. Of course, there were signs that my uncle was not the man people admired on TV, but I doubted my instincts until I started spending more time with him on the trail. My head was so messed up from the accident that I had trouble trusting what I was seeing in front of me. I was so confused and afraid. I was simply trying to hang on. My uncle took advantage of me, treating me like his queen on a chessboard, moving me around as he saw fit, waiting to deal a final blow to his Democratic opponent.

"I remember thinking, What will happen to me after he gets what he wants, or, worse, if he doesn't? As bad as the days could be, nights offered no shelter from my mind. I had all the time in the world to wait while my rage boiled to the surface. It would get to the point where I remember saying 'Fuck you' aloud. Knowing my uncle could bring me to such a point that I would utter my inside thoughts only added to my disgust."

When they returned to Cassie's condo, she retreated to the bedroom without saying a word. Bill could hear the sound of shuffling. When she reappeared, there was something tucked under her arm. She sat down and patted the cushion next to her. Bill smiled, feeling like the family dog being allowed on the couch. Cassie dropped a photo album on her lap.

"I was always trying to think about things that brought me joy. There was none to speak of at that time, so I kept returning to my most precious experiences. The one that usually did the trick was picturing myself deep in Muir Woods. I would gaze toward the sky, tracing the redwoods toward the heavens. I listened for the bubbling creek that ran between the moss-covered giants. Sometimes, if I was calm enough, I could feel the sting from dipping my toe in the frigid stream. Memories like these got me through many sleepless nights."

Cassie flipped through the pages until she found what she was looking for. "Ah, here it is." There were several pictures of her, including one standing inside the trunk of a mighty sequoia. Even with her hands locked with her friends, fully stretched, they were not close to being able to bridge the gap. Cassie's smile left no doubt that this moment would be fossilized, even without the photo to memorialize it.

"You look so happy," Bill said, pointing at the photo. "Who's that?"

"That's Kayla. My parents invited her to come with us to California. I couldn't believe my parents let her go." Cassie closed the book and sighed. "But as time passed, I lost my ability to escape to these places. My uncle's betrayal seemed to deplete what few coping tools I had left in my toolbox." Cassie leaned back on the couch and pulled her knees to her chest. She curled her toes around the edge of the cushion. "I recall one night in particular where I swore I was dying. I could feel my palms getting sweaty. My heart was racing. I felt like I was going to be sick."

"It sounds like you were having a panic attack," Bill said.

Cassie looked at him in a way that conveyed the message, *No shit, Sherlock*, before replying, "I know that now, but it was the first time something like that ever happened, even after the accident."

"Sorry, it can be hard to turn it off sometimes. Let me flip the 'No Fare' switch in my cab." He pretended to flip a switch over Cassie's head.

Cassie smiled. "You are such a dork." With that, Cassie got up to go to the kitchen, dodging the Nordstrom Rack and Banana Republic shopping bags they had dumped on the floor. Bill could hear the beeps as she preheated the oven. He wasn't sure what the plan was for dinner, but it hardly mattered. The unfinished granola bar from the car ride had failed to satiate his growing hunger.

"So, what did you do?" Bill asked, loud enough that she could still hear him in the other room.

She returned with a bottle of Pinot Noir and two glasses. Pouring a glass for each of them, she continued, "What I always did. I called my grandfather. It was probably like 2:00 a.m. As far past too late to call as possible."

Cassie harked back to her conversation that night. The phone rang several times. As she was about to end the call, she heard her grandfather's voice. "Hello. Cassie? It's uh, well, it's late. Are you OK?"

The only suitable response to the question was a resounding no. Cassie was anything but. The next ten minutes were dominated by tears and her occasional declaration, "He's a fucking monster." Her grandfather waited for the worst of the storm to pass.

"Oh, Cassie. I'm so sorry. Can I come to get you? You can stay with me for a while."

Overcome with congestion from the crying spell, she responded between heavy breaths. "I . . . I . . . can't. I have school."

"Of course. I can get you this weekend. How does that sound?"

"I have a campaign event."

"Jesus, Cassie. Are you running for office, or is he?"

Hearing him jump to her defense brought a sense of calm.

"That's just it. He only cares about winning this election. Since I started joining him on stage, I have been bullied nonstop. It's disgusting, some of the crap they say."

"Who's they?"

"Good question. Everyone and anyone. They hide behind their computer screens, drop a bomb, and then walk away. You can't even defend yourself because that's just what they want, someone to engage, someone to allow them to lean into their anger."

"That's awful. I've heard about cyberbullying but never seen it. I guess old people don't have the energy, or maybe they just don't know how to use the internet."

Cassie giggled. Even in the worst of times, her grandfather could find a way to make her laugh. "You know what I keep thinking about?"

"What's that?"

"Do you remember that time I played in a summer hockey league? I think I was like ten years old."

"I seldom missed a game or practice."

"Remember that boy picking on me while waiting in line for a drill? He was telling me how I sucked at hockey. He followed me from line to line, offering insult after insult. Finally, he pushed me down to the ice. When I got back up, I cross-checked him in his facemask."

"How could I forget? You could hear the gasps from the parents sitting in the stands."

"Lately, it's all I can think about."

"Did the cyberbullying make you think about that?"

"I think so, but it was less about the altercation with that kid and more about what happened afterward. Remember how the coach suspended me and the boy for two weeks for the fight?"

"Your father was pissed. You were inconsolable. You kept saying how it was so unfair. And you were right."

"Exactly! I was too young at the time to understand. Now I do. My dad called the coach over, looked me in the eye, and said, 'Cassie, he's your coach, so if he says you're suspended, it's his call.' Then, my dad told me I had the right to defend myself and that he was proud of me. He turned his attention to the coach and began to undress him. He told the coach that giving us the same punishment was unfair and sent a bad message that it is OK for a boy to lay his hands on a girl. He never raised his voice. At the time, I thought it was just about the suspension; I thought it was about hockey. All these years later, I realized it was so much more. My dad protected me, not from the stupid boy on my team but from the dangerous idea that it might be OK for a boy to mistreat me, especially physically. He loved me enough to stand up to the coach and ensure I was there to hear it. He wanted to plant the seed, the expectation that I deserve a safe, healthy relationship."

"He really loved you. He was a great dad."

"It made me think about what my uncle would have done in that situation. My guess is he would have said something like, he's only giving you crap because he likes you, or being bullied is part of growing up and building character."

Seeing that Bill had almost finished his glass, Cassie presented the bottle. "Refill?"

Bill nodded.

Cassie's story moved Bill, and he began to understand how he'd grown so close to Chuck. As Cassie refilled Bill's glass, he said, "Sounds like your father really supported you. I'm sorry you lost him at such a young age, but I'm glad you, at least, have had your grandfather to lean on."

"I'm not sure I realized how much speaking with my grandfather relieved my anxiety in a way that my prescriptions never could." Cassie was interrupted by a series of beeps from the kitchen. "Oven's preheated. Be right back."

Bill took the opportunity to use the bathroom. When he returned to the living room, Cassie was already back. Bill sat down and put his arm around her. Pulling her closer, he kissed her gently on the cheek. "So, did you ever get a break from the road? Wasn't there anyone to push back against your uncle?" Bill asked.

"Not really. I continued attending my uncle's campaign events. But somehow, I managed to go through the motions. I think I put myself in a state of semi-hibernation, like a fish at the bottom of a frozen pond. I was awake and aware of what was happening around me, but only in the most basic sense. After what happened, I was wise enough to avoid the internet. The more I was around my uncle, the more I saw how he acted differently depending on who he was talking to. Now that I am older, I see how skilled he was at manipulating people with his charm. He could make you feel like the most important person in the room if it allowed him to pass go and collect his $200. I want to say it never worked on me, but there is video evidence to refute that." Cassie nodded in the direction of the

DVD, which sat on the far edge of the coffee table. "I suppose some people could think critically and see through his hall of mirrors. Unfortunately, the majority were more interested in hearing what made them feel good, no matter the truth."

After dinner, Cassie decided to take a hot bath while Bill scrubbed the pots, pans, and dishes from their casserole. Since they began dating, they had been trying to learn to cook. They even took a couple of cooking classes at Mount Allure University before realizing that following a printed recipe was something they could do at home. Having someone looking over their shoulder was hardly worth the $100 per class. They agreed to alternate between their places with the host cooking. The only rule was no repeating dishes. Fully aware that it was amateur hour in their kitchens, they agreed to steer clear of more challenging dishes like paella. Regardless of the result of their experiments, both agreed it was a significant upgrade over their microwaveable meals in a box.

After drying the last pots, Bill sat by Cassie's feet on the edge of the jacuzzi. Only her head, neck, and knees could be seen, the rest of her body obscured by a healthy froth of bubbles.

"Care to join me?" Cassie said, extending a soapy leg in his direction.

"You know I want to," Bill said. He considered it momentarily. "But I need to get home. Tomorrow is family day, and I have to prepare some content."

"I understand."

"I'll call you tomorrow. Thanks for dinner," Bill said as he scooped up some foam and put it on Cassie's head like a fluffy hat.

"See ya," Cassie said before sliding further beneath the water.

CHAPTER 33

OF ALL HIS job responsibilities, Bill's least favorite was family day. For every caring parent, spouse, friend, or sponsor, there was one who didn't care in equal measure. Bill, complete with his "My Name Is" nametag, greeted visitors in the lobby. While he knew he should reserve judgment based on appearance, he had been around long enough to know that his instincts were seldom wrong.

On this night, the deadbeat prize went to the parents of Shelby Marshall, who had turned fifteen only a week before she ended up at Maybrook. Like many girls her age at the center, she carried comorbid diagnoses of addiction, depression, and generalized anxiety disorder. Such a diagnosis was as inane as identifying someone as being from the human species. It was her eating disorder that made her more unique. It wasn't uncommon to see bulimia, but it remained underdiagnosed at the facility. Kids were skilled at hiding their midnight excursions in the bathroom. It didn't take long to learn how to gag in relative silence. Hiding bloodstained eyes and dilated pupils when under the influence of street drugs was more difficult than sticking a finger down the throat in the privacy of one's bathroom.

The first couple of times Shelby was caught kneeling over the toilet, she passed it off as a stomach bug or something bad she ate. She couldn't be sure if her parents bought it or if they were in denial. Perhaps they figured she would grow out of it if they ignored it. The stomach bug was plausible, making it easier to wrap themselves in the comfort of their defense mechanisms.

The group therapy had started a few minutes late. The certified drug and alcohol counselor was making his typical speech about addiction. Its purpose of scaring the hell out of families was thinly veiled. Like a truck mowing down pins in a bowling alley, its impact was overkill, and its message was complete. His monologue always began the same way:

"There are thirty patients in this room. Sadly, years of statistics tell us that only ten of you will survive your addictions. Some may die from an opiate overdose or a DUI or alcohol poisoning or an unfortunate cocktail of uppers and downers." He paused for effect and looked around as if demanding eye contact before continuing. "For every one of those, three more will die from the long-term assault of the addiction on their bodies. Cirrhosis of the liver, fatty liver, kidney damage, dementia, blood disorders, HIV, cancer."

Some families and, less commonly, patients would dismiss the message as hyperbole, the same ones most likely to contribute to its veracity. Having gotten their attention, he offered a lifeline. "That said, everyone here has it inside of them to be one of the thirty-three percent who become and remain sober. It truly is up to you. As we say in meetings, 'It works if you work it.'"

The monologue was followed by a deeper dive into the recovery strategies that were applied at the facility. Families were reminded to be aware of "dry drunk" behaviors. These were tendencies and actions that were strongly correlated with future relapse. They weren't the same for every person. For some, it could be who they choose to spend time with. For others, it could be lying, making excuses, sleeping late, or skipping medications.

The drug counselor was fielding questions from families when Shelby's parents finally appeared. Bill's anger had been building. He stood in the nursing station with arms crossed. Cassie's stories had a cumulative effect on Bill, and he lately found himself more protective of the innocent and the victimized. He was further aggravated when Shelby's guardians approached the sign-in sheet, laughing and carrying bags from Burger King. Shelby's father was still chewing as his wife searched her purse for her identification. After being buzzed in, Bill approached them.

"Hi, Paul Marshall." Shelby's father extended his hand. Given his proximity, he spoke much louder than was warranted. He was more arrogant than confident—at least, that's how Bill saw it. They shook hands.

"Nice to meet you. You're late."

"Ran into some traffic."

"But you still had time to hit the drive-through."

"Excuse me?" Offended, Paul took a step back. "Who do you think—"

Bill cut him off. "How do you expect your daughter to value her sobriety and health when you so clearly do not?"

Shelby's mother joined the fray. "How dare you speak to us that way."

"Look, I am paid to try and help your daughter. With insurance, we are lucky if that gives us three weeks. So, you'll have to excuse me if I don't have time to tiptoe around your feelings."

Out of view, Barbara was enjoying every minute of the dressing down.

"How do you think Shelby will feel when her parents are the only ones who are late and that grabbing a bite to eat was a higher priority than her future and health?"

"We will tell her we hit traffic. She will understand."

"Can I ask you a question?" Bill did not wait for a response. "If Shelby didn't tell you she was using and lied to you when you asked her, how did you know?"

"It was obvious. Anyone could see."

"So, what makes you think your daughter, who has lived with you for fifteen years, cannot read you like a book? It's not just what you say. It's what you do over and over and over that counts. Look, I don't know you well outside of the couple of family sessions over the phone. But I know Shelby can't be successful without trusting that her family has her back and best interest in mind, not just today or tomorrow but every day. Do you want her to be her best self? That is what it takes."

With that, Bill escorted them to the group room. They tossed their Burger King bags in the trash before entering. Bill followed them in, smiled at Shelby as if to say, "I get it," and sat at the front next to the addiction counselor, who had since yielded the floor to Miranda Keys, one of the facility's social workers.

No fanfare or neon sign overhead marked the slight change in Bill's perspective. Shelby was a troubled child, and Bill had been the victim of more than one of her tirades, including a deep dive into every one of his perceivable flaws. She once mocked him in group therapy for having a degree from a school nobody had ever heard of. She referred to him as "Dr. Cracker Jack," since his degree was worth the same as one of the prizes in a Cracker Jack box.

He recalled another time when he had to redirect her for being in a boy's room. Her response was to unload an impressive string of insults and curse words on him. All of which she managed without repeating a word and seemingly without even taking a breath. All of that fell away as Bill looked across the room and saw the look of defeat and hopelessness in her eyes. Where before he could put her suffering into words, now he could feel her pain. The difference between the two was becoming tangible for the first time.

CHAPTER 34

CASSIE AND BILL often talked late into the night. Sometimes, Bill would get home at three in the morning only to drag himself to work by nine that day. Cassie talked about her love for her parents and how she credited them and her grandfather for all her best qualities. She shared what she was learning at night school, what she liked, and who and what annoyed her as she progressed toward completing the degree that she had started years before. In turn, Bill talked about his dysfunctional but well-meaning family, especially his complicated relationship with his troubled brother when they were younger. Cassie opened up in ways she hadn't since her existence was fractured into a life before and after the event. She shared her doubts about meeting her parents' expectations now that there was no way to receive their validation. She described how it felt like their sudden passing interfered with the natural progression where one learned such confirmation was not required. Similarly, Bill spoke of how he was probably too concerned with his parents' approval. Bill thought about his estranged relationship with his brother. Cassie's abrupt loss of her parents made him pause. Amends did not always wait for those to be ready to make them.

Following a long day of wine tasting in the Hudson Valley, Cassie and Bill returned to his place just after eleven at night. While they were both exhausted, neither could fall asleep.

"You awake?" Cassie whispered to Bill.

He rolled over in bed to face her. "Yeah. How about you?"

"No, I am sleeping. I talk in my sleep, wiseass."

"Something bothering you?" Bill stroked the sleeve of her silk pajamas with the back of his hand.

"I don't know. Well, maybe, it's just, do you think antidepressants help?"

"I do. Absolutely. Meds are especially critical for things like bipolar disorder or schizophrenia. It's the only thing that helps. You can't talk someone out of hearing voices with psychoanalysis or Rogerian therapy." He continued. "But I also think drugs like SSRIs help a ton of people with major depression and anxiety. I guess I see it as taking the edge off so people can begin to work through issues. It's hard to ask someone to reflect on their thoughts and behaviors when they can't even get out of bed."

"I think you're right, but I wasn't so sure when I was a teenager. I guess I'm less sure about psychotherapy, even now. I hated agreeing with my uncle on anything, but if I am being honest, I can't deny I had the same unfavorable opinion on therapy, although for very different reasons. No offense."

"That's all right. I'm probably not the best defender of the practice right now. We probably agree on more than you think."

"I got some relief from psychotropic medications, but only in that they helped me shuffle back and forth between school and home. After the accident, I attended weekly therapy sessions with this woman, Sarah Roberts, or maybe it was Robbins, I can't remember. She was a licensed social worker. Even then, I knew opening up about my grief and loss would hardly move the needle in easing my pain, but I didn't see much point in trying out other therapists. Short of anyone being able to reanimate my parents, attending sessions was mostly another way to fill an hour on my calendar. I figured it was better to have someone other than myself to talk to. Don't they call that psychosis when you do that?"

Conditioned like one of Pavlov's dogs, Bill couldn't help respond-ing to the query. "That's one possibility, yes, but believe it or not, sometimes people with high-functioning autism do it too. It can sig-nify superior intelligence," Bill said before realizing the question may have been rhetorical.

"Have you ever gone to therapy?" Cassie asked.

"I did briefly as part of my education. It was highly recom-mended as part of becoming an effective technician."

"Really? I guess that makes sense, but I meant on your own accord. I just thought with all the struggles you had with your fam-ily as a kid . . ." Cassie didn't finish her sentence.

"Funny you should ask. We went to family therapy when Colton started to struggle."

"That's good. Did it help?"

"I wouldn't know. I sat in the waiting room."

"Wait, what?" Cassie was not sure she heard correctly.

"My brother and my parents met with the therapist for an hour every week while I either did my homework or browsed whatever magazines were available in the lobby."

"You're shittin' me. Why weren't you part of the sessions?"

"I'm not exactly sure. I never thought to ask, even years later. I think my parents just thought I didn't need it. I excelled in school, had good friends, and seemed unaffected by the turbu-lence at home. Maybe they just thought it was sparing me from some pain."

"But . . . you were affected, right?" Cassie asked, her eyes wide with concern.

"I assume so, but all these years later, I can't really say how."

"That's terrible." Cassie put her hand on his shoulder and gently scratched his neck.

"Water under the bridge, as they say. Anyway, look how well

I turned out without it." Even in the dark, Cassie could tell he was smiling.

"Jury's still out on that," Cassie teased.

"I agree. At least your uncle tried to get you the help you needed. Although, from everything you've told me, it's hard to be sure about his motives."

Cassie clarified. "My uncle may have gotten me therapy, but he wasn't shy in his criticism of me being on medications. He would comment on how exposing the body to such foreign substances was unnatural. It's funny, given the much greater impact that alcohol and his binge drinking had on his behavior. He was what you would refer to as a functional alcoholic. When he was sober, he was OK but could be quite the opposite when he wasn't. He never missed an opportunity to criticize the help he hired, and . . ." She paused as if replaying a scene in her mind. "I remember one night in particular. I heard him yelling at a landscaper about the trimming of hedges not being up to his standards. I will never forget the fear I saw in the man's eyes. He just stood there taking it. I thought it strange, at the time, that he didn't defend himself. Of course, now I understand he was probably afraid of losing the generous money he made working his property. Knowing my uncle, I'm sure he paid well—not so much out of kindness but because he thought doing so would keep the help from stealing. He always assumed those with less coveted what he had. He made no effort to get to know those who worked for him, even Maria, his longtime maid. After almost a decade of service, he didn't know if she was married or had children. Even back then, I could see relationships with those around him were largely transactional, with those below him restricted to exchanging funds for services. At the same time, those at his perceived level were seen as competition or people to be leveraged to increase his social or economic status."

Bill grabbed an extra pillow that had fallen on the floor, folded it, and tucked it under his head to prop himself up as he looked her in the eyes. "Can't say any of this is surprising. If his autobiography were based on good deeds, it would be a short story."

"No doubt about that. It might even belong in the fiction section."

Bill appreciated her wit.

Feeling a slight chill, Cassie pulled the blanket up, tucking it under her arms. "When I first moved in, my uncle was supportive, or at least feigned concern. I could not tell the difference without the benefit of history in our relationship and being so young. I spoke to my best friend, Kayla, almost daily, but seeing her regularly was more difficult. I remained in contact with a few of my old hockey friends from school but failed to see that our bond would not be strong enough to weather the erosion created by distance. I had to learn that proximity was important in relationships, especially those based on shared interests instead of values.

"I especially missed my grandfather. I spoke to him often but seldom got to see him. Had I not been acutely aware that my uncle had no interest in me, I would have thought he was jealous of my grandfather. He seemed to find endless excuses why he couldn't drive me to see my grandfather on weekends. Sometimes, I would eavesdrop when they were on the phone. My uncle would explain that the following weekend might be better for us to get together, the goalposts always moving. I learned to stop asking to see my grandfather for fear of feeding my uncle's temper.

"When I think about it now, I'm convinced that running for office left my uncle exposed in ways that were previously foreign to him. For the first time in his life, he received as much negative feedback as positive. He could not comprehend the criticism he received from pundits and polls. The anger festered within him, slowly building. What had become a desire and expectation that he would win had become a necessity. As the pressure grew, so did his self-medicating with the bottle. As was typical, he found some solace against his doubts by chastising and belittling others. The safer the target, the more he attacked. He did not hesitate to criticize me whenever the opportunity presented itself. I was such an easy mark. I was utterly dependent on him for everything, and that knowledge, when mixed with the lack of inhibition from being inebriated, made him cruel."

Cassie could feel her eyes swell. Her nose tingled as it sometimes did before the floodgates opened. She managed to quell the storm. "I did my best to distance myself from him. This became increasingly more difficult on weekends. Having a license served little purpose since I had no car, and he rarely let me use one of his four vehicles. Occasionally, I would tell him I was going to Kayla's only to take a detour to see my grandfather. It felt wrong keeping my visits secret, but I suspected my uncle might be trying to isolate me from the only real family I had left." Cassie patted her watering eyes.

"Hey, hey, come here." Bill pulled her toward him and embraced her in a tight hug. "I'm so glad you had your grandfather, someone in your corner. I can see how much your grandfather means to you." A sliver of doubt entered Bill's mind before taking root in his heart. What her grandfather did was morally reprehensible, but knowing all Cassie had been through, Bill felt genuine gratitude toward the grandfather.

"I-I . . . I'm sorry." Cassie's tears broke through the levy and began to track down her cheeks. "It's just that, most of the time, I can think about things and look at them as if they happened to someone else or lock them away where they can't hurt me. Other times, it's not so easy."

Lying on her back, Cassie wiped her eyes again, this time with each sleeve drawn into action to meet the tears that were falling with greater frequency.

She recalled the nightmare that happened on a cool, late summer night so many years ago. She was sitting at the desk in her bedroom doing her algebra homework while listening to her playlist on headphones when her uncle entered her room with purpose. She caught him out of the corner of her eye and turned to face him.

"Take off those fucking headphones!" He was angry, but his words were muffled. As she took her eyes off him to remove the headset, she felt an immediate pain in her left shoulder. A coffee mug adorned with Yosemite National Park bounced off her before the handle shattered on the edge of her desk. In a small victory, it was empty of any liquid. She was in a state of shock. Her mind doubted what the pain in her arm was so clearly telling her. As she met his gaze, she stared into nothingness. It was as if nobody was behind his eyes; his humanity was replaced with a rage that seemed out of proportion from even the worst offense.

"What, what are you—" Cassie couldn't put the words together.

"How many times do I have to tell you not to leave your dishes in the sink?"

Cassie inspected her red and soon-to-be swollen shoulder and looked back at him, hoping the mark would register and snap him back to reality, that the immediate horror of what he had done would quickly be followed by deep regret and concern. Instead, he turned, slammed the door behind him, and mumbled something to the effect of, "Don't let it happen again." Cassie dropped the shattered mug in the waste bin beside her dresser and started crying. The tears were a mix of pain, sadness, and fear. He had been drinking, but that was nothing new and had never before resulted in violence. What little sense of security she had in her new life had now been discarded along with the broken mug at the bottom of her trash can.

The following day, she threw on a long-sleeve shirt, ensuring the now angry black-and-yellow baseball-size mark on her shoulder remained out of view of curious schoolmates. She was always led to believe that people who were the subject of such abuse often blamed themselves, asking what they did to provoke such an act of betrayal. In contrast, Cassie fully and correctly laid the blame on her own flesh and blood, the person who was supposed to be her protector. The next punch came that same morning when he poured her a cup of coffee and slid it across the island.

"Sorry about last night. It's been a rough few days in the market and the campaign. Just try to make sure you clean up after yourself." He took a sip from his coffee, satisfied with his apology, fully confident there was nothing more to say.

Cassie rolled over and slipped a leg between Bill's legs, looking straight into his eyes. Her tears had abated. "Sitting on the bus as it pulled away from my uncle's mansion, all I can remember was wondering what hurt more, the bruise on my arm or the disingenuous and disconnected response that followed. I never told anyone about that night, not my grandfather, Kayla, or even . . ." Cassie paused, realizing she had never mentioned it before, "or even my friend who he'd assaulted. Given what happened, she would understand my discretion more than anyone. Now that I was a victim of my uncle's violence, I had a new understanding of the complexity and fear that she had about reporting the incident. I was so frightened. What would happen if I told someone? Would child services be contacted? Would I be removed from the home? Was that a good or bad thing? I had no experience or knowledge of state custody but had little reason to doubt the stories I heard on the news and saw in countless movies. I couldn't remember many positive stories. Although it ended well, *Annie* could have gone either way. For a time, my decision to remain quiet seemed the right call, as weeks had passed without further incident. His constant nitpicking cooled. Had it not been for the deep imprint the abuse left on my mind and, for the better part of two weeks, my arm, I may have even wondered if I'd dreamt the whole event."

That night, Bill learned that Cassie's Uncle Davis was not just a rich, selfish, arrogant prick but truly dangerous.

CHAPTER 35

THE FOLLOWING MORNING, Bill met with forty-two-year-old Rebecca Combs. It was their fifth session since her arrival at the MPF, yet it was likely the first time he was truly seeing her. Something in him had changed. It was as if he had access to a part of his brain that had previously been walled off. He paged through her chart while waiting for her to appear for her session. There were plentiful notes about her medication trials and clinical impressions. It wasn't a heavy lift to diagnose her bipolar condition. Rebecca didn't just alternate between the poles but touched their limits. Her decline was rapid. A fifteen-year career as a senior administrator at the same medical center was undone in less than twenty-six days. The unraveling began during a weekly team meeting when, without so much as a word, she rose from her chair, got down on all fours, and crawled to a heating vent on the floor.

"Do you hear that?"

Her colleague's reactions ran from shock to surprise to pure confusion.

"Hear what?" asked an intern from one of the local universities.

"It's beautiful!" Rebecca said. As she rose to her feet and approached her boss, he looked like he had seen a ghost. "Dance with me," she said, grabbing his hand. He did not move.

"Rebecca. Are you OK? I don't hear anything. I think maybe you aren't well."

"Don't be such a chicken. Hey, I know! Who wants to go skinny-dipping?" Rebecca's eyes grew wider.

"Rebecca, why don't you . . ." One of her female colleagues jumped in to intervene. Before she could reach her, Rebecca grabbed the bottom of her sweater and attempted to pull it over her head. She struggled mightily, a consequence of forgetting to remove her glasses first. With one final tug, she was free, her glasses flying halfway across the room.

During the chaos, her boss texted the VP of human resources, who called 911. Since starting Vraylar, the old Rebecca, who was once married and held a master's degree in hospital administration and had a meaningful career, returned. What didn't follow was almost everything she had built. Her husband left about a year after the incident at the office. Rebecca had been wildly unfaithful and had developed a passion for shopping on QVC. She'd even signed up for an expensive time-share in Thailand despite never having been there or expressing interest in going. The marriage may have survived a single event, but it proved too much to overcome in combination.

Rebecca entered the office. "Hi, Doctor."

"Hey, Rebecca. Have a seat."

Rebecca folded her hands on her lap as she sat on the couch.

Bill tucked his binder between the recliner's armrest and his leg. "So, how are you feeling?"

"I'm feeling better, Doctor. The medication's side effects seem to be lessening."

"Good. Good. You have made incredible progress. Without question, the medication has helped. But I'm afraid I have fallen short as your therapist."

"I'm not sure what you mean," Rebecca said, perplexed. Bill flipped open her chart and turned it around so she could see.

"I fumbled the ball." He pointed to the address on her intake form.

"I'm afraid you've lost me."

"How do you like living at . . ." He paused, pulled the binder closer, and put on his reading glasses. "323 Violet Lane."

"Like it? It's a complete nightmare. You know it's a boarding home, right?"

"I do now. I knew it was in Scranton, but I had failed to notice that it was a boarding home until I took a second look the other day. I'm sorry."

"That doesn't require an apology, Doctor."

"I think it does," Bill said, leaning back in the chair. "We have spent the better part of the last couple of weeks talking about your depressive and manic states but never once talked about where you live. I fear I have been only looking at half the story. You've lost so much to this illness. Not once have I asked you about your living situation."

"Well, no, but—"

"Rebecca, you live in a shithole; excuse my language. It would be a crime for us to treat the chemical imbalance in your brain, educate you on your condition, and then send you back to that place. Worse, now you have the faculties to truly see what's around you. I am not sure any medicine in the world can overcome that. If you weren't depressed going back there, I would question your state of mind."

"I appreciate that. But I'm not sure I have a choice. I lost my home and most of what I had in my spending spree."

"You said you're still on good terms with your ex, right? Would you be amenable to me asking him to come for a family session this weekend? I will see what social worker is assigned to your case. They are great at finding people outpatient aftercare. I'm not sure how much they dabble in real estate, but we need to find you an apartment. I think if we all work together, we can make it work. We have you on the right treatment plan. Let's get you into a place where you can fully realize its benefits. It's a step in rebuilding the life you deserve. It's important that you remember that all of those things you accomplished in your life were not a mirage. It's not just who you were; it's who you are."

Rebecca teared up. She had fully expected to be stabilized and released back to a world with nothing but the slowness of time and a clear mind to interrogate all she had lost.

Dr. Taggart looked at his watch and rose from his chair. "Looks like we are about out of time. But how do you feel about the plan?"

Rebecca stood, stepped toward Bill, and hugged him tightly. "I think it is a lifeline. Thank you."

Bill offered her a Kleenex as she left his office. He smiled inside, feeling a warmth and a sense of accomplishment that had so often eluded him.

CHAPTER 36

WITH EACH TALE Cassie shared, Bill's righteous judgment of Chuck weakened at the edges. The stories Cassie's grandfather shared about the abuse were true. He must have felt an incredible duty to intervene, likely and justifiably thinking he was the only one who could help her. Bill had learned all about the diffusion of responsibility, where nobody responds to someone in distress when there are multiple witnesses, assuming someone else will intervene. His old friend did not wait for someone else to act. Cassie was another brother in arms, fighting a very different battle. How could he abandon her at such a time?

It was the dog days of summer. Taking advantage of a lull in the oppressive heat and humidity, courtesy of an early afternoon thunderstorm, Bill and Cassie decided to hike through the state forest a few hours from Maybrook. When they reached the trail's peak, they were rewarded with a stunning view of the valley below. As promised by TripAdvisor, a majestic hundred-and-fifty-foot waterfall could be seen in the distance. They sat on a boulder shaped as if it were made for that purpose, a prize for their effort. No words were spoken, as they would only diminish the moment. When they finally returned to the trail, Cassie reminded Bill how happy she was just before slipping on an algae-covered stone. In one moment, they were holding hands. Next, she was flat on her back on the side of the trail. Bill was relieved to find her laughing hysterically.

"That was a hallmark moment. What a klutz." Bill always

appreciated Cassie's ability to be self-deprecating. Such a trait usually spoke volumes about a person's empathy for others.

They laughed as Bill extended his hand to pull her back up. When they returned to Cassie's condo later that evening, they showered, washing away the great outdoors. Exhausted from their adventure, they ordered a pizza and melted into the cozy sofa. Slightly rejuvenated from the food and a few bottles of Vitamin Water, Bill asked Cassie a question that led them down a path he could not have expected.

"I know your uncle lost the election, thank god, but what happened after getting that bump from your speech?" Cassie grabbed a stack of cheap napkins the pizza shop provided and wiped the grease remnants from her hands.

"After everything he did to me and my friend, we came up with a plan. My friend knew a reporter named Isaac from prior campaigns. We figured we could leak some of my uncle's bad behavior. The reporter agreed to meet me at the Nook, an all-day breakfast joint about twenty minutes from my house. Best omelets in the world, by the way. We should go. Anyway, I figured there would be no chance I would run into my uncle, who had a meeting on the opposite side of town. I remember noticing Isaac sitting at the counter. I knew it was him from the hat he said he would wear, appropriately a newsboy cap."

As Cassie's mind returned to the diner, she could still picture Isaac from that day. He was short and round and, given his small stature, was well beyond an acceptable weight. He wore a suit that was probably a size-and-a-half too big, perhaps to make himself look smaller. He was writing on a yellow legal pad. His brown shoes were weathered from his many years following the story of the day. His wedding ring appeared to be smothering his ring finger. The only way it was coming off was with the digit itself. As Cassie approached, he set down his pad to take a gulp of black coffee.

Cassie sat on the weathered red vinyl stool next to Isaac, who made brief eye contact and nodded. She removed her fleece jacket and put it across her lap. Isaac tapped his index and middle finger on the bar to get the waitress's attention. He held up his cup, suggesting he would like a refill.

"And can you please get a menu here for my friend?" He paused as he turned toward Cassie. "Cassie?" Cassie nodded, confirming he got the name right. "Welcome to my stomping grounds, Cassie. The coffee's shit, but they have the best breakfast."

"I heard that, Isaac," the waitress said as she served a soda at the far end of the bar. As she came over to refill his cup, she playfully challenged Isaac. "You mean the coffee that is so bad that you drink a pot and a half of it every time you are here."

"I told you, I need the caffeine."

The waitress finished his thought. "I know, I know, the story doesn't wait for sleep."

Isaac held up his mug as if he were giving a toast.

The waitress wiped the counter next to him and smiled. "Can I get you something, honey?"

"Maybe just a water and some fries."

"Ketchup?"

"Sure."

"You got it, sweetie."

Isaac took another sip and began. "So, I understand you have something you want to tell me—something about your uncle's campaign." It was more of a statement than a question.

"That's right. I'm told you can be trusted."

"Normally, I would disagree, but in the case of Passion, yes, she is good people; I would never cross her." He laughed. "Truth is, no good reporter exposes their sources, not if they ever want to get another tip, but I appreciate Passion's faith in me. We go way back, you know. So, I'd ask for your story, but it seems the whole world knows it since you gave that speech several weeks ago." He took another sip of coffee and decided to add a bit more sugar. "I understand you've been on the receiving end of a lot of internet abuse since then. It's a shame. Amazing how authenticity is punished when it should be rewarded."

"It wasn't exactly authentic. I was encouraged to do it, you know, to help win an election."

"Well, either way, the pain in your voice was genuine, and the plan seemed to have worked." He looked at his watch. "Just over two months left before the vote, and your uncle has a slight lead or is tied based on the margin of error. Then again, the polls are often shit in predicting things."

"Look, I don't have much time, and this is not about me."

"Yes, of course. So, how can I help, Cassie?"

"It's really about how you can help the State of New York."

"Go on . . ."

"My uncle is not how he portrays himself in his stump speeches."

"A phony politician is certainly not news. If he were truthful, well then maybe you'd have a story."

Cassie tried her best to hide her frustration. "Look, my uncle hates women. I mean, I have seen him bring female staffers to tears. He attacks them personally. It is the complete opposite of how he treats men. He took his niece and used her grief to try and win votes. Even after being bullied and asking to be removed from campaign events, he has continued to force me to participate."

"Cassie, don't get me wrong. I am sure your uncle is a grade-A prick, probably more than any recent politician. He was a self-serving, power-hungry, cruel businessman. Nothing made me change the channel from CNBC faster than seeing his mug. But I am afraid that hardly makes a story. That your uncle is sexist and not the warmest fellow is not a secret to anyone. I think it is already baked into the polling. Clearly, it is not enough for the public to discard him. I'm not sure what Passion thought you had, but I am afraid it's not news, certainly not front-page worthy, and frankly, that's all that's worth printing these days." He put down enough money to cover his dinner and Cassie's fries. "I'm sorry, Cassie. You ever have something I can run with, you know where to find me." He tipped his hat, put on his trench coat, placed his pen and pad in his small leather briefcase, and headed for the door.

Cassie made eye contact with Bill, her expression of disappointment similar to the day she exited the diner. "When I left, it dawned on me that the material left at Isaac's feet never really had a chance of seeing the light of day. Worse, I was pretty sure my friend knew it too. My friend's assault, the only arrow I had, remained in my quiver. A promise is a promise, and I wasn't about to betray her wish to remain silent. I was a little idealistic, or maybe just hopeful. It was a Hail Mary, plain and simple. I feared it was over. My uncle would be elected. He would get away with all of it, using his flesh and blood as a punching bag and for personal gain, squashing the egos of competent women while advancing the careers of far less talented men, and, worst of all, the rape of my friend." Cassie squinted, her brow furrowed. Uttering the word "rape" had further awoken something that seemed to have been hibernating.

"That must have been deflating, but I think you're right," Bill said. "The only thing that may have made it to print was what he did to your friend. You haven't told me her name; I will never ask. I respect that you've honored your friend's wishes. I can't imagine how hard it must have been to sit on that knowledge, knowing it might have stopped your uncle."

Bill's empathy was genuine. Playing back what patients said was part of the rhythm of psychotherapy. But Bill began to understand that while he excelled at saying the words, he was often remiss when attaching empathy to them.

"It was torture," Cassie said. "For the next several days, I was on autopilot at school. I warmed my seat, only participating when called upon. I racked my brain for anything to stop my uncle from winning the election." Cassie walked over to the window and gazed into the distance. The streetlights had turned on. "I remember my level of obsession gave me some pause. I tried to remind myself that I was performing a public service. I knew it was too dangerous to confront my uncle publicly, and Isaac was unwilling to put pen to paper without naming names. That left only one choice. I asked myself, who would be less likely to be concerned by the inconvenience of proof? I figured maybe those disgusting, slanderous campaign commercials weren't so bad after all. I can still feel the chill that ran down my spine. I knew what I was about to do conflicted with everything I was raised to be. Not only was I discarding the values my parents instilled in me but I was doing so to the detriment of my own blood."

Cassie sat back on the couch beside Bill. "I opened my laptop and began typing, repeatedly highlighting and erasing the first few sentences. I remember thinking, How did the bullies who victimized me online make it look so easy? After I finished, I checked the thumb drive that my friend had given me. It was a copy of a cell phone video of my uncle verbally abusing a staffer."

Cassie turned around to face Bill. "You know what? Wait here. I'll be right back." Still in her robe from showering, Cassie reappeared from the bedroom carrying a legal-sized manila envelope. She handed it to Bill, who delicately reached in to retrieve its contents.

"What's this?" Bill asked, unsure where this was going.

"You'll see."

Bill was stunned by what now lay in front of him. It was a copy of the aforementioned letter.

"It's the only copy I made. It's been under lock and key for so many years. Kayla kept it hidden at her house until a few years ago. She even took it with her when she moved to Oregon for a teaching position. Can you believe that?"

Bill read the letter in silence.

To whom it may concern.

It is imperative that Davis Ripley not be afforded office in the New York State Senate. This is not about politics. Frankly, I am an independent. This is about character or, more specifically, the lack thereof. Davis is emotionally abusive to female staffers. He berates them and comments on their looks and lack of intellect. All his senior advisors are men for a reason. Despite the well-documented cyberbullying his niece has received following her public appearances, he continues to make her participate against her wishes.

I am enclosing some campaign correspondence between Davis and his chief strategist, Amos. Note Davis's line saying he deserves to get something out of taking Cassandra in. He openly asked the point of being her guardian if she couldn't help him win the seat. To prove this is authentic, you will also see a draft of a daily schedule from two weeks ago, including a complete listing of hotel reservations and speaking engagements on official campaign letterhead. Finally, I am enclosing a thumb drive. What you will see shouldn't require any commentary. Just watch and know that it is his typical treatment of women. Hopefully, this is enough to convince you that the information is authentic.

I will not be going public. Nor will I provide additional information. I can only hope that this will be enough to keep Davis from office. Please do not mistake this as an endorsement of your candidate.

Like most people, I have little to no faith in politicians. I hope you

make the most of this opportunity to do some good in office, although I won't hold my breath.
Anonymous

"Wow! You had some balls, Cassie."

"It's amazing what some teenage angst and suffering will do for you. I Bubble Wrapped the thumb drive, applied some Scotch tape, and tossed it into the envelope. I printed the Democratic headquarters address on a label to ensure it could not be traced. There was no return address. I plastered the envelope with so many stamps that it looked ridiculous. I didn't want to risk being seen at the post office. I dropped it in the mailbox outside the public library several blocks from school the next day."

"So, what happened?" Bill sounded like a kid eagerly awaiting the end of a good bedtime story.

"Initially, nothing. It had been almost a week since I mailed the letter. I was alarmed. I hoped that I had used the correct address. I was freaking out, asking myself all sorts of questions. Did they toss it out with the junk mail? Was it sitting unopened on an intern's desk? I remember thinking everything could be undone by a simple oversight or a casual decision not in my favor. I was prepared to accept that I had lost when I went to bed that night. But the following day, I awoke to pounding from my uncle's den. 'What the fuck!' I remember him shouting. I went downstairs, feigning concern. I asked him what was going on. My uncle, deeply absorbed in the content of his television, either did not hear me or chose to ignore me. With him, it was never easy to tell. He yelled again, 'What the fuck!' The local news was looping the worst parts of the video. The verbal tirade and abuse of the sobbing staffer could not be spun. There could be no justification for his behavior. It would be difficult, if not impossible, to suggest it was taken out of context."

"That must have been surreal to see the contents of your thumb drive all over the television," Bill said as he tried to imagine himself in her shoes.

"It was like an out-of-body experience. My uncle dialed Amos in a panic. I stood in the doorframe of the den. I had no idea what Amos was saying, but it was clear he had also just learned about it. It seemed he was trying and failing to calm my uncle. He kept screaming things like, 'I wanna know who did this. You find out who did this! I will fucking end them. Do you hear me?' He was seething. Sweat was dripping from his forehead."

Bill looked again at the letter in his hands, amazed by its power. Oddly, he felt he was holding a historical artifact.

Cassie continued. "My uncle ended the call and slumped into his office chair, staring at the broadcast. The news got worse. The letter, briefly appearing on the screen, will forever be burned into my brain. The anchor read the note as a copy of the itinerary was shown on-screen.

"Within a couple of hours, national broadcasts were running the story. While it was state politics, my uncle was a national figure, and the story was too juicy to ignore. CNN already had a few 'experts' weighing in on the authenticity of the letter, who may have sent it, and why. Everyone agreed it must have come from within his campaign. There was consensus that it was likely a female. By the time Amos arrived at the house, my uncle had already pushed back a glass of Scotch to calm his nerves. There wasn't much time left until people cast their votes. My uncle demanded that Amos find out who did it. Amos just kept repeating that they needed to do damage control and worry about the leak later."

Cassie took a deep breath. "That was the first time I ever heard my uncle scream at Amos. I went from being concerned to terrified. With his temper, I knew collateral damage was not out of the question. He yelled something like, 'Let's do both. Can't we fucking chew gum and walk at the same time?'"

"My uncle called me into the room. I tried sounding oblivious to what was happening. He asked if I knew anything about the story, pointing wildly at the TV. 'Jesus. No,' I said. 'What is this?' I hoped my brief dabbling in theater in my preteen years was paying off.

"He blamed my friend, the same one he assaulted, saying she couldn't be trusted and that she never liked him after he rejected her advances. I had to swallow my disgust. I couldn't afford to show any loyalty to my friend. He was a master of manipulation and was likely probing for some sort of tell. I told him I didn't know and couldn't imagine who would want to do such a thing. I suggested it had to be someone in his office, given that they had the video and documents. I made it sound like a revelation. 'You think?' he snapped back, following it with disparaging remarks about the lack of critical thinking skills taught at my school. I remember Amos putting his hands out, trying to get my uncle to bring it down a notch.

"I was giddy inside from having successfully gotten under his skin. At that moment, my fear mostly dissipated. I felt I was safely disregarded as the source of the leak. When I think about it," Cassie paused momentarily, "I'm not sure whether I should have been relieved or irritated that he thought I lacked the intellect to pull off such a stunt."

"Keep going, I'm listening," Bill said as he got up to go to the kitchen.

"After that, it was all about damage control, including a steady stream of television appearances across local and national stations. My uncle tried to sell it that he was only human and had a moment that most people didn't have the misfortune of having on camera. Once again, he found a way to pull me into it. He said a chauvinist wouldn't have taken me in and included me in the campaign because he wanted to share my brilliance with the world. He had more difficulty explaining away the lack of women in senior positions. I was relieved I was not asked to participate in the media appearances. Amos convinced my uncle that it would be too heavy-handed and likely be interpreted as a political ploy."

Bill returned from the kitchen, carrying two wine glasses and a bottle of pinot grigio.

"This is insane, Cassie. It sounds like something you would read in a political thriller. You must have been freaked out about your uncle discovering the leak. I mean, rationally, I don't know how he would, but fear isn't usually rationale, especially as a teenager."

Cassie ran her finger around the edge of the glass, her eyes following the path, putting herself in a quasi-hypnotic state to a place she did not want to go. "The fear was real and justified. Just over a month after the negative story broke, I was on the phone with Kayla when I heard the front door slam. It was a Friday night, and my uncle was home early. It was sometime after eleven in the evening. The few restrictions my uncle placed on himself during the week were swiftly dismissed once the weekend arrived. He was like a werewolf succumbing to the pull of the moon."

Bill's wine remained on his coaster, untouched as he anticipated the horror that was about to unravel.

"I abruptly told Kayla I had to go and hung up. I turned out the light and retreated to the closet, irrationally hoping he might be tricked into thinking I wasn't home. It was difficult to call his bluff when we both knew I had yet to make a real friend in the months since coming to live with him. It might sound strange, but my mind began to race. *I should have taken up running. Maybe he would assume I was out running. Why didn't I take up running?* I realized how irrational my thought process was and knew it was driven by profound fear and a drastic search to find myself any protection against what was scaling the steps. That was the last time I . . ."

Cassie paused. The remainder of the sentence lay precariously close to the cliff's edge.

Bill wondered if Cassie knew what happened to her uncle and whether she might divulge the answer to the mystery that started him on his journey. Instead, Cassie briefly returned the unspoken words to storage, where she temporarily recommitted to keeping them locked away. "Anyway, not long after that night, I went to live with my grandfather," Cassie said, changing gears.

Bill had cast a line into Cassie's waters the first night he heard her sing. He had watched the hook sink to the depths, where it would remain unseen. His faith that he would be rewarded with a bite was not unwarranted. She had revealed so much since the night they met. Their relationship had long ago crossed the boundary from superficial to authentic. They had professed their love for one another. Still, there was an invisible line between them. On one side was the mystery behind Cassie's uncle's passing. On the other side was the unspoken origin of Bill and Cassie's relationship. The longer the truth remained unearthed, the more the fissure beneath them widened, threatening to create a gap that could no longer be negotiated.

Every time Cassie made herself vulnerable, the protective layer that afforded him protection from the worst of his guilt became thinner. The intoxication he enjoyed from the excitement of falling in love could no longer overcome the cold sobriety that the truth demanded.

Looking into Bill's concerned eyes, Cassie felt safe. It was time to get it off her chest. As Cassie flashed back to what she had endured that night, her eyes widened, dilated with rage. If tears were shed reliving what happened, they were undetected, burned off from the fire within.

Her uncle's footsteps grew louder in accordance with his level of intoxication.

Fuck, she thought, he is shitfaced.

He opened her door surprisingly delicately. "Cassie," he said with a noticeable slur as he placed an odd emphasis on the second syllable in her name. He flicked the light on. Then off. Then on again. "Cassie, oh Cassie? We're both too old for hide and seek." He laughed unconvincingly. He turned off the light again and tiptoed to the walk-in closet door. "Next time you want to hide, I suggest you turn off your phone, you dumb bitch. I can see it under the door." He laughed again. This time, it sounded sinister. He opened the door, grabbed a lock of her hair, and pulled her out of the closet. She instinctively grabbed her hair between her scalp and his hand to relieve some of the worst tension. The one-day class she took at the YMCA a few years ago was paying dividends. However, she could do little to avoid what came next. She voluntarily got to her feet to further relieve the stress on her hair and head.

"Let me go! You fucking drunk."

He picked her up off the floor as if she were a bag of groceries and threw her on the bed. Her head snapped back as there was not enough time to brace herself. Now, on her back, she bent her legs, positioning her knees between her core and her enraged attacker. He began removing his belt. She pushed hard on her feet, trying to propel herself to the floor on the opposite side of her mattress. He reflexively lunged for her shoulder, his belt dangling from the two remaining loops.

His balance was highly compromised by the hours of drinking. He missed the intended target. The heel of his palm landed squarely across Cassie's left eye and part of her ear. Her studded earring was forced sideways, cutting into her ear lobe. She screamed out in pain. Her eye socket felt hot as blood rushed to the area of impact. Her uncle paused momentarily, his belt swaying half-on and half-off his waist. He had a confused look on his face as if he knew this was foreign territory. His mind was a mix of cloudy cognition, anger, and perhaps, in the depths, the realization that he could stop, that he should stop.

In Cassie's eyes, the respite only exacerbated the fear. A terrifying new prospect had now involuntarily taken root in her imagination. Is he going to rape me? In the next moment, she incredulously pictured herself blowing a rape whistle. How fucking ridiculous is that? she thought. She couldn't believe her mind would conjure such a useless fight response. Even if she had a whistle, who would hear it? The thousands of square feet and acres of land that separated her from the nearest help would drown it out. Her uncle finished undoing the belt and folded it over. Cassie prepared to fight to the death if necessary. She pictured herself clawing out his eyes until nothing was left but empty sockets. Even if this were to be her last night, she would be taking something with her, something that he would carry with him for the rest of his time on this planet. She flexed her right hand and rereleased it as if to remind her it was still functional and could be relied upon to execute her plan.

The belt was now being raised over her uncle's head, loading the potential energy for a downward strike. He jerked suddenly. The belt began its downward arc toward the good side of her now bruised face. Surprisingly, he stopped the momentum just as quickly. Holding it above her face, he slowly released one finger at a time until the belt fell toward her face. Cassie instinctively blocked it on the way down, and it harmlessly grazed her shoulder before sliding off the bed behind her. Her uncle had an otherworldly look. He had a crooked smile across his face as if saying, well, that was fun. Now what? Without saying a word, he made his way slowly back downstairs. He would likely pass out on the couch in front of the television, as had become a habit after nights of bingeing. Cassie sat in bed and pulled her knees close to her chest. Without being aware, she rocked herself slightly back and forth, her body's attempt at self-soothing. She retrieved her phone, which had fallen on the floor and bounced partially underneath her bed. After several minutes, she made her way to her dresser and flicked on her phone's flashlight. The intense light bounced off the mirror. The shadows morphed into various shapes and configurations as she tilted the phone toward her eye and ear, which now throbbed like a ticking clock. A line of blood appeared between her piercing and the earlobe. She watched the blood pool before giving way to gravity and dripping on the hardwood floor at her feet. Her eye was swollen and beet red.

She was not surprised to see a black eye the next day. A feeling of dread and shame overcame her. It was bad enough that her insides were scarred, but now it was visible to the world and worse, to her uncle. She could deny him the satisfaction of knowing he had left an imprint on her mind, but an eye swollen shut confirmed he'd gotten the better of her.

It was a trophy for him if he chose to see it that way. Unlike her feelings, which could be stuffed deep down and starved of any light, the black-and-blue mark left at the hands of her uncle would be on full display, not just for the day but probably for the next several to follow. In a small blessing, her uncle was nowhere to be found when she got downstairs, with his favorite car missing from the garage.

It was the weekend, meaning she did not need to worry about being seen by any of the help. She could hide in her closet and wish it all away until forced to confront the world again. When her uncle returned, he said nothing to her. It was as if she were invisible. He spent much of the weekend out of the house. He left her cash on the kitchen island, a common practice that indicated she needed to order delivery if she wanted to eat. It hardly mattered, as she found she had little appetite since Friday night's violence. On Sunday night, her uncle finally said something to her. He called her to come downstairs and meet him in his den. Cassie wore the same pajamas she had on the night of the assault, drops of blood staining her top. She figured that if she couldn't hide the wound on her face, there was no sense in hiding the other evidence. She tried to turn it into a badge of courage, as if to say, I am still here.

Upon her entering the room, her uncle, who was parked in his leather chair at his desk, lowered the copy of the *WSJ* he was reading and, as if reciting the weather, informed Cassie that she would not be going to school on Monday, or, for that matter, not until the black eye was gone.

"I won't let you tear down what I have built. You are lucky I took you in. I provide for you, and despite this, you are ungrateful. We have to do better. You should be able to go back to school in a few days. Think of it as a few well-deserved days off. And I will inform Amos that you could use a break from the campaign; I'm sure you won't mind that." He displayed a disingenuous smile and, as if to say no response was needed, went back to reading his paper.

Cassie polished off her half-filled glass. "Like I said, I moved in with my grandfather after that."

Horrified, Bill embraced Cassie.

"I-I . . . I just can't believe what that fucker did to you. I am so sorry, Cassie. I wish I could take away your pain. I know I don't have that ability."

Cassie separated from the hug, looked him in the eyes, and took his hand in hers. "That's not true. You have helped me to trust again. Until we met, I had kept life and the people in it at arm's length. I built a life based on safety over substance and predictability over spontaneity until I no longer dreamed of wanting anything else. He took that from me without my even knowing it until many years later. I can never get back the time he stole." The anger in Cassie's eyes gave way, pacified by the warmth of contentment and gratitude. "I am so lucky to have met you," Cassie said, pulling him toward her and kissing him softly.

Having to work early the next day, Bill left just after midnight. Any remaining reservations he may have had to come clean dissipated into the warm midnight air. He was only ten minutes away when he tapped her number on his phone.

"Miss me already?" Cassie said as she picked up the call.

"Actually, I had an idea. How would you feel about a road trip next weekend? I thought I could find a nice bed and breakfast within driving distance."

Cassie took a deep breath. "Geez, after a tale like that, your first thought is to plan a romantic getaway?"

"I know, it's shit timing. I just thought you could use a change of setting."

"Sure, why not? I'm off this weekend. Let's do it."

"Great! You should know that you are the bravest person I have ever met, and believe me, I've seen the full gamut from cowardice to selfless heroism. I wish I had half of your strength."

"That's nice of you to say. I sure as hell don't feel that way. But I appreciate it."

Bill wanted time to plan exactly what he would say on their road trip, how he would say it, and how he would convince her of his remorse for his dishonesty. He thought it was strange that honesty was always the best policy but that we would tie ourselves into knots to evade it.

CHAPTER 37

FOLLOWING CASSIE'S horrifying revelation, Bill felt like he was swimming against the current for the next few days. Despite his best efforts, he was pushed back downstream, returning time and again to the same place, the only tangible difference being his gradual decline in energy. His sole comfort was his belief that it was not visible to others, that the quality of his work was not suffering.

As Bill sat in his office watching children from one of the residential treatment centers make their way to the cafeteria for lunch, he heard Barbara's voice just outside his door. His mind scattered like the leaves that curled and fluttered with a distant but approaching summer thunderstorm. Despite having taught the technique of mindfulness to his patients, he found himself unable to master it. Not knowing what genuinely being in the present felt like, he could never be sure when his clients were getting it or only pretending. He could easily spot a dry drunk who was not using but exhibited many unhealthy behaviors that often led to relapse. His peers celebrated his ability to identify and act on the issue. It seemed strange that something that should be as easy as relaxing, focusing on what was in front of him, remained foreign to him all these years later.

"Hey Barb, got a minute?" asked Bill.

"What's up?" Barbara asked as she plopped herself in the seat in front of his desk.

Bill realized that despite his almost two full years in upstate New York working at the MPF, he only had one person he could confide in, and, in this case, she was not an option. While he appreciated her biting sense of humor, stoicism under pressure, and compassion for others, he failed to let himself believe she was a friend. At that moment, he told himself to make more of an effort to expand his inner circle.

"Do you ever wonder if we are helping anyone?"

"Strange coming from you, Doctor. You're the one who is always telling everyone else that we are here to make a dent, to point people in the right direction. We are not here to save anyone."

"No, that's not what I mean."

"Sorry, I'm not following."

"It's just that we go to school, learn from books, listen to lectures on how we should understand people, their motivations, their histories. We follow the latest research on treatment approaches. We tell people how to think about things, work toward closure, and process grief and anger. But we discharge people back to the same abusive environments that brought them here in the first place. We tell them not to self-medicate their depression, but when they leave, they return to the same life with the same triggers. I would argue that if they weren't depressed returning to those environments, they could only be seen as delusional."

Bill, now on a roll, continued his train of thought. "I don't know, it just seems like we ignore the whole reality of people's lives. What if their anger is justified? Like that teenager in our care that ended up killing himself. He was medicated. We counseled him. But we could never remove the trauma he experienced. How can you tell someone they have a future after they were violated with a broom handle because of some dumbass kids feeling it was acceptable to haze a freshman member of the wrestling team? How do you sincerely tell that child to forgive and convince him to release the anger before it eats him alive like some kind of flesh-eating bacteria?

The violators will get counseling to help them process the guilt, assuming they ever have any, and when they turn eighteen, they'll have a clean slate with their whole lives still in front of them. They get to start anew. But that poor kid is gone, and if we are being honest, it makes sense. That stain. The anger. At best, he would learn to compartmentalize his life into the before and the after, but it would always be there. As his life progressed, it would pop up again and again in his dreams, as insecurity and fear in relationships, in being overprotective of his children, should he ever have the courage to bring them into such a world where someone could be inexplicably traumatized by people he thought were his friends."

"Doctor, I get it. I do. We put our professional hats on, but we were once kids at the end of the day. We have known cruelty. We have witnessed injustice in ways that the most creative people can't conjure. But this might be a good time to remember the twelve-step motto about accepting things you cannot change."

"Maybe you're right. But let's be honest. If you had it in your power to decide, would you rather that poor boy still be here or those three bastards who, if they take the hand being held out, will know love, will have new experiences, and see beauty in the world as it reveals itself to them? If we had to make a choice, all of us, I mean one hundred percent, would choose the innocent. But instead, we ask the violated to process their anger by diffusing it. All the while, none of us believe they should be able to let things go."

"OK, so what's your point? Should we do nothing? Should we let their anger consume them and hope it does not manifest in violence or self-destruction? Nobody can change the evil that happens; we can only help those victimized by it to put the pieces back together again."

"But what if that kid hurt one of his attackers instead of himself? He would receive the same punishment under the law for committing an act that in a thousand lifetimes would never have happened without him being pushed to unimaginable psychological limits. Is that justice? Is that fair?"

"I think you're talking about an eye for an eye. I think that's out of our hands. It's not our place to say."

"Barb, please don't tell me it's in God's hands."

"No. I can't be sure there is a god when such things are allowed to happen to people. You know that astronomy guy on TV, Dr. Neil deGrasse Tyson. He famously said something like, God can be all-good or all-powerful, but not both. Either he is all-good but does not have the power to stop all evil, or he has the power to stop all evil but doesn't, implying he is not all-good. Either way, maybe no force can prevent such things." Barbara got up from her chair. "Let me give you some advice. Take a few days off. You must have tons of vacation time. That kid's death is weighing on you. We've all been there. We never know what case or event will push us past our limit."

As she turned to exit, Bill stopped her. "Barbara?"

"Yes, Doctor."

"You don't think less of me, do you? You know, for saying these things as a clinician."

Barbara smiled. "Frankly, Dr. Taggart, I would think less of you if you didn't."

Having no more appointments, Bill decided to call it an early day. He would take her advice and put in for some vacation time. As he put the car in drive, he thought about the Neil deGrasse Tyson point again. He was amazed by how obvious the logic was while acknowledging that he would never have thought of it himself. Almost everything Barbara said was correct—everything but the source of his sense of injustice and moral doubt. Yes, he was upset by the tragic suicide of the teenager. Still, the basis of his cognitive dissonance came from what to do about Cassie's grandfather after everything Cassie had shared. His mind and heart were engaged in a tug of war—one where they seemed of equal strength, unable to break a stalemate by pulling the other over the line.

CHAPTER 38

WHEN BILL RETURNED to his townhouse that night, he thought about what he had said to Barbara about justice and fairness and began to see his brother in a new light. He thought about the photo Cassie shared of her and Kayla in the Redwood Forest. After shedding his coat and depositing his keys and wallet on the end table, he headed straight to the bedroom, knowing precisely what he wanted to do. Getting on his hands and knees, he began searching under his bed. Even with the light from the fixture overhead, it was too dark to make out the labels he had affixed to the plastic storage containers. He tapped the flashlight on his phone and scanned the area. After shuffling some bins around, he found what he was looking for. He flipped the lid on a green Rubbermaid tote. Inside were some old yearbooks going back to middle school. Curious, he opened the cover of his eighth-grade yearbook. Unsurprisingly, the majority of messages from his classmates lacked a personal touch. "*Have a great summer. Good luck in high school*" was only occasionally interrupted by more creative zings or references to events that, while he could no longer recall, must have seemed important at the time. Bill realized that the birthday cards passed around the MPF shared the same absence of creativity and sincerity.

Bill returned the yearbook to the bin and retrieved what he had been looking for. It was a photo album from his childhood. He had taken ownership of it following the passing of his parents several years earlier. Some pages were slightly stuck together from years of disregard and living with the dust bunnies. There were pictures of him and his brother at Disney World. They looked happy. Bill's smile revealed several missing teeth as he waited for his adult teeth to close the gap. It was not surprising that the number of pictures would decline as the boys grew older, but the precipitous drop was jarring. Bill figured there was not much anyone in the family wanted to remember in the later years, let alone capture for posterity. As he went to place the book back in the container, a single loose photo slid to the floor. He flipped it over. It was a photo taken when they were both in high school. They were sitting on a sea wall in New Jersey. He couldn't be sure but thought it was from one of Colton's going-through-the-motions college visits. The contrast between them was apparent. While Bill feigned a smile, Colton was staring at the horizon, looking overwhelmed by the turmoil and vastness of the ocean. The photo was a stark contrast to the photo at Disney World. It could have been two strangers from two separate images combined into one. Bill could not remember when the photo was taken, but he knew it had to be after the event, which marked a turning point in his relationship with Colton.

Bill had just celebrated his fourteenth birthday. It was a swelter-ing day, even for mid-July. A heavy downpour had barely lasted five minutes. Steam from the scorched asphalt made its way back from whence it came. Bill hopped on his Raleigh 10-speed and rode five miles to his friend's house across town. He was the last to arrive. His friends Chase, Devon, and Shannon were already waiting with their bikes.

Chase waved when he saw him approaching. Shannon gazed at his Swatch watch, unfazed that they had not been in style for quite some time.

"Nice job, you're only fifteen minutes late this time," Shannon said, laying on the sarcasm.

"Thanks. I may always be late, but you will always have a girl's name," Bill said with a straight face.

Chase and Devon chuckled.

"Bite me, Bill," Shannon said, too impressed with the quick come-back to be angry. Shannon had heard it all by the time he entered the sixth grade, so it no longer registered with him. The same couldn't be said when he received magazine offers from *Tiger Beat* and *Seventeen*, which seemed to increase in frequency with every birthday.

"Let's go," Chase said.

The four boys headed two blocks to the cul-de-sac that marked the beginning of the woods behind the neighborhood. They ditched their bikes behind the hedges and went down the hill on foot. In just a few minutes, they arrived at their fort, a decaying shed-sized building, once part of the paper mill. The place gave each of them a respite from something or someone in their lives, even if only temporarily. For Dr. Taggart, it was the regular conflict at home between his brother and his parents. It was an escape from serving as a vessel for trading secrets between the warring factions. "Don't tell Mom," and, "Don't tell your brother, but . . ."

After skipping stones, talking about the latest video games they hoped to get, and shooting the breeze about their classmates, they returned up the hill. They would have been surprised to see Colton and his friends had it not been for the telltale giveaway of Megadeth cranking from the speakers of his friend's shit-bucket Dodge Omni. The car rattled so much from the oversized speakers that it wouldn't surprise anyone if the doors were to have fallen off mid-song. The last remnants of a sunset were quickly fading in the distance.

"What are you guys doing here?" Bill asked, hoping it was not to give him and his friends a hard time.

"Nothin'," Colton said. "See all these cars lining up? It looks like the Pinkstons are having a party."

The cars continued to park along the street in increasing numbers. "So?" Shannon said.

"So, we thought we might participate," Noel said.

"Join them? They don't even know you. Why would they want you to join them?"

Colton and his friends looked at one another, indicating they were up to no good.

"No invitation needed. I'll show you what I mean. Follow me." Colton and his friends made their way into the woods and down the hill. Bill's fear was all too familiar when Colton had one of his ideas. Against his better judgment, he followed with his friends.

Colton stopped just short of the old mill by a tree with an orange X spray-painted on its trunk. A few feet from the roots, he reached into the cavity in the main trunk and retrieved something. Bill figured he must have marked the tree to return later for his treasure.

"Oh shit!" exclaimed Shannon. "Why do you have a gun?"

"Quiet nerd, it's only a BB gun. We come down here sometimes for target practice with old, discarded beer cans."

"Can I see it?" asked Devon, the most daring of Bill's friends. Colton handed him the small pistol.

"Hey, dumb shit, don't point it at people." Colton grabbed it back, confirming that the safety was on.

"You'll shoot your eye out," Shannon said with a laugh, referencing *A Christmas Story*.

Noel announced his exit and returned to his Omni to pick up his girlfriend. The vibrating thump of the base faded as it disappeared into the distance.

It was almost entirely dark. The party had begun. The occasional beams from the cars of late arrivals splintered between the trees. The loud chatter blended into a chorus of white noise, creating a single voice. The only exception was the baritone laughter of one of the partygoers, which rose above the rest. A small bonfire had been started. Several men and women circled it as they conversed over beer and wine.

"Colton, what are you planning on doing with that BB gun?" Bill asked. The way it was asked made it clear that whatever the answer, he should reconsider.

"I'll show you, little brother."

With the ease and familiarity of screwing in a light bulb, he worked his way through some of the thick, entangled summer brush. He stopped at a thicket, stood up, aimed the weapon at the sky, and pulled the trigger.

"Shit! Forgot the safety. Hold on."

He flicked it off, lowered the barrel, and pulled the trigger again. It was surprisingly silent, barely making a noise as the projectile disappeared into the night. He aimed and fired again.

"What was that?" a confused male voice shouted from the party's direction.

"Holy shit! Did you just shoot somebody?" Without hesitation, Chase, in complete darkness, scaled the hill back up to the cul-de-sac and was halfway down the street before Colton could even reload.

"What a pussy," Colton's friend said.

"Yeah, it's just a BB gun. It only leaves a little mark. Hurts for maybe a second."

"How do you know?" Devon asked.

"Because we tried it to see how it felt. It stings like a bee for a second or two, that's all."

Devon took the device and aimed it in the party's general direction, the projectile cutting through the thick, humid air.

"What the fuck!"

The pause in the party's conversation, followed by some incoherent mumbling, suggested people were comparing notes, trying to figure out what was happening to them. Someone, clearly not one of the victims, opined that it could be the mosquitoes. After a few misses, Colton retrieved the weapon and switched his focus to the general vicinity of the bonfire, where he found greater success.

"Ow! I just felt it too," another partygoer said.

Bill and Shannon, while not participating, remained frozen in place, unable to process what was happening around them.

"What—what are you doing? Why are you shooting people?" Shannon's question faded as if he needed to validate that this was indeed happening.

Bill finally noticed that Chase had disappeared. He'd never said anything as he slipped into the shadows and back to the world where things made more sense. Before they knew it, flashlights began to bounce off the foliage and trees around them.

"I see them! Over there," a man shouted, pointing in their general direction.

"Fuck!" Colton's friend said in a half-whisper.

It was every delinquent for himself. The boys scattered deeper into the woods, trying to avoid being caught in the beams of light crisscrossing like searchlights at an airstrip. They hoped the din of the insects would help cover their escape.

Bill found a deep recess between two enormous rock formations farther down the hill. A thick mixture of pricker bushes, weeds, and an entangled mess of vines and shrubs surrounded it. He dove in, catching a few thorns on his leg. He winced in pain as he got as low as possible.

Several seconds later, he heard someone shout, "I got one!"

"Great," shouted another. "Keep looking. I saw at least three running away."

Bill remained utterly silent, not daring to move. He guessed almost twenty minutes had passed when he heard Colton's voice.

"Bill. You can come out. They're gone."

Bill hesitated.

"Did you hear me? They left. Come on out!"

With that, Bill made his way back through the thick brush, managing yet again to get victimized by the pricker bush despite his best efforts. He followed Colton's voice to the street where they'd initially gathered. When he stepped into the open, he felt panic set in. Three men, probably in their late twenties or thirties, stood beside Colton and Shannon. They had been caught.

"Sorry, bro, they made me trick you," Colton said.

Bill wanted to say, "Sorry" or, "I didn't do it," to the men who now held his fate in their hands. Instead, he just stared at his feet.

One of the men said, "No, it wasn't him. He's too short. The other one must have gotten away."

For the first time in his young life, Bill's short stature was to his benefit. The men threatened to call the police unless Colton agreed to take them to his house and tell his parents what he had just done. Plenty of anger and f-bombs went around at the Taggart house that night. But the only thing Bill remembered was the empty look in the eyes of his parents, one that suggested they had no answers to the problem in front of them. They were exhausted, numb, and unable to conjure a coherent response. The men from the party left, unsatisfied. Still, Bill suspected they may have empathized with the parents, believing that engaging the authorities would only be kicking them when they were down and that they would maybe never get back up. They could return to their party and friends while the Taggarts were unlikely to escape their dysfunction.

The childhood memory repeated as Bill lay in bed later that night. He flipped his pillow over, tucked his arms underneath, and stared at the ceiling. He was sure that was the last he'd spent time with Colton. He put distance between them, both in proximity and emotionally. If Colton were in one room in the house, he would be in another, if not out of the house altogether.

Bill continued to thrive in school. His parents praised him, mainly his father, who laid it on thick when Colton was around. Bill was convinced it was a means to further emphasize his accolades as a contrast to Colton's failures and to validate his ability to raise a respectable son. *See, the problem is you.* He couldn't remember if he ever uttered the words but thought maybe he had.

Initially, Colton showed little concern about getting the cold shoulder. However, as the relationship between Colton and his parents further decayed, this began to change. Colton took shots at Bill whenever possible, attacking his ego. If Colton were hurt by his withdrawal, he would never have verbalized it. It was easier to tap into anger, which came much more naturally. Colton was particularly effective in painting Bill as a pawn, a product of others' wishes rather than his own.

As Bill rolled onto his stomach, he wondered if it were true. It was time to start putting his life in order. It was time to be brave, even if it were only a fraction of what Cassie had demonstrated in her life. He would put truth and accountability before all else in his work and personal life. His weekend getaway with Cassie was only a few days away.

CHAPTER 39

CASSIE, MAKING GOOD on her promise, decided to drive to Bryn Wood Rehab to surprise her grandfather. It was a gorgeous summer day. Despite being August, the weather was hot but not humid. The sun burned bright and high in the noon sky over the valley. She stopped by the café to grab a coffee, a small but meaningful perk of working there.

She checked in at the front desk and received a warm welcome. The Bryn Wood staff had come to know Cassie and appreciated that she tried to regularly visit, unlike some other tenants' families. After her departure, her grandfather would brag about her until her next visit.

She sat under the same evergreen tree Bill had frequented during his first few lunch breaks at the pond. Having been told he had a visitor, her grandfather wondered if it was his doctor friend before dismissing such a possibility. After all, it had been several months since they last spoke. When he saw Cassie waving from across the pond, he smiled and waved back. She began to get up to walk over to meet him before he waved for her to stay seated. He had become skilled at using his cane and navigating the trail over the small wooden bridge on the pond's edge. The koi clumped together like a single organism as they raced across the water's surface, hoping to be fed. When he stopped before Cassie, she stood, leaned over, and hugged him firmly.

"Hi, Grandpa"

"Hi, angel." It had been a while since he called her that. She thought it was a sign that he was extra pleased to be in her company.

They talked about his rehab schedule and his annoyance with a new patient in the room across the hall who was obsessed with eighties television. Her grandfather joked that hearing *The Love Boat* and *Magnum, P.I.* themes would likely cause him to have another stroke, one that he was not sure he would want to return from should he be subjected to those shows much longer. His complaint was tongue-in-cheek.

She updated her grandfather on school, her work, and even the joy she had rediscovered in singing at the café, something she had abandoned after her early years doing musical theater.

Mostly, she spoke about the new love in her life. She talked about the sense of peace she felt around him. She described how being with him made her feel like the best version of herself. Being happy had become effortless in a way that she had not felt since the innocence of childhood. Cassie even went so far as to mention the possibility of the m-word.

"How long have you been seeing this fellow?"

"Fellow?" She laughed.

"Sorry, gentleman."

"That's not much better." She smiled.

"OK, the dude."

"Ugh, never mind," she said. "It's been over six months now."

Her grandfather put his old, wrinkled, and scarred hand on hers. "You don't know how happy that makes me, Cassie. You deserve it. I mean that. I had long hoped for this." He was about to ask if she had a picture when she abruptly changed the topic.

"So, have you heard from your visitor friend?" she asked, somewhat afraid of the answer she figured was coming.

"No, no, can't say I have." He looked sad, though he had come to terms with it.

"You said he was a doctor, right?"

"Yes, that's right."

"Weird. Well, it's his loss, Grandpa. He sounds like a flake."

"Flake, and you make fun of me for saying gentleman. Who says flake?" He giggled.

"You know what, I have a picture of him. The nurse took it for us last fall. I tried to send it to you, but I don't know how to email or text it. I wanted to send it, but I kept taking new pictures of the wall or my face."

"Why didn't you ask someone to help?" She knew the answer before she finished the question.

"No way, I'm not going to admit to someone that I don't know how to send a photo. They might think I have dementia."

"Fair enough."

He scrolled through his iPhone photos. It did not take long, as he only had a few of him and Cassie and a bunch of pictures of him feeding the koi.

"Here it is. The fella that went missing."

He handed her the phone.

Cassie stared at the photo on her grandfather's phone, her mind temporarily unable to process what her eyes had revealed. She may have accepted it immediately when she was younger, when the world was much smaller. When her heart caught up with the evidence presented, she felt a familiar feeling: the anger that comes from betrayal. The feeling was recognizable but seasoned by what only the passing of time and life experience can bring. While the accident that took her family could be blamed on the random actions of a stranger, this was from someone she thought she knew, someone she loved. She spread her index finger and thumb on the screen to confirm this was not some bizarre coincidence or a perfect doppelganger. Then she dropped the phone, which bounced on the grass beside the sidewalk.

"Cassie, what's wrong? You look like you saw a ghost."

Cassie was present in her body only. The rest of her was someplace else, a mixture of calculations, formulas, probabilities, explanations, theories, emotions, and doubts.

"Cassie! Cassie, you're frightening me. What's wrong?"

"I . . . uh . . . I . . . I have to go, Grandpa."

Without a second thought, she turned and walked briskly back to her car. Her back turned to her grandfather; he could not see the tears that had begun to fall. He called after her but to no avail. Before he could even pick up his phone, she was backing out of her parking spot.

He immediately dialed her number. No answer. He called again—same result. The third time, he left a message insisting she call him back. He texted the same message. He gazed into the koi pond before him. Like the humans that fed them, the fish had slowed a bit from waves of unforgiving heat and humidity. It was almost 4:00 p.m., and a late afternoon storm was brewing in the distance, as if right on schedule. The contrast between the battleship gray and the bright blue sky was beautiful and ominous. The branches from the trees above began to wave in the bright sun, as if giving fair warning to those beneath to seek shelter. Chuck took the hint and turned back toward the center.

Cassie raced down the highway back toward her home. She found herself doing what she insisted she would never do while driving: scrolling through her call history. She found Bill. Her finger hovered over his picture. She wanted to call him but had no idea what to say. About an hour later, she was home despite having no recollection of how she got there.

She cycled through scenarios of what she would say to him and how he would respond. By the time she was done, she had assembled a tapestry of dialogue. The common thread was that regardless of how she imagined the conversation, it would be rife with anger, disappointment, and betrayal. More than anything, she wanted him to feel her pain. In a perfect world, she would transfer it to him and walk away forever, unburdened by the betrayal.

She pulled a new bottle of pinot grigio from her wine chiller and poured herself a generous glass. The liquid courage was unnecessary, but she knew she had to take off some of the edge before calling Bill. The phone rang three times with no answer. She wasn't about to leave a message; what she had to say wouldn't translate well. As she raised her finger to disconnect, he picked up.

"Hey! I was just thinking of you. I thought this weekend we could—"

"I need to see you," she said, her voice shaky.

"OK, I have a staff meeting tonight. I can come after that."

"No, no, I need you to come now."

"Is everything OK, Cassie? You're scaring me."

Cassie thought, Scaring you! Fuck you and your feelings.

"I'm fine. When can you get here?"

"I . . . uh . . . if it can't wait, I will leave now. I will make up some excuse."

With that, Cassie disconnected the call.

On the ride down to her place, Bill feared the worst. Did she find out about him and her grandfather? No, it couldn't be. That would mean the universe was conspiring against him. He was going to come clean in less than forty-eight hours. He replayed the prior weekend when they last saw one another. Did he do something? Did he say something wrong? He almost hoped he had. That would be much easier to repair. He could not think of anything. His heart began to race, his dread increasing with every mile.

When he knocked on her door, he was surprised to see how quickly she answered, as if she were waiting on the other side.

"Oh, hey." He leaned in to give her a peck on the cheek.

She reflexively took a step back.

"Is something wrong?" Bill looked frightened, anticipating that his world would be turned upside down.

Despite her insistence to herself that she wouldn't, she began to cry, her tears made of a mixture of despair, broken trust, venom, and the loss of the only thing she'd felt sure about since she was a child.

"Cassie, what's—"

"I need you to listen to me. I don't want to hear a word from you. I don't want to hear excuses. Understood?"

"Yes."

"Why didn't you tell me you knew my grandfather?"

"Cassie, I—"

She put her hand up, reminding him she did not want an explanation, at least not yet. "Is this some kind of weird game to you? Do you get off on stalking people? You broke my grandfather's heart. He kept telling me about this doctor who befriended him, how he looked forward to your visits, and how you became fast friends. And then, you just stopped visiting. I tried to explain it away, even if it was bizarre. I figured his work took him somewhere else, or he got busy with family. I never in a million years imagined it could be you."

"Why would you?" Bill said in an unwelcome attempt to convince her not to feel foolish.

In response, she gave him a glance that suggested his words no longer had substance, as she would grant them no credibility. "Am I an unwilling participant in some fucked-up psychology experiment? I have given everything I have to you. Do you know how hard that was for me? Everything I have ever loved has been taken from me.

Everyone I ever trusted has disappointed me or taken advantage." She was crying heavily now. It was a struggle to get the words out.

"Who are you? Are you even a doctor? I'm not even sure your hospital ID is real. Did you ever love me?" She retrieved a tissue from the box on the end table and wiped her eyes, now inflamed red and purple around the edges. Her nose was running as if she had a full-blown cold.

"Cassie, please. Please let me explain."

"No! No. I need you to leave now. Lose my number. I don't want to ever see or hear from you again."

He took a tentative step forward and reached out his hand.

"Cassie! You have to let me—"

"Get the fuck out! Now."

Bill paused as if observing a brief moment of silence, a time-out of sorts, to reset the table so he could begin to attempt to explain. A simple look into her eyes made it clear that no such time would be granted, and he turned and left without looking back. The door shut behind him. What started as a typical day had become the worst day of his life. August 18th. A date he would not soon forget.

CHAPTER 40

KNOWING SHE COULD not leave her grandfather in such a worried state, Cassie called to explain her behavior and why she'd left so abruptly the day before. She apologized profusely. Her explanation was based on truth, similar to how movies are based on a true story. The photo he shared looked like someone she had a relationship with that didn't end well. That part had a thread of truth. The added part about being overwhelmed with school stress was complete fiction. Cassie's grandfather accepted her apology even if her explanation didn't seem to fully justify such an intense response.

A couple of months passed. Cassie dealt with things by diving into her schoolwork and working additional hours at the café. She seldom sang on open mic nights, as it reminded her too much of Bill and the circumstances around the first time they met.

Bill fell into a full depression. He had lost the best thing that had ever happened to him. He was overcome with guilt and hated himself for his cowardice. He called out sick the next day, returned to the office for a few days, and then took a week of vacation. Most of that time was spent lying on the couch, seldom changing or showering. He rarely felt like eating, and when he did, it had become a habit to have food delivered so he needn't venture out into a world he believed no longer had anything to offer him. He came close to calling her. He wrote letters he never sent. This was not some college thesis that would make a difference if he presented the correct logical argument and supported it with facts. He had to honor her request to disappear.

Bill could compartmentalize enough at work that people either failed to notice or chose not to engage. On one occasion, Barb asked him about his weight loss, which he explained as a new diet and finally making good use of his gym membership. The night became a comfort to Bill. He wished it were winter so the days would be shorter. He forced himself to at least stay up until the summer evening sun finally fell behind Maybrook's mountains. With the benefit of time, Bill began to see the wreckage that he left behind and, in many ways, helped contribute to. He was overcome by guilt for not coming clean to Cassie right from the start.

He thought of the twelve-step motto: "Give me the strength to accept the things I cannot change, change the things I can, and the wisdom to know the difference." He realized the saying he had heard so many times in group—and thought only applied to the addicts in the room—now applied to him as well. It was time to take his own medicine, to practice what he preached. His suffering acted as a mirror in a way it never had before, asking him to reconcile what he practiced within the walls of the MPF with what he actually believed.

He'd lacked the courage to confront what was necessary for what was convenient, similar to how he'd failed to understand what happened with his brother and reach out when he was hurting the most. Now he realized that, in some ways, he was all that his brother had back then. Maybe he wasn't just sharing secrets about his exploits to burden him. Perhaps he was finding his way, the only way, to keep his brother in his life. Bill was not so naive as to think he could have reversed course for his brother or his family, but had he been less concerned about self-preservation and more empathetic, it might have made some difference. He rolled out of bed and looked in the bathroom mirror. It was time to start making amends. He knew it was too late for a redo with his patients that he may have failed, especially Kyle, wherever he might be. He hoped the same was not true for Cassie and his brother.

Colton's number was still in his phone, but he hadn't dialed it for nearly five years. Bill's father had passed away during the final year of his doctorate program, followed by his mother about six years later. She was a common point between two lines; without her, Bill and his brother drifted further, running parallel lives within sight of one another but seldom crossing. Bill was grateful that Colton had been clean and sober for the better part of two decades and was a successful insurance agent. He took a deep breath and clicked on the number.

"Hello?" Colton picked up right away.

"It's me, Bill." He wondered if he was still on Colton's contact list and, if not, whether he could recognize his voice anymore.

"Hey. I haven't talked to you in a while. Did something happen?"

"No, nothing like that. I just wanted to catch up," Bill said.

Colton hesitated before responding. "OK, so what's up?"

They indulged in small talk for several minutes, discussing everything from the weather to sports to how they were doing at their respective places of work. Unable to switch the topic gracefully, Bill decided on a direct approach. Something he had become well versed in as a therapist.

"It's great catching up, but I hoped to clarify some things. Some things about the past."

"OK, but I am not sure what needs clearing up," Colton said.

"Maybe you're right. It's just some things I want or maybe need to know. Do you hate me?" Bill meant to ease into the conversation, but his nerves led the words to cut in line.

"Hate you? Geez, that's quite a question. How long have you been sitting on that?"

"Probably for a long time. I'm just not sure I knew it until recently."

"To answer your question: no, I don't hate you. Not now, anyway."

"So, you did hate me?"

"Probably. I hated everything and was so angry that everyone fell under the same umbrella. It's all water under the bridge. We aren't kids anymore. Just because we are very different doesn't mean we hate each other. Where's this all coming from? Why are you asking me this now, after all these years?"

"I was cleaning out the crawl space in my townhouse, sorting through some old boxes, and found a letter you wrote. I don't know why I have it. I don't remember ever seeing it before."

"A letter . . . to who?"

"Well, it's less of a letter than maybe a train of thought you put to paper."

"Hmm, I must admit, I am curious about what I had to say. I'm guessing it wasn't pleasant."

"I'll read it."

"I fucking hate him. Mr. Perfect. Always kissing ass, trying to make me look bad. I hope that piece of shit gets hit by a car! Better yet, they can all die in a crash together! Fuck them."

"The rest talks about being frustrated over a girl you liked who didn't want you in return."

"Jenny," said Colton.

"Jenny?"

"Jenny Kohler. She was in the grade between us."

"Oh, yeah. I remember her."

"She was funny and smart. We had an elective course together. She must have looked at me like some alien from another planet. I had nothing in common with her. We were going in different directions.

But I am guessing that is not the part you are talking about."

"No, not really."

"I don't remember writing that, but I'm not surprised. If you are asking if it was about you, it was."

"I knew you were angry with me, but I never thought you truly hated me that much."

"Look, I took everything personally back then. I thought the entire world was against me . . . including you. I was a dick to you most of the time, but I would still ask you to cover for me and make you promise not to say anything to Mom and Dad. That couldn't have been easy. And I know Mom was asking you to report back on my activities. Dad just wanted me out of the house as soon as possible. No wonder you disappeared to friends' houses so much. I may have felt abandoned back then, but I was hurting and unable or unwilling to consider what others may have been going through. So, while we are on the topic, what about you?"

"Me?"

"You may not have written it down, but I am guessing you weren't too fond of me either."

Bill paused. He hadn't anticipated being on the receiving end of his question. "At times, I worried about you. Sometimes I felt sorry for you. But mostly, I resented you. I blamed you for turning the family upside down. I never stopped to think about why you acted the way you did. I don't ever remember even trying to talk to you about what you were going through. You may have been a shitty older brother, but I didn't make things any better." The memories came back into focus with greater clarity. "Dad was so hard on you when you started to go down the wrong path. It took me a while to see how he poured gas on the fire. I guess I just thought he was the adult in the room and was infallible, that if things were going bad, it had to be because of you. He harped so much on how you were ruining his life that I thought if you stopped pushing buttons, we wouldn't have all the problems we did."

"He just didn't know how to handle me. His love was, I guess, what you would call conditional."

"I'm fairly sure I studied so hard in school just to make sure Dad would be proud of me and that he would love me. I can see how that only added to Dad's disappointment with you. I am sorry I didn't see your side of things. I shouldn't have remained on the sidelines so much or stayed away from home. You must have felt abandoned."

"It's OK. It wasn't your responsibility. Being put in the middle without a compass and expecting you to navigate was never fair. You were only a kid. Anyway, I have long since forgiven Dad. I only wish we could have mended fences while he was still with us. I wish we could have had a talk like this when he was still around."

"You're able to forgive and forget that easily?"

"I never said it was easy. That's why it never came to pass while he was still alive. I don't want you to carry that same burden, thinking I hate you. It took me far too long to learn that anger only hurts the one holding it."

"It's funny. I went into counseling for a living, and sometimes I don't even know why. I have been so quick to judge, always following logic as if life were a flowchart with predictable and explainable paths. I've heard so many stories of suffering, abuse, and pain, but I'm not sure how much I have been listening. I don't think I've appreciated the emotional toll it takes on someone. I managed to complete all those years of schooling, able to recite every theory and diagnosis in the DSMV while barely understanding what it means for someone who lives with its labels."

"I guess neither of us had the best model for empathy," Colton said. "You know what, neither did Mom and Dad."

"But if we know that, I guess it's not too late to start learning," Bill said.

Colton laughed. "Yeah, maybe we can figure that out together."

"I'd like that," Bill said.

CHAPTER 41

CASSIE GRIPPED THE pillow tightly, momentarily holding it over her face while she tried to slow her breathing. Things had been so bad at home that it was hard to imagine them getting worse. Yet, they did.

The bottom had one trap door after another. Since losing a close election, Cassie's uncle seemed truly lost and vulnerable for the first time. It made him even more dangerous. He had never learned to lose gracefully, having never really experienced the sting of defeat. This anomaly was an albatross because it was such a public failure. There was no spin to put on it. Despite benefiting from a bump after introducing his niece on the campaign trail, the letter leaked to the media closed the gap and, in the end, being a blue state, Democrats got people to the polls and took greater advantage of absentee voting.

Davis was coming home later now. More time at the bar meant more time to drink. When he was home, he completely ignored Cassie, only speaking to her when absolutely necessary. The quiet felt like a new tactic with its own, if not detectable, violence. The digital clock on her nightstand read 1:43 a.m. The soft yellow-green glow of the numbers marked the countdown to the inevitable. She peeked out from beneath her pillow, having managed to calm her nerves, if only a little.

With each passing minute, her plan became more real. What was once a passing thought that crept into her head only to be quickly suppressed by her more rational self had now been set in motion by its inertia.

Since losing the election, her uncle unceremoniously dumped his housekeeper, Maria. His isolation was nearly complete. He avoided media requests for interviews and let calls go to voicemail. Once the votes were cast, the fickle nature of his 'friends' and believers became evident. Their lip service and promises faded with the late autumn breeze. It hurt for someone so fueled by atta-boys and public praise.

Cassie couldn't be sure, but she felt his resentment of her grow after the election. He was sold that she would make the difference. Now, she was just a mouth to feed, an anchor hanging around his ankle that he could not shake. In his view, the only remaining benefit was the annual tax credit. His superficial interest had been replaced by pure indifference. Cassie would have been happy with that development, but it was periodically contrasted with her becoming the unwanted focus of his rage.

Cassie heard the familiar slam of the storm door. It was now 1:56 a.m. Her heart was in full gallop. All her senses were heightened, tuned to the fight or flight response perfected over millions of years. At these times, all the sophistication that came from human endeavors fell away, leaving only the animal to react to the simple binary truth of survival or death. The next sound was of keys sliding across the kitchen island and the unmistakable crack of a can being opened, no doubt a beer to keep the buzz going.

What followed was several minutes of silence. She tried to picture where her uncle might be in the house. Had he parked himself on the living room sofa? She did not hear the TV. A moment of panic rose in her chest. Was he upstairs already? Did she space out and miss it? Her thoughts were outpacing her ability to process them. She took a few deep breaths, focusing on her stomach as it moved in and out. She heard the refrigerator door open and close again. He was still downstairs.

Moments later, the familiar creak on the stairs told her he was on the fifth step, or maybe the twelfth. They had a similar reverb after releasing pressure. She closed her eyes and asked her parents to watch over her. He stopped outside her bedroom. She could see his boots cast a shadow in the moonlight under the door.

He paused, leaving her to wonder if it was for her benefit, ensuring he created the maximum tension.

The door partially splintered from the heel of his boot, and a crack formed beneath the doorknob. Simply opening the door was not dramatic enough. He grabbed a folding chair from the closet. Raising it over his head, he brought it down towards her stomach. She flinched, drawing her arms up under the blanket, preparing to block the worst of the blow. He stopped short before striking her, revealing a misplaced smile.

"I knew you were up, bitch! You think you are so smart. I know what you are going to do before you do it. You are as predictable as you are plain."

He turned the chair's backrest facing away and straddled it. Placing his arms over the backrest, he leaned forward. The alcohol in his breath was only moderately less potent than what was coming through his sweat, a familiar combination of body odor and a sickly sweet fermentation that always made Cassie queasy.

"I thought I asked you to do the laundry."

He hadn't.

"I thought we agreed you would clean the bathrooms."

They didn't.

Even if he had asked and Cassie had made good on his demands, the result would be the same. It was a test she could never pass—a labyrinth without an exit.

He stood up, pushing off the back of the chair. His balance was compromised from intoxication.

"Well, I guess it's the belt then, huh."

He undid his belt buckle and released it one loop at a time. He made sure to make eye contact the entire time. His heart was racing, his excitement building. It was a power that could not be described. It filled a void in ways that all his business accolades and TV appearances could not. He needed the drink to give him the courage to tap into his dark side. He knew it was wrong but could not control it or perhaps did not care to.

Before he completed undoing his belt, Cassie threw off the covers and dashed for the door. He managed to grab the tail of her shirt, slowing but not stopping her momentum. She reached the top of the stairs before feeling the tug on her hair, pulling her backward. Her uncle put her in a headlock, the sweaty crux of his elbow against her throat. She summoned all of her strength, which, given the possibility of pending death, had reached new levels. She elbowed him as hard as she could in his groin. It was not a direct hit, but close enough to give her the space she needed to slide out from his chokehold. Angrier, if that was possible, he lunged at her face with an open hand as if trying to tear skin from bone. She dodged the offering with little difficulty.

Her uncle seemed dumbfounded by her dexterity, unable to see how his intoxication had dulled his reflexes. His momentum carried him toward the stairs. He grabbed the banister to restore his balance. Cassie and her uncle were now side by side. There was no time to consider the pros and cons or make a list of options as she did before leaking to the press. She was afforded only a moment to make a decision. She stuck her leg between his, positioning her foot directly behind his back leg. She lowered her shoulder and launched into his chest. As their eyes met, she swore she saw fear and surprise as he fell backward down the marble staircase. A sickening cracking sound could be heard as his head and shoulder connected with the unforgiving steps. He somersaulted a few times before his body rolled to the side, sliding to the floor below. The only sounds were those from the trauma inflicted on the way down. He was silent, likely unconscious too quickly to put words to his pain.

A trail of blood traced the last part of his path to the floor. A pool of red was slowly but steadily expanding from beneath his head and neck. The contrast of the blue-white marble and red was startling. Momentarily, Cassie convinced herself that he had slipped and fallen. She thought, He was falling anyway; I was just trying to protect myself from going down with him.

The nausea that followed told a different story. She didn't need to check on him. He was dead. She was certain. Her heart began to race, suggesting a panic attack was imminent. She took a few deep breaths, focusing on her stomach going in and out. She'd learned this trick to ward off anxiety in her many psychotherapy sessions. She knew the best she could hope for under these circumstances was to avoid full panic.

Regaining her composure, she knew she could not go downstairs. Her uncle's blood was everywhere, and she would surely leave footprints. She decided to exit from one of the unoccupied upstairs bedrooms whose window exited onto the garage's roof. She had used the route before to evade her uncle. She felt for her car keys in the fleece jacket on her bedroom floor. It was almost 4:00 a.m. It would still be dark for the next two hours. She knew her grandfather was an early riser. He often complained that no matter what time he went to bed he no longer had the ability to sleep in. This was frustrating because he was always tired, had nowhere to be, and answered to no schedule.

When she finally pulled into her grandfather's driveway, she had no recollection of how she got there. She knocked on the door with increasing force, a direct reflection of her building anxiety and fear. When he opened the door, she collapsed into his arms. He did not think he had ever heard someone cry with such abandon, even during the war. He held her tight while she unleashed a year's worth of tears into the shoulder of his sweater. Once she regained some composure, he put his arm around her and led her inside. She collapsed on the couch in the TV room. Now under the light from the lamp on the end table, Cassie's grandfather could see the scratches on her neck. His heart dropped, taking the air in his lungs with it.

Cassie recovered long enough to put together a string of words.

Her grandfather, already knowing the answer, asked, "What happened?"

There was another gasp and heavy sobbing. Her grandfather waited for the wave to pass.

"He's dead."

"Who's dead?"

"My uncle."

"What are you talking about? Did you call 911?"

"No! Please, you can't call them, please promise me! He's dead."

"How do you know he's dead!"

She paused and looked him straight in his eyes. "Because I killed him."

The admission made it even more real. Voicing the words created a fear in her that she had never experienced. Even dead, her uncle could still terrify her in ways that even the worst of his violence in life could not duplicate.

Her grandfather sat across from her on a loveseat. He put his hands on his knees and took a breath. He replayed what she'd communicated in his head a few times to confirm that he was awake and heard what he'd heard. Cassie stopped crying. Her eyes were locked on her grandfather's. At that moment, she waited to see what the rest of her life would be like. Would he be disgusted with her? Would he turn her in? Would he help her?

"OK . . . OK," her grandfather said. "It will be OK, but I need you to tell me exactly what happened. Everything, do you understand?"

Cassie nodded.

CHAPTER 42

CASSIE WAS STUDYING at the school library when she received a call that her grandfather had a setback, not from another stroke but what looked to be a minor heart attack. Cassie found that description odd. How could any heart attack be minor? She packed her books and raced to the hospital about twenty minutes from the rehab facility.

When she arrived at his room, he was reading a paperback that looked like it had seen better days. Its jacket was barely attached, and many of the pages were dog-eared by the numerous patients who had read its story. He smiled when she walked into the room and pulled up a chair beside his bed. He looked pale. Oxygen was feeding into his nose, and an IV was in his arm.

"Hi, angel." She leaned over to kiss his forehead.

"Hi, Grandpa. I was petrified when they called. Please tell me you're OK."

"OK. I'm OK." He smirked.

"You are such a wiseass. I'm serious."

"I'm fine, just a minor heart attack."

There it is again, she thought, minor. Someone should address that terminology. They caught up on things since they'd last talked on the phone. There was nothing exciting to report on either end. Both were stuck in their routines. Cassie had been going out more with Kayla, who was a tremendous support following her breakup. She even had coffee a couple of times with Passion, who had recently moved into a marketing position she enjoyed. Passion was in therapy and genuinely appeared to be rebuilding her life, even if it was not always a linear journey. She was glad that Davis was dead, but it left her with mixed feelings, knowing that her justice had likely died with him.

"I'm glad you came, angel. I've been wanting to talk to you."

"OK." Cassie sat back in her chair, unsure what was coming.

"It's just that, well, something about that day you left in a huff just doesn't seem right."

"Huff? Grandpa, you need to update your terminology." She smiled.

"I'm serious, Cassie. Don't try to knock me off course. It won't work. You should know that by now."

"OK, but I'm not sure what you mean."

"You looked like you saw a ghost when I showed you that photo. It was like you didn't just know someone who looked like him; it seemed like you knew . . . him. Is there something you aren't telling me?"

Cassie's eyes became heavy, and she gulped, took a deep breath, and successfully fought back her tears. She looked at a poster of the muscular system on the opposite wall as she weighed how to respond. She didn't want to burden her grandfather after his cardiac incident, but they had always had a relationship based on complete trust, where anything could be said without fear of judgment.

"OK, look, it's going to sound impossible to believe, but I do . . . er . . . did know him."

Her grandfather scooted up in bed, surprised to find that his suspicions may have had some merit. "You knew him?"

"Yes. I more than knew him. He was the relationship I told you about. I didn't want to say anything. I figured it had been a while since you last saw him and that maybe it was better that you let time do its thing and slowly put him in the past, frankly, where he belongs."

Her grandfather was focused on her every word.

"I can't figure out why he looked me up and went out of his way to meet me. I've been racking my brain to try and make sense of why he stalked me, but regardless, he preyed on my trust, and worse, he cut you off completely without any explanation. You must have mentioned me for some reason, and then he looked me up and liked what he saw. I don't understand any of it, but it is creepy, and I'm over it. I don't want you to worry about it, Grandpa. You are better off without that imposter in your life."

Her grandfather sighed and looked into Cassie's eyes. "I think I might be able to help fill in some of the blanks. There are some things you need to know. You are missing some pieces of the puzzle."

"Grandpa, I appreciate it, but I am still trying to get over the betrayal, and frankly, I don't need or want to know. I just want to forget. Sometimes putting the past in the past is the best path forward."

"Maybe." Her grandfather paused. "Maybe sometimes. But, other times, it might be the worst thing you can do. You need to know why he may have sought you out. I don't think it's what you think."

"Does it matter, Grandpa?"

"I think it does, yes. It matters a lot."

Cassie sat back in her chair. "OK, fine. So, what is this great revelation?"

"I'm getting older, Cassie. I've had a stroke. I've got bum parts from the war. And now, I've had a heart attack."

"Grandpa, you're as strong as an ox, you're—"

"Cassie, stop." His firmness was unlike him and startled Cassie. "I need you to listen carefully. I love you more than you know. After your grandmother passed, you are the only motivation I have had to keep going. You are the most extraordinary person I know. You deserve to be loved unconditionally. It was important to me that you had a model in your life after your parents were taken from you.

You have had much suffering in your life. At the time when you needed the most support." Her grandfather wiped away a tear that had breached his eyelid and rolled down his cheek.

"Grandpa, please. It's OK."

"He abused you. I saw it too late. I failed you, Cassie."

"Stop it! Don't you do that. Everything I am, I owe to you. I love you, Grandpa. You are the most important person in my life. Please know that." She reached out to put her hand on the bedrail.

He put his hand on top of hers, the IV sticking out of the back of it. "I know. It's just that. The best thing I could do for you was to ensure that what happened could never be traced back to you. No matter how unlikely, the possibility has always been in my mind. What if that bastard somehow came back to hurt you from the grave."

"I don't know what you mean. Where are you going with this? What does this have to do with Bill?"

"I told him, Cassie."

"You told him what I did?"

"No. God, no! I told him what I did."

"But you didn't do it. You weren't even there. Oh my god! Oh my god! That's why he sought me out? To confront me about what happened all those years ago?"

"Cassie, I think I greatly burdened him with that confession. I think he was trying to find out if it was true, and verifying your existence was part of that. Although, it sounds like he found out some even more important things than that."

"Please, that just makes it worse! The whole time I was laughing at his jokes, bathing in the warmth of his compliments, holding his hand, sleeping in the same . . . God!" Cassie leaned back into her chair again, putting her hands behind her head as she processed the implications. "Grandpa. Why would you do that? What if he tells someone?"

"If he tells, and they choose to investigate a closed case and drag an old man to court, that's fine by me. If he doesn't, it stays buried forever. Either way, it will never come back on you if it ever comes to light. Do you understand?"

"I didn't ask you to do this, Grandpa."

"You didn't need to, and I knew you would never approve. Sometimes, you have to do things to protect the ones you love. Although I plan to leave everything to you when I'm gone, I don't have much to give. This was the best thing I could do to be certain you could live the life you deserve."

Cassie sighed. "This is a lot to take in, Grandpa. I understand and appreciate why you did what you did, but I am still mad at you for doing it."

"That's fair. So long as you know how much I love you."

"I love you too, Grandpa."

"Regardless, it's good that he is no longer in my life. No matter the reason, his feelings were based on a lie."

"Let me ask you a question. You have to tell me the truth."

"OK. Sure. What is it?"

"Before you knew about all of this, about him, how did you feel around him? Did you, well, did you love him?"

"I don't think that matters, does it? I do know what happened. It can't be erased."

"I think it matters more than just about anything, Cassie. Did you ever stop to think that he really did love you? That the time you spent together, what you built together, was real?"

"He should have told me. I had the right to know that we did not meet randomly."

"You're probably right. He should have told you. But doing so means he would have to give words to a terrible burden I unfairly placed on him. Once he saw that you existed, he had to start considering that what he was holding onto was the truth, not just some faulty neurons firing in the head of an old fart. I was hurt that he stopped coming to see me, but I never blamed him for it. Don't you think when he fell for you that made it all the more complicated?"

"But we met based on a lie."

"Cassie, I met the love of my life laid out in a hospital bed, covered in shrapnel wounds. We don't always get to choose how we meet the one. I just happened to meet mine in the middle of a war zone surrounded by death and young men slowly dying in beds just meters away. What if I was to have said she only cared for me because it was her job to do so? What if I never considered the possibility that both could be true? You are smart, Cassie, probably the smartest person I know, but you are your own person and need to make your own decisions. I can only tell you what I have learned in my life."

Cassie smiled faintly. "OK, Grandpa. I don't know, but I heard you. You are something. You know that."

"So are you."

CHAPTER 43

THE BRIGHT MORNING sunlight woke Bill early. He reminded himself, yet again, that he should invest in some room-darkening shades. He made a feeble attempt to go back to sleep. His efforts to shorten what had become long, directionless weekend days had failed. During the week, Bill stayed late at work—not to catch up on cases but to avoid being alone at home. There was too much time to think. Hiding in his office allowed him to avoid interacting with patients while retaining the benefit of listening to chatter in the halls. The sound provided an alternative to the silence at home, a void that welcomed the deafening dialogue in his head.

He begrudgingly rolled out of bed, plopped on the couch, and booted up his laptop. It was early September, almost two months since he last spoke to Cassie. It was time to get off the fence. Letting life happen, a passenger in the car's back seat left him with no hope of gaining control again. He typed in the search engine "Forgiveness in Japanese." It returned, 許し *Yurushi*. He ripped a sheet of paper from his MPF-branded pad and copied the symbol. It took him a few tries to get it right. He wondered how someone could write an entire sentence in under an hour. He grew to admire Japanese culture, the characters in their language, their traditions, and even their storied relationship with the living jewels he had come to appreciate. He added some additional content in English and folded it multiple times until it resembled one of the paper footballs he used to make in grade school. Next, he called the café and asked if Cassie was there, ready to disconnect should he hear anything to the effect of "hold on."

"She doesn't come in until 6:00 p.m. tonight. She's doing a show. Can I take a message?"

"No need, I will try again later. Thank you."

Mission accomplished. He knew she would be at the café tonight. The fact that she was performing gave him some cover to sneak in during her set while the stage lights partially blinded her. He knew exactly where to sit.

It was eight-thirty at night when he arrived. He waited in his car until it was dark. The same creepy feeling he had when he started searching her social media months before had returned. He considered putting the car back in gear to let the past be the past. Instead, he leaned back in his seat and put on Fates Warning's "A Pleasant Shade of Gray" to distract him from allowing any additional doubts to take root in his mind. After it was dark, he lowered the passenger side window. He turned off the music and listened intently, waiting for someone to open the door. A few minutes later, a young couple entered. While there was no way to be sure it was her, he could briefly hear a female voice over the microphone. Just as quickly, it was silent again as the door closed.

It's time, he thought. Time to get a backbone. He was relieved that the table in the back corner was available. It made sense, given it was probably the worst spot in the café to see the stage. Being partially obscured by a wooden beam, Bill had to lean slightly to his right to see. It was her. He felt a jolt in his heart that was a strange alchemy of sorrow, hope, loss, and love. One thing he had resolved was that he would not leave with the feeling of regret. He would put his cards on the table and trust the results to a higher power. He closed his eyes to recite the prayer in his head: "God grant me the serenity to accept the things I cannot change, the courage to change the things I can, and the wisdom to know the difference." In doing so, he felt a connection to a faith that had been dormant for many years. He was here to try and rekindle the most important relationship he had ever experienced. He would be vulnerable. He would leave, not knowing the outcome of his plan. It would be out of his hands. It was momentarily freeing for someone who had always tried to find the answers through science and logic.

Cassie sounded as angelic as ever, her raspy voice adding depth to her effortless command of range. She announced a new cover, "Chosen" by Generdyn. It was a beautiful song, albeit unknown to the audience. Had she not credited the artist, nobody would have been the wiser.

Bill was happy to see she was still sharing her voice with the world, even if he was no longer part of it. She played a couple more tunes before taking a brief break. The café raised the lights slightly but not enough to drown out the candles on the tables. Bill glanced at the bar for anyone who might recognize him. He was happy to see Amber was not there. He remembered one of the men but only knew him as a customer. It was unlikely he would recognize him or pay him any attention. Once Cassie left to use the restroom, he approached the stage. He had seen her enough times to know that her guitar case was likely to be next to the step leading to the stage. He approached cautiously and tossed the note in the case as if it were loose change offered to a street performer.

Just as she made her way up the steps, Cassie saw someone exit into the night. She thought she recognized the silhouette for a moment before convincing herself otherwise. Cassie closed her set with "My Mind & Me" by Selena Gomez. Her unique rendition resulted in a standing ovation. She thanked the crowd and took a bow.

Exiting the stage, now out of view of the audience, she leaned down to place her guitar in the case. She noticed a tightly folded triangle piece of paper with her name in block lettering. Sitting on the step, she used the key to the café to cut a single piece of tape. She figured it might be a note from a new fan. At first, she denied what her eyes told her, figuring maybe the stage lights were playing games with her vision. She glanced into the audience for a moment before refocusing on the note. There was no denying it; the Japanese symbol stared back at her. She had no idea what it meant, but she knew it could only be from one person. Beneath the symbol was written, *Tomorrow, 10:00 a.m.*, with a familiar address. It was the drive-in theater from their first date.

The lights were up now as the café was closing for the night. She scanned the crowd as they prepared to exit; unsurprisingly, he was nowhere to be found. She left from the back door of the café, where staff took their smoke breaks. She was alone. Her phone was bright against the otherwise very dark night. She typed the Japanese word in the browser. It returned "Forgiveness or Mercy." She stared into the starless sky and thought about what her grandfather had told her. For the first time in her life, she got on her knees and asked for her parents' guidance. She prayed for an answer. There was no shooting star, no breeze to indicate a sign from the heavens. However, in its place, she felt a warmth and a wanting in her heart. Her stubbornness had only brought her isolation. Without her knowing, her pride had made her a prisoner, controlled by the inability to trust—only this time it was her own doing.

The drive-in would not be open for several more hours. The sign advertised two movies. One of them was *Honey I Shrunk the Kids*, only the "Sh" was missing, so it read *Honey, I runk the Kids*. The other movie, *The Revenant*, while not new, had at least come out in the last six months. As Cassie drove down the long dirt road that led to the drive-in's gate, she could already see Bill was out of his car and leaning against the back bumper. She felt surprisingly nervous, like her first time there, but somehow different given the circumstances. That magical night was about potential. It had revealed endless possibilities, all of which, while unpredictable, shared the common theme of hope and excitement. Would this be a new beginning or the beginning of the end?

She parked and exited the car.

"Thanks for coming," Bill said.

"You asked me to come." Cassie hadn't intended it to come off as biting as it did.

"In any case, thanks for, um, hearing me out."

"Forgiveness."

"I'm sorry?"

"Your note. I looked it up. The English spelling was thoughtful. Not sure how long it would have taken me to figure out the meaning of the Japanese character."

"You failed to give me the same courtesy when we first met." He smiled.

"But what fun would that have been?"

"Well, you look great."

"Thanks. But do you want to tell me why we're here?"

"It's pretty simple. I should have come clean from the start. When I first met you."

Cassie pulled the paper out from her back pocket and unfolded it.

"So, you want me to forgive you? Why? Why should I forgive you?"

"Because I believe we belong together. I believe you believe that."

"You know how hard it was for me to trust someone again, and you broke that trust. I am better on my own. I always have been. You just reminded me of that."

She stepped forward, grabbed his hand, and turned it over so his palm was toward the sky. She unfolded his fingers and deposited the note along the love line she once traced, jokingly telling him it wasn't there at all. She folded his fingers over the paper and looked into his eyes. Bill dropped the paper into the long, dried grass along the dirt road. He slid his fingers between hers and put his other hand over hers.

"Please, Cassie. I am sorry I met you the way I did. If I could take it back. I . . ."

Cassie retrieved her hand. "But you can't." She began to sob.

Bill's eyes welled up too. He could see he was losing her again.

"And I can't either," she said under her breath.

"You have nothing to take back, Cassie."

Cassie wiped away her tears. "What are you going to do about my grandfather? I suppose you are going to turn him in."

"No. Even if this is the last time I ever see you, I will never reveal his secret, Cassie. I hate what your uncle did to you. I hate that he robbed you of your childhood. I hate that he violated your trust when you needed it most. I hate that it, in some sick way, led to our meeting. I became a therapist to help people. How does it help anyone to put a good man, a war hero, in jail because he ended the life of someone who destroyed so many others? It's not about justice. It's about what it really means to help someone. I have a chance to do that by ensuring the one person you have left, who you can still trust, is there for you, for however long that may be. If I can't be that, if you won't let me, that is the only way I can help you, to continue to love you from afar."

Cassie stepped toward him and embraced him in a tight hug. She was crying heavily. Bill could no longer fight back his tears.

"I haven't been honest with you either. You say you love me."

"I do. I do, Cassie, more than I can ever express."

"No. You wouldn't if you truly knew me."

"I do know you, Cassie."

Cassie loved Bill. All the turmoil and doubt she had experienced in her life could not occlude this truth. All the love that life had shown her, from her parents to Kayla to Passion to Bill, all the pain from the accident, the assault of her friend, and the abuse at the hands of her uncle had led to this point. Someone who had all the reasons in the world not to place her trust in anyone again found herself at a crossroads, a decision point that would alter the rest of her life one way or the other.

She was surprised at her calmness. Knowing what she needed to do brought her a sense of clarity she had not known for years.

"I'm glad you didn't turn him in. That would have been a mistake."

"I know."

"No, I'm afraid you don't."

She stepped back from him and stared into his eyes. "My grandfather didn't kill my uncle."

"How do you know that?"

"Because I did."

She watched his eyes upon saying the words, hoping that they were, as they say, the window to the soul. She looked for a sign of how this impossible news would be received. The same question arose: Would it be a new beginning—one where he would grant her the same grace he was willing to give to her grandfather—or would it be the beginning of the end, one that put bars between them?

"Oh my god. Oh my god, Cassie."

CHAPTER 44

THE SUN SHONE BRIGHTLY as Chuck positioned himself at the edge of the koi pond with a piece of bread in hand. He was happy to be back at the rehab to finish his therapy. One of the nurses walked by as she began to start her workday.

"Hi, Chuck. You're looking particularly radiant today, young man."

Chuck loved the humor in calling him a young man. Her conviction almost made him believe it.

"I'm waiting for a visitor," he said with excitement.

"I see. Well, enjoy!"

"I will, I will." He tossed an offering into the pond, which resulted in a flurry of splashing and bobbing from his fish friends. His eyes smiled, followed by his lips.

It was the first time he had ever had two visitors at once. His two favorite people in the world approached. One of Bill's hands was locked with his granddaughter's, while the other held a carrier of iced coffee made just as he liked it.

ACKNOWLEDGEMENTS

To all those who have encouraged me through the years. Your support has allowed me to put words to paper.

To my family, Martha, Marvin, and Mark.

A special thank you to Greg Lutz, Ronnie Connely, Liam Sheehan, Waqas Khan, and Dr. Marlene Kolodziej for your friendship and belief.

To my four pawed friends (past and present): Seamus, Wyeth, Brad, Pelle, and Dewey.

Made in the USA
Coppell, TX
24 July 2024

35139671R00185